KADE'S TURN

KADE'S TURN

A COMPANION NOVEL IN
THE KATHLEEN TURNER SERIES

TIFFANY SNOW

Published by Montlake Romance, Seattle

www.apub.com

Amazon, the Amazon logo, and Montlake Romance are trademarks of Amazon.com, Inc., or its affiliates.

ISBN-13: 9781477830666
ISBN-10: 1477830669

Printed in the United States of America

For Ian, with my thanks.

PROLOGUE

From a certain point onward there is no longer any turning back. That is the point that must be reached.
~ *Franz Kafka*

K ade Dennon was naked.
Of course, that's how he always felt when he had to leave his
weapons behind. His job today required he be at the Indianapolis courthouse, which necessitated a walk through a metal detector. This morning, however, he'd managed to throw a wrench in the gears at security
that disabled the system long enough for him to sneak in a gun taped
to his back. So while he wasn't armed to the teeth the way he usually
was, he felt less naked than if he'd had nothing.

He said a few choice words when he ripped the tape from his skin
while standing inside a stall in the men's bathroom. Shit, that hurt.
Blane was *so* buying dinner for that one. An expensive dinner. Steak
dinner. Kade shoved the gun into his ankle holster.

The big guy in charge of security—what was his name, Hank, maybe?—had done a careful pat down on Kade, eyeing him suspiciously, but not saying anything. Kade had just given him a thin-lipped smile before moving on.

Now Kade sipped hot black coffee out of a Styrofoam cup and kept a casual eye on the entrance. The courthouse was an ideal location to arrange a clandestine meeting since so many people came and went, on both sides of the law. Which was why he was there to see exactly who spoke to James Gage Jr.

Kade snorted in disgust at the mere thought of that pansy-ass. He was nothing but a spoiled pretty boy who clung to his dad's coattails and had achieved nothing of his own. Not to mention he'd probably shit himself if he even knew Kade was watching him.

Bored, Kade glanced at his watch. He'd gotten there early. They'd since fixed the metal detector and now the line to get in the courthouse was slightly backed up. Shifting his weight, he leaned against the wall and looked casually back at the entrance, making mental notes of those in line.

Hello. What have we here?

Kade's gaze swiveled back to the spot in line where a woman stood waiting. She had the most unusual shade of hair he'd ever seen. He couldn't see her face yet, she was a little thing, but her hair stood out in the crowd. It was the color of the sunset, golden with a hint of rose.

Without even thinking about it, Kade moved from his position by the wall, drawing closer into the crowd just to get a better glimpse of her. He was close enough to hear the security guard when he spoke to her, his voice booming out.

"Kathleen! How's it going on this fine day?" Hank asked her.

Kathleen. Kade liked that. But he still couldn't see her face or hear her reply to Hank. Her voice was too soft to carry.

Someone stepped in front of Kade, temporarily obscuring his view, and he had to tamp down his irritation. Moving again, he finally caught a glimpse of her face as she turned away from the metal detector.

For a moment, he couldn't breathe. She was beautiful, her face and smile radiating youth and innocence. Even from where Kade stood, he could see she had blue eyes. Of course she did. Her skin was the color of cream and was flawless, a hint of pink in her cheeks betraying the chill in the air outside. She looked like a fairy-tale princess who'd just stepped from the pages of a storybook.

Kade stopped in his tracks. He'd unconsciously taken several steps toward her. What was he going to do, ask her out? Yeah, he could see how that would go:

"Um, excuse me, you don't know me, and if you did, you'd probably run screaming in the opposite direction, but can I buy you coffee or dinner, then take you to my apartment and spend the next several days in bed with you?"

As a pickup line, it wasn't one of his better ones.

Kade watched as she walked away down the hallway and turned a corner out of sight. It didn't matter. He could tell without even speaking to her that she wasn't his type, his type usually being the kind that wasn't looking for more than a quick hookup where names were optional. A step above having to pay for it, but not by much.

Kathleen looked like the kind of girl who liked flowers and slow dancing, who'd no doubt never had a hard day in her life, or any cause to ever, ever hold a gun. She was the kind of girl you fell in love with and brought home to mom.

That caused a long-buried pang to echo through Kade and he pushed the thought aside. Christ, what was he doing? Going all gooey-eyed and maudlin just because he saw a pretty girl? Obviously, he'd gone too long without killing someone.

Maybe Junior . . .

But no. Blane would get pissed if he killed that little snot. Not that he couldn't make it look like an accident, but Blane would know and then Kade would have that to deal with.

Kade took another sip of coffee, then tossed the rest in a nearby trash can. As he did, he heard screams and commotion coming from down the hallway where Kathleen had gone.

He followed the crowd, moving quickly through the press of people until he was able to see what the problem was.

The girl, Kathleen, was being held hostage by a man wearing a rumpled suit and a desperate expression. He held a knife to her throat.

Well, fuck.

Kathleen's face was as white as paper, her eyes wide and scared as she gripped the lunatic's arm, trying to keep the knife from her throat. The guy was terrified, too, but he was also deranged. A dangerous combination. Kade doubted he even realized how close the knife was to her skin. He was too focused on the crowd of onlookers and the security guards scattered in front of him.

Kade glanced through the crowd and saw Blane standing to one side. Their eyes locked and Blane gave a short, quick nod.

Kade crouched and pulled his gun from its holster, careful to keep it hidden from those around him as he stood back up. His eyes narrowed as he surveyed the situation. Kathleen was lucky. She was short. Kade could get a clear shot if he was careful and quick. If Kathleen had been taller, there wouldn't have been anything Kade could have done.

Out of the corner of his eye, Kade saw Blane moving, slow but deliberate. Kade would tap the guy to the head and Blane would grab the girl, followed by a hasty retreat out the back exit. Problem solved.

The guy's knife slipped, nicking Kathleen. People in the crowd gasped at the sight. The bright gash of red blood against her ivory skin made Kade forget everyone around him. Cold fury took over and he instantly raised his gun to take aim—

Kathleen moved suddenly and Kade's finger twitched. He'd been a split second from pulling the trigger, but now she was free, the knife embedded in the man's side. He crumpled to the ground.

Security guards swarmed around the man, obscuring him from view. There were shouts for an ambulance and the crowd started talking and moving again, filling the hallway with noise and mayhem. But Kade only had eyes for the girl.

She had retreated to the wall, as far as she could get, and now stood looking shell-shocked. Her mouth was agape, her eyes unblinking as she stared at where the man had fallen, as though surprised by her own actions. As Kade watched, her knees seemed to give out and she slid down the wall to the floor, dropping from sight.

Kade pushed through people to get to her. Was she okay? Had she been hurt? When he finally reached her, he could see from where he stood that Kathleen's entire body shook with tremors, her chest rising and falling with rapid, short breaths.

She was in shock and hyperventilating.

"Put your head between your knees," Kade ordered.

Kathleen didn't seem to hear him, her attention still on the crowd around the man. Kade could hear her gasping breaths. Her little hands were curled into fists at her side.

The last thing he needed was her passing out on him. Reaching down, Kade pushed on the back of her head and neck, forcing her head down between her knees. She fought him at first, *how cute*, but he kept pushing and then held her there.

Her hair was soft, the locks slipping through and over his fingers like silk. Her neck felt fragile and delicate in his grip. Too delicate. But then again, she'd just escaped from that guy like a pro. Maybe Kade had pegged her wrong.

After a few moments, her breathing slowed and the tremors eased. When she pushed back on his hand to sit up, Kade reluctantly released her, allowing his fingers to trail slightly through her hair as she sat back. Then she looked up at him with wide, innocent eyes as pure blue as the summer sky.

And he was lost.

Crouching down next to her, he asked, "Are you all right?" Now that he was closer, he could smell her perfume. It was like spring after a thunderstorm, and Kade knew he'd never smell that fragrance again without thinking of this moment and the color of her eyes.

Kathleen just stared at him, open-mouthed, before finally nodding. Kade wondered if he should get the paramedics over to her. She was obviously still reeling and in shock.

Reaching out to the still-oozing wound in her throat, he brushed away the warm blood. It felt almost intimate, her blood on his fingers. Soft was too dull of a word to describe her skin. "You're bleeding," he said. No shit. Nothing like stating the obvious, but he had to give some excuse as to why he'd touched her.

"Just a scratch," she murmured.

Kade smiled a little at that. Sounded like something he would say, actually.

"Nice move," he complimented her, wanting to prolong the conversation. She just looked confused. "What you did to get away," he said. Had she hit her head?

Kathleen just shrugged like it wasn't a big deal. "Thanks," she said, then jerked her chin to indicate the guy on the floor. "Will he be okay?"

Well, that was certainly *not* something Kade would say. Who gave a shit if he was going to be okay? He'd used her as a human shield. He was lucky Kathleen had done what she had or his brains would be splattered all over the hallway right now, courtesy of Kade. It still wasn't a bad idea, the motherfucker.

But still, she seemed worried. Kade gave an inward sigh. Innocent, naive, and way too soft-hearted. Nope. Not his type. At all. He needed to keep thinking about that and not how he felt as though she held a magnet inside her body that was focused solely on reeling him in.

"Yeah," he assured her. "The wound isn't deep and the medics got here quickly enough." Kathleen was too tiny to have caused any serious damage with the knife, and Kade thought it more than a little amusing that she thought she might have really hurt him.

She closed her eyes in relief. Kade knew he had to take the opportunity to leave. If she looked at him again with those eyes that made him wish she'd be impressed by his hand-to-hand combat skills or his aim at fifty yards, he'd do something stupid and no doubt juvenile, like ask if he could buy her dinner, or ice cream, or a car, anything just to be around her a little while longer.

God, he was really losing it. With one last glance at her, memorizing every last detail, Kade stood and melted into the crowd.

$\sim$

One Week Later

He could kill her so easily.

Kade Dennon stared down at the sleeping woman. She was a plant. She had to be. There was no other explanation for it.

She'd bolted from Blane's house in the dead of night into a car waiting at the curb. She'd known enough to wipe the hard drive he'd coerced from her, had pretended innocence and gotten Blane to sleep with her, had run off once she'd realized Kade was on to her, and had hid here with a known prostitute.

And she'd fired a gun at his brother.

Kade's hands curled into fists. If Blane hadn't shoved him, following Kade down as they'd hit the deck, she might've shot him.

The switchblade was in his hand before Kade had made the conscious decision to pull it. A flick of his wrist exposed the razor-sharp edge.

Blane's weakness: women. This one in particular seemed to have gotten under his skin, and Kade could see why.

She was beautiful in a too-innocent-to-be-true kind of way. Kade had been taken in as well, from the moment he'd first spotted her in the courthouse, so he could hardly blame his brother. It appeared this particular woman—this Kathleen Turner—had managed to squeeze between the armor of not just one, but both brothers.

That alone was a compelling reason to kill her, and the events of tonight just added to the list against her continued presence among the living. She'd taken the code from the drive and then fucked his brother. Now she knew that he and Blane were working together, which was a threat to not only Kade, but Blane, too.

And the list kept growing.

Blane would be pissed, but he'd get over it. Yeah, Kade was just supposed to check on the girl, make sure she was there in this chick's apartment, but Blane didn't have to know she was dead. Kade could break the news later. A quick flick of his knife and it'd be done.

The more he considered it, the more logical it seemed, until there wasn't any reason Kade could think of *not* to kill her. Yeah, she had the code, but he'd gotten a look at her neighbor's apartment and seen the computer equipment. Kade would bet a thousand bucks she was in on the TecSol plan, too. He'd hack into her stuff and get what he needed. Easy-peasy.

A pillow over the face would be less messy, but it was also more personal and took longer. A slice to the carotid was efficient and slightly more merciful, in Kade's opinion, not that he cared much. It was a shame she was so pretty, but as she'd already proven, beauty was only skin deep.

Kade slowly drew back the covers she'd pulled to her neck. Luck was with him, she was sleeping on her back with her head turned to the side. Her hair was in the way, but it only took a moment to move the silky strands aside. There it was. If he looked closely enough, Kade could see a faint pulse underneath the delicate skin.

She made a slight noise and Kade froze, holding his breath. It had always amazed him how people could sense another human being's presence at times, no matter how silent he was. Science said there were five senses, but experience had proven to Kade that there were really six, though not everyone listened when their intuition told them things their mind didn't want to believe.

The girl made another noise, something like a whimper, and Kade watched in disbelief as tears leaked from her eyes to slide down her cheeks.

She was crying in her sleep.

But wait, was she asleep? Maybe this was a ploy, a tactic to get him to relent. Kade reached with the hand not holding a knife and gently touched her cheek with the backs of his fingers. It was like brushing against warm velvet, the track of her tears wet on his skin. She didn't so much as flinch at his touch, which told him she really was sound asleep.

Kade frowned, softly wiping away her tears until he caught himself and jerked his hand away. What the fuck was he doing? He was here to kill her, not comfort her. But she'd stopped crying and part of him was glad of that, though he refused to dwell on it.

Back to business.

He held the knife to her neck, finding just the right spot before the artery split on its way to the brain. Then, inexplicably, he hesitated.

Maybe the girl had gotten caught up in this without her consent. She was young and tiny. What defense did she have against people like the Santini brothers if they wanted to use her? They could have threatened her, hurt her, done all matter of vile things to ensure she did as she was told. Was Kade going to deliver her final judgment for a sentence that may not have been of her choosing?

Kade was familiar with being made to do something against your will, and there were few he hated more than those bullies who forced others to do their bidding. He'd once been a victim of men such as those, and he'd vowed to never let it happen again. But he was stronger, colder than the woman who lay innocently oblivious beneath his blade.

Slowly, he withdrew the knife. Another flick of his wrist and the blade disappeared.

He'd let her live, for now, and dig into who she was, her past, her friends, every move she'd ever made, every mistake she regretted, every guy she'd fucked, every friend she'd betrayed—Kade would find out. And so help her, if she wasn't everything she appeared to be—what he couldn't help hoping that she was—then she'd pay, and pay dearly.

CHAPTER ONE

Two Months Later

K*athleen is in danger."*

Blane's words ricocheted inside Kade's head as he drove. It took about seven hours to get from Buffalo to Indy. A quick glance at the clock said Kade would make it in six.

He didn't want to go, but Blane had left him no choice. Kade couldn't refuse Blane's plea for help, and wouldn't. If his brother needed him, then he'd be there, no matter what. It had always been that way, and it always would be that way.

Alone in the dark silence of his Mercedes, the road nearly empty of cars, Kade allowed himself to acknowledge the ridiculous surge of anticipation inside him at the thought that he'd get to see her again.

Her. Kathleen. A woman who'd haunted him since he'd first set eyes on her. He remembered now how close he'd come to killing her that one night, the night she'd run from Blane's house, and a chill ran down his spine.

She'd become his obsession after that night. He'd found everything out about her that was possible to know, determined to dig up something that would prove she was a fraud, something concrete he could take to Blane.

But there was nothing.

Born an only child, she'd been raised by two seemingly happily married people. Her father was a cop who had died in the line of duty; her mother a stay-at-home mom who'd passed from cancer not long ago. Though she'd grown up in a small town, she'd left soon after the death of her mother to move to Indianapolis, selling the family home and using the money to try to make a dent in the mountain of bills left from her mother's cancer treatments.

She'd done well in high school and even spent some time at college, studying prelaw of all things, before her mother had taken ill. Then she'd left to go back home and care for her. Working as a bartender in the small town of Rushville, her time had been consumed with work and nursing her mother, friendships falling by the wayside. Not one of the popular kids in school, by all accounts she'd been quiet and reserved, though everyone had seemed to like her well enough. *Kind* and *sweet* were the adjectives most often used to describe her.

Such an out-of-character thing for her to do, selling the home and moving away from everyone she knew. It puzzled Kade. Why had she done that?

Kade had been intrigued by her, absurdly glad that she'd come across him holed up in the law office that night he'd been snooping around. Of course, she'd been on a date with James-the-douche, but God, she'd felt good in his arms. He'd thought it was pure coincidence, a twist of fate, then she'd shown up again the day he'd been following that tech dude Mark.

Wincing a little at the memory of Kathleen cracking him over the head with a chair, Kade's lips twisted at how she'd gotten away that day. She'd listened to that little voice inside her head warning her that Kade was dangerous, and had taken steps to escape. From time to time, Kade had wondered which "guy on TV" he supposedly looked like because those teenage girls had swarmed like flies. He'd even had to scrawl a dozen or more illegible autographs—he'd drawn the line at posing for photographs—before he'd managed to extricate himself.

Seeing her do the dead-on Britney impression on Halloween in an honest-to-fucking-God schoolgirl costume had just sealed Kade's fascination and infatuation with her.

He'd been betting that night, betting she was a do-gooder bleeding heart who'd do what had to be done to protect her friends rather than put them in danger by asking them for help. That bartender had looked like he might interfere, so Kade had showed her his gun. As he'd expected, she'd gone all martyr, waving away help. Not that Kade had complained. Do-gooders were the most easily manipulated, they were so predictable. She'd been half-crocked, too, which was probably why she hadn't put up a fight when Kade had kissed her.

The kiss.

Kade had replayed it over and over inside his head. If it had been a photograph, the image would have been worn and faded from too much handling. Her taste, her scent, the feel of her body in his arms, the softness of her lips and warm slide of her tongue against his . . .

His cock twitched at the memory and Kade cursed under his breath, shifting uncomfortably in his seat. He shouldn't dwell on it, especially if he was going to be in close proximity to her. The last thing he needed was to be sporting a constant hard-on for his brother's girlfriend.

Which was why he shoved the memory aside and concentrated on why he was here as he neared Kathleen's apartment building.

From what Blane had said, it looked like Kade might be pulling bodyguard duty for Kathleen, which really sucked. He'd had to do that a couple of times before and didn't like it. Throwing himself in the path of a bullet meant for someone else just wasn't Kade's thing, even if that someone was five-foot-nothing, weighed half what Kade could bench-press, and made Cinderella look like an ugly stepsister.

Habit made Kade park a block away from Kathleen's apartment building, the instinct for secrecy too ingrained for him to pull up to her door. Glancing at his watch, he saw dawn was still a ways away. Might as well case the joint ahead of time, get a look at the surrounding area and possible escape routes and hiding places. He automatically checked his gun and magazine before sliding it into the holster attached to his hip.

Kade shrugged into his black leather jacket as he exited the Mercedes, locking it before pocketing the key. He never carried more than one key if he could help it. Keys made noise, even inside a pocket.

The neighborhood was a shitty one and Kade kept to the shadows as he walked, mentally mapping the streets and layout inside his head. It had snowed recently, but the pavement was clear. There were two flophouses within three blocks of where Kathleen lived and a stretch of corner run by a pimp with half a dozen whores. Not exactly the best place for a single woman to live alone.

Kade was on his way back to her apartment when he heard someone coming, and coming fast. The running footsteps grew closer and he melted further into the shadows, waiting. A woman turned the corner and light from the streetlamp fell on her face.

Kathleen.

She was running, her arms tightly gripping a dog, and she glanced behind her every few steps.

Well, she certainly was never boring, that was for damn sure.

Kade didn't even think, just stepped out from where he'd been hiding and let Kathleen run full bore into him, grabbing her arms to keep her from stumbling back and falling. She screamed and he covered her mouth with his hand, stifling her. Struggling, she let go of the dog and started pushing against him.

Kade jerked her closer, making her unable to fight him, and she finally looked up, her body stilling when her terrified eyes locked with his. It felt as though an electric shock went through Kade at the touch of her blue gaze, but he kept his reaction carefully hidden.

"Nice to see you, too, princess."

Her knees buckled and Kade had to tighten his hold, bringing her body more fully against his, so she didn't collapse altogether. The feel of her was like a hit of acid after being sober for too long, overwhelming and addicting. The object of his obsession was suddenly back in his arms, the scent of her hair teasing him with memories he'd tried to forget. She even had the same look in her eyes as she gazed at him.

I trust you.

"Someone's chasing me," she gasped, breathless from running.

Kade scrutinized her. She was obviously terrified. Her eyes were so wide the whites were showing and her mouth was pinched with fear. Her body trembled against his and he didn't think it was from the cold.

Drawing his weapon, Kade pushed Kathleen behind him. "Stay close," he ordered.

She didn't argue, just picked up the dog—when had she gotten a dog?—and did as he'd said, scurrying behind him. He felt her clutch a handful of his jacket as he headed back to her apartment. The gesture seemed to awaken a part of him he'd thought only Blane could touch— the protector rather than the killer.

Kade's eyes scanned the area for anything that wasn't supposed to be there, even as another part of his mind processed the unbelievable fact that Kathleen implicitly trusted him to keep her safe. He wanted to reach back and take her hand, pull her up next to him so he could wrap an arm around her, but that would be unwise. If there was someone out here, he might need both hands free, so Kade resisted the urge to shield her body with his.

But he saw no one and nothing on the way back. When they reached her apartment building, Kade holstered his gun. "There's no one around," he said.

"I saw someone earlier," she insisted, then pointed to a small knot of trees and bushes. "Over there."

Kade walked to where she'd indicated, crouching down to look at the ground. The snow was trampled here, the footprints large and heavy, pressing the tread of work boots into the ground. Someone had been here all right, and for a while. Kade glanced up and saw a direct line of sight into Kathleen's front window. Cigarette butts littered the area and Kade reached for one.

"What is it?" Kathleen asked, hovering over his shoulder.

"Cigarette butts," he replied, showing her one, then he stood. "Let's get you inside."

This time, he didn't hesitate to shield her body with his as they went up the stairs, though Kade would bet the guy was long gone by now.

Kathleen tripped on the top step and Kade moved fast, snagging her around the waist and hauling her backward against him, which was a big mistake.

Her scent clogged his throat as the silky strands of her hair brushed his neck. He had the insane urge to lean down and bury his face in the crook between her neck and shoulder and see if her skin there was as soft as he'd imagined. Kade tightened his hold ever so slightly. She was so small, seemed so fragile, her bones half the size of his, yet she was brave and strong. He admired that. She'd climbed out of the window of a burning house, fought and shot a man who would've killed her—and stood up to Kade when others would have quaked in fear. The bite of that stinging slap she'd given him in Blane's study still made him grin with reluctant admiration.

All these thoughts assailed Kade in the span of a second while Kathleen paused to catch her breath. She tried to move, but Kade's grip was locked tight and she had to tug on his arm.

"Thanks," she said.

Kade abruptly released her, startled that he'd been reluctant to do so. This was really becoming a problem.

Following her inside, Kade locked the door behind him, then glanced around curiously. The last time he'd been here had been a quick in-and-out, just long enough to leave the envelope with the money on the table. He hadn't lingered to look around, so he took the opportunity now.

She had a Christmas tree in her living room, shining gaily with festive lights. There were a shit-ton of ornaments on it, family ones by the look of it, their dates stretching back to before Kathleen had been born.

"Would you like some coffee?"

Kade glanced at Kathleen, who was now standing in the kitchen, nervously shifting her weight from one foot to the other. She'd taken off her coat and now stood clad in a T-shirt and pajama pants, looking as pure and innocent as it was possible to look without clutching a teddy bear.

Their eyes met and it seemed a thousand unsaid things passed between them. Her cheeks flushed and Kade wondered if she remembered the kiss they'd shared . . . the one he couldn't seem to forget. And perhaps she did because after a moment, she began to fidget. Kade bit his tongue to keep from telling her to stop, instead saying, "Sure. Coffee." Despite the tension between them, he could pretend everything was normal as well as she could.

She started a pot of coffee and disappeared into what Kade assumed was the bathroom, from the sound of the running water.

He had to get a grip. Kathleen belonged to Blane. Regardless of whether the relationship was just temporary—and which of Blane's relationships weren't?—they didn't poach each other's chicks. Frankly, the issue had never come up before. It wasn't like he and Blane shared the same taste in women. Kade thought of Blane's ex, Kandi, and grimaced. He had no idea what Blane saw in her that kept him coming back for more. She was cold enough to freeze a man's dick.

Shoving Kandi aside, Kade's thoughts shifted back to Kathleen. Part of the problem was she trusted him, thought he might be a *nice guy.* Kade could tell by how she'd softened toward him. The fear he'd initially seen in her eyes when they'd first met had faded. And the nicer she was to him, the harder it was going to be to keep a tight grip on his self-control. He needed her to hate him, to *loathe* the very sight of him. If she despised his very presence, it would certainly help keep some much-needed distance.

The last thing he wanted was to make another pass at Blane's girl-friend, especially now that Kade actually *knew* she was his girlfriend.

He shrugged off his jacket and tossed it over the back of a chair, then settled on the couch just as Kathleen emerged from the bathroom. She didn't glance his way as she poured two cups of coffee, merely asking, "How do you take it?"

"Black."

A moment later, she was handing him a steaming mug before curling up on the couch as well, though as far away from him as she could get. She'd brushed her hair and it gleamed golden in the soft light of the encroaching dawn. A whiff of mint said she'd brushed her teeth and her face had that fresh-scrubbed look. She was beautiful, still a fairy princess come to life, though her face was paler than usual for even her fair complexion and dark shadows marred the fragile skin beneath her blue eyes.

Whatever was going on was serious enough to make her hand tremble as she sipped her coffee.

"Why are you here?" she asked.

Ah, shit. Goddammit. Blane hadn't told her. Nice. Kade reached for the condescension he was so talented at dishing out.

"Wondered when you'd get around to that," he replied. "What's the matter? I can't drop by for a friendly visit?"

She gave a delicate snort. "The last time you were here, you'd been paid to kill me, so no, a friendly visit never crossed my mind."

"That's not precisely true."

Her eyes locked with his and Kade knew she was thinking about the money he'd left. The money she'd used to pay off fucking hospital bills instead of padding her bank account. He'd watched her credit card statement. She hadn't even gone on a shopping spree, instead sending nearly every dime to the creditors.

"Trust me, I wouldn't be here if I didn't have to be," he added, which was one hundred percent truthful. Resisting temptation had never been his strength. He took a sip of the coffee, which she'd made just how he liked it. Strong, but not bitterly so.

"Then why?"

Kade just looked at her over the rim of the mug. She was smart. She'd figure it out.

"Blane asked you to come, didn't he?"

"Ding-ding-ding." Give the lady what's behind door number one.

Kathleen's face grew red at his mocking, and Kade had a brief pang of regret before he shoved it aside. No kindness. No mercy. Or he'd do something they'd both regret and Blane would kick his ass, or at least try to.

"Why?" she asked.

Kade glanced away. "I'll let Blane tell you that," he said. The asshole. As if Kade was going to do his dirty work for him. "Where is he, by the way?"

"Asleep."

So Blane was sleeping here. Fucking at her apartment, Kade could see, but actually spending the night . . . Blane never did that. Was he here because he cared about the girl? Or because of what he'd mentioned on the phone, that she was in danger? Kade chose to believe the latter.

"It appears there's no end to the trouble you cause my brother," he said.

Out of the corner of his eye, he saw her stiffen. Good.

"He put his life on the line for you once before. Are you going to require he do it again?" Kade turned to look at her. Kathleen's face had gone completely bloodless, her mouth falling open in shock as she stared at him. *Time to seal the deal*, he thought.

"Find another rich guy to screw."

The words were bitter on his tongue and he knew they were unfair, but it didn't matter. In an instant, the softness in her eyes was gone, replaced by furious anger as her cheeks flooded with color.

"What's between Blane and me is none of your business," she retorted. "I don't care about his money, not that you'd believe me or that I even care what you think! I don't even know why you're here. Why don't you just get out? Go on! Get out!"

Tears were shining in her eyes and it was like a knife to Kade's gut. He struggled for control, to keep his wits about him, when all he wanted to do was pull her into his arms, press his lips to her eyes, and soak up the tears he'd caused. But he couldn't do that, so he unleashed his frustration in anger.

Looming over her, he watched with grim satisfaction as she shrank back, fear in her eyes. "Don't . . . push . . . me," he gritted out.

To her credit, she didn't cower, though it was obvious she was afraid of him. His gut twisted, but Kade told himself it was better this way, better she be afraid of him. She didn't have to know he'd sooner cut off his hand than hurt her. No one had to know that.

The door to her bedroom flew open and Kade knew without looking that Blane was there. The relief in Kathleen was nearly palpable as she jumped up and hurried over to him. A twinge went through Kade, which he ignored.

He could hear them talking and saw Blane wrap an arm around her for a hug. Jealousy spiked hard, taking Kade by surprise, and guilt followed close on its heels.

" . . . I doubt you took a gun with you," Blane was saying as Kade silently approached the couple.

"I thought about it," Kathleen said, "after I left."

Kade rolled his eyes. Typical. "She was running," he interrupted, leaning back against the counter. "Said someone was chasing her."

Kathleen started at his proximity, but Kade carefully avoided making eye contact with her. If he did, he was afraid Blane would be able to see everything he was hiding.

"Did you find anyone?" Blane asked, curving his arm over Kathleen's shoulders. She slid her arms around his waist and rested against him. Jealousy again bit deep.

"No," Kade said. "Just some cigarette butts. Looks like whoever it was had been there a while, with a good view of the apartment." He couldn't stop his gaze from flicking to where Kathleen's arms encircled Blane. It was almost as though she wanted Blane to protect her from Kade, which was the reaction that Kade had been going for, so why did it make him feel empty inside?

"Why is Kade here?" Kathleen asked Blane, looking up at him. "He said you asked him to come."

And that was his cue. "I'll step outside for this," Kade said. "Take a better look around now that it's getting light."

He felt Kathleen's eyes burning a hole in his back as he walked out the door.

Walking to his car gave him time to think. It had been a close thing, but he'd managed to pull it off. Kathleen hated and feared him. How well that boded for bodyguard duty, Kade didn't particularly care. He'd keep her safe whether she liked it or not, whether she cooperated or not.

Kade again saw the look in her eyes when he'd gotten in her personal space. The trust had been gone, replaced by fear . . . and hurt.

Cursing under his breath, he slid into the driver's seat of his car, then reached behind him to the seatback pocket and pulled out the packet of cigarettes and lighter he kept stashed there. A habit he'd picked up the first time he'd seen Blane smoking on a visit home from Afghanistan. Kade lit a cigarette and took a deep draw.

Blane had kicked the habit, mostly, and Kade didn't often light up either. Some occasions just called for something to steady the nerves, and carrying a bottle of vodka around in his car wasn't a smart idea. The cops around here hated Kade and it wouldn't take much in a traffic stop for them to haul him off to jail.

After a few minutes, Kade flicked the cigarette out the window and drove to Kathleen's lot, parking next to Blane's car. When he entered the apartment again, Blane must've broken the news to Kathleen because she looked decidedly unhappy. She didn't say a word before disappearing into the bathroom again and a moment later, Kade heard the shower start.

"I see that went well," he deadpanned.

Blane shrugged. "She'll get over it."

"So you want to tell me what's going on?"

"It's this case I'm on," Blane said. "Somebody with either a vendetta or motive is trying to get me to throw it and they're using Kathleen as leverage."

"What happened?" Kade asked.

"A sniper shot at her last night while she stood in my office."

Kade's blood ran cold and his fingers itched for that cigarette.

"Luckily, I spotted the sight on her and pushed her out of the way," Blane continued, "but I can't be at her side constantly. Someone's been following her, taking pictures, leaving creepy notes. I don't know what they'll try next."

"So you decided to call me," Kade interrupted, a sinking feeling in his gut.

"Yeah. I just need you to play bodyguard for a couple of weeks. It shouldn't take longer than that to get through this case. Stay here, take her to work, go where she needs to go—just keep her alive."

"Fuck," Kade groused, shoving a hand through his hair and turning away from Blane. Be constantly with Kathleen, day and night, for two weeks? It would be torture to be so close and unable to touch her, and Kade wasn't into self-denial.

"You're the only one I trust," Blane said. "I know this isn't your thing, but I need you. Will you do it?"

"Can't you just break up with her?" Kade asked instead, staring unseeing out the window. "Surely you can go a couple of weeks without sex."

"It's not just about that," Blane said. "And I'd like to keep the relationship intact, if I can."

"Why?" Now Kade turned. He wanted to see Blane answer this and gauge what, if any, feelings he had for the girl. Obviously, he wanted to keep her alive, but that could just be Blane's inherent protective streak coming out.

Their eyes met, green to blue.

"I like her, Kade. I care about her."

A moment passed, Kade understanding that Blane was leaving a lot unsaid there, but even those words spoke volumes. Blane had fucked a lot of women, but rarely had he spoken of them in terms of a "relationship," much less voiced any feelings he had for them.

Kade gave a curt nod.

Relief crossed Blane's face, adding more guilt to Kade's steadily growing pile. Blane reached for his shirt and pulled it on, doing up the buttons as he spoke.

"Try to be nice," he said to Kade. "She says you hate her and think she's a white-trash slut."

Kade shrugged. "If the shoe fits . . ."

"You really think I'd date someone like that?" Blane asked incredulously. "Give me some credit for my taste in women."

"One word: Kandi."

Blane put on his shoes and pocketed his keys, ignoring Kade's remark, though Kade could tell he'd hit a sore spot by the way Blane's jaw clenched. He was holstering his Glock when Kathleen emerged from the bathroom. She was wearing a fuzzy pink robe, her hair wet and trailing down her back.

Kade would bet his Mercedes she wasn't wearing anything under that robe.

The thought was unbidden, but now images of her naked body crowded through his mind. How she'd looked cradled in his lap in the hotel in Chicago when he'd saved her from Stephen Avery. The rosy tips of her nipples tempting him as they'd peeked through the blanket covering her, watching it slip from her shoulders to reveal the curve of her waist, the fullness of her breasts . . .

He was jerked from his thoughts by the sound of them arguing and his ears perked up.

"You know I need my job," she was saying. "Both of them."

"I told you I'd take care of you," Blane said.

"It would be foolish of me to quit my job," she replied. "You'd better go. You're going to be late for court." She was changing the subject, which obviously Blane caught on to as well. He pulled her to him and kissed her.

Kade's hands curled into fists, the green monster digging its claws in deep, and he forced himself to look away. He was a horrible person, a horrible brother, lusting after Blane's girl. Even as he thought this, he couldn't deny the burning desire to yank Blane away from Kathleen, make him stop touching her, stop kissing her.

Which put him in a real shitty mood.

Blane left, finally, and the silence in the apartment grew thick. Kade didn't speak. He didn't have anything to say. And frankly, the less interaction, the better.

"You should be protecting Blane," Kathleen said, grabbing his empty coffee mug and loading it in the dishwasher. "The case he's on has got people all riled up."

"Blane can take care of himself," Kade replied. As if Blane would allow Kade to provide a protective detail for him. Please. He'd look at Kade like he'd lost his fucking mind.

The cat jumped up on the counter and Kade absently scratched behind its ears. Kathleen didn't reply, just poured herself another cup of coffee and went to her bedroom, closing the door behind her.

Kade let out a deep sigh, pressing his fingers into his tired eyes. Shit, he was exhausted. If he sat down, he knew he'd be out like a light, so he remained standing. He wouldn't put it past Kathleen to sneak right by him and leave his ass passed out on the couch.

The television held little appeal, so he inspected the ornaments on the tree while he waited, taking a moment to go grab his suitcase out of the car. He hadn't put up a Christmas tree in his apartment . . . ever. There didn't seem to be a point.

Stomach growling, he pulled open the refrigerator, then frowned. What the hell did she eat? There was a package of bagels and a bit of cream cheese, some tired-looking grapes, and leftover Chinese takeout. Nice. He opened the freezer, his gaze lighting on a bottle of vodka—a cheaper brand than the kind he drank—and two containers of ice cream. Grabbing one, he looked at the flavor. Rocky Road.

Finally, Kathleen came out of the bedroom. She was wearing black slacks with a wide black belt, and a pale, ivory blouse made of some kind of thin, feminine material. It made her skin look like cream, the neckline a modest V that made her appear sexier than if it had been low-cut.

She'd curled her hair, the rose-gold waves tumbling over her shoulders and down her back. Black boots were on her feet and she grabbed a black peacoat and her purse. She didn't look at Kade and she didn't speak. Kade noticed she didn't eat any breakfast either, though he didn't blame her for that, considering the shit in her fridge.

Kade followed her outside, his eyes scanning the area and his palm resting on his gun while she locked the door. Getting in his car, he followed her little Honda to Blane's law firm.

To his surprise, she went to Blane's floor and settled herself in Clarice's seat. Kade guessed she was filling in temporarily and he scoped out the place before settling on the sofa across from her desk.

He sat up but rested his head back against the cushions. Maybe he could grab a quick power nap. Even if he hadn't been awake for over twenty-four hours, being in this place would put him to sleep. The boring monotony of the business world was like a shot of Novocain to his brain.

"You'll be here all day?" he asked, not bothering to open his eyes.

"Yep," he heard Kathleen say.

"Okay, then I'm going to get some shut-eye. Wake me if you want to leave." Not that she'd be going much of anywhere today, given the forecast.

"All right."

Kade was out inside of thirty seconds. When he woke, hours later, Kathleen was gone.

CHAPTER TWO

At first, he thought she'd just gone to get lunch or was on another floor. So Kade got up and headed into the bathroom to splash some water on his face and wake up. He'd slept longer than he'd intended, but he felt a helluva lot better.

When he returned, Kathleen still wasn't back. He glanced at his watch. It was after one. The skin prickled on the back of his neck, and he knew before he looked that her coat and purse would be gone.

Fuck.

Kade clenched his fists to keep from smashing one through the computer monitor. The firm's logo dancing merrily across the screen seemed to mock him. She'd taken advantage of his trust, leaving like that. And she must've been quiet, too, because Kade wasn't a heavy sleeper, which meant she'd intended to be sneaky.

He was so going to kill her, *if* she was still alive.

His cell rang and Kade yanked it out, muttering another curse when he saw it was Blane calling.

"Yeah," he barked into the phone.

"We're on a lunch break," Blane said. "Thought I'd check in on how Kathleen is doing."

Kade hesitated. He didn't want to lie, but neither did he want to tell his brother that his pain-in-the-ass girlfriend had managed to ditch her bodyguard in the span of a few hours.

"She's fine," he said. That was true. She'd been fine the last time Kade had seen her.

"Are you two getting along okay?"

"Like peaches and cream." The words fell out of Kade's mouth without him thinking first and he winced at the crude slang.

Blane seemed stunned silent, then said, "Really? That's the image you wanna go with?"

"Yeah, sorry. Just popped out. We're getting along fine," Kade back-tracked. "So when'll you be back?"

Blane sighed. "I'm not going to make it back to the firm today. Odds are we'll be at this for a while this evening. Tell Kat I'll call her later."

"Will do."

Kade ended the call, then dialed Kathleen's cell from memory. He'd never let himself program it into his phone, but he couldn't forget a number if he tried. It rang five times, then went to voice mail. He didn't leave a message. Where would she have gone? Somewhere for the firm?

With that thought in mind, he headed downstairs, running into one of the paralegals. His memory supplied the name.

"Lori, hold up," he called out as she walked past the elevators.

The woman stopped and turned, waiting as Kade approached.

"Mr. Dennon," she said, her voice calm and polite despite the flush in her cheeks. "What can I do for you?"

"I'm looking for someone," he said. "Kathleen Turner. Seen her around today?"

Lori frowned. "Not for a while. I thought I saw her leaving earlier this morning. Have you asked Diane?"

Kade shook his head. "No, but Kathleen's supposed to be filling in for Clarice, not doing runs. If she got bored, would she have gone to Diane for things to do?"

Lori shook her head. "Huh-uh, no way."

That seemed odd. "Why are you so sure?" he asked.

Glancing around, Lori sidled a bit closer and spoke in an undertone. "Diane *hates* Kathleen. She makes her life miserable and if Kathleen had a couple of days respite by filling in for Clarice, there's no way she'd willingly come back to Diane no matter *how* bored she was."

Kade frowned. "Why does she hate Kathleen?"

Lori shrugged. "I don't know, she just does."

"Okay, well, thanks. If you see Kathleen, tell her I'm looking for her."

"Will do." She gave him a smile and headed toward her cube.

So Diane hated Kathleen. It didn't surprise him. Kade had never liked Diane. She was a petty woman with a mean streak. The fact that her outlet for that mean streak was currently Kathleen just pissed Kade off. And if Blane knew about it and had done nothing, then that pissed him off even more.

Kade headed to the parking lot, unsurprised to see it had begun to sleet. And what was Kathleen driving in the snow and ice? A fucking Honda Accord. Just what Kade needed, to call Blane and tell him that his girlfriend had been killed in a car accident.

Fuck it. He was starving. Might as well drive around town, see if she'd gone to a Starbucks or something, and grab a bite to eat while he was at it. There was nothing he could do until she decided to show back up at the firm. Then there'd be hell to pay.

Kade tried calling her at least half a dozen more times as the afternoon went by, the weather and the roads growing worse every hour, but each time it went to voice mail unanswered. Worry gnawed at him, as well as frustration at his inability to do anything to find her. This would be the last fucking time she got away with something like this, that was for damn sure.

What if she was hurt? What if she'd been kidnapped, taken somewhere to be raped and left for dead? The nausea those thoughts produced made the sandwich he'd eaten turn to lead in his gut.

Images assaulted his brain until he could barely think straight. This was why it was a bad idea to care about anyone, he reminded himself. If you cared, then you gave them power over you—the power to hurt you, destroy you. It was a bad idea, caring about the girl. Look at what she'd done to him already, sweating it out in his car as he waited in the parking lot, glancing at his watch every three minutes.

By the time five o'clock rolled around, Kade had worked up a good head of steam. She had to know he was back here, waiting for her, she just didn't give a shit. Anger warred with worry as he chain-smoked his way through the rest of the pack of cigarettes.

A car pulling slowly into the lot caught his eye. A blue Honda Accord. It was her.

Overwhelming relief filled him, followed by furious anger. Kade pushed open his door as the car pulled into an empty space and he flicked away his cigarette. He approached the vehicle, watching as Kathleen carefully stepped out, her gaze on the slippery ice-covered asphalt.

She was alive. Fabulous. He was going to kill her.

The second she'd slammed the car door, he had his hand on her arm and spun her around.

"Where the *fuck* have you been?"

She gasped in surprise, her back flat against the car as she stared up at him.

"I-I'm sorry," she stammered. "I had some errands to run. And you were sleeping. I didn't want to wake you."

Bullshit. She was too goody-two-shoes to be anything less than truthful and Kade could tell immediately that she was lying to him. It shouldn't have bothered him, but it did.

"Errands that took all fucking day?" he prodded, wanting her to tell him the truth, to trust him.

"It's the weather! Traffic is horrible. I didn't mean to be gone so long."

Kade stared at her. That part looked to be true, but she was still lying about where she'd been. He changed tactics. "I had to lie," he growled, "and normally, I wouldn't care. But I had to lie to Blane when he called to check on you." He leaned closer to her. "I detest lying to my brother."

Fire sparked in her eyes. "Then don't," she snapped. She pushed away from him, but Kade grabbed her arm again, pulling her to a halt. He leaned down so their faces were mere inches apart.

"If you pull something like that again, I'll save someone the trouble and kill you myself."

His hissed words seemed to get through to her. Her eyes were wide and fearful and Kade saw her throat move as she swallowed. That knot in his gut felt like lead. In spite of himself, he hated to see her afraid of him.

"Let's go," he said, tugging her with him toward his car.

"Wait! Where are we going? I wanted to see Blane." She tried to pull against him to stop her forward momentum, but wasn't nearly strong enough.

It shocked Kade how much he hated hearing her say Blane's name.

"Blane can't come. He said he'd call later."

Kade unlocked the passenger door and none-too-gently shoved her into the seat. In another moment, he was sliding behind the wheel.

"What are you doing?" she asked. "I can take my car and you can follow me."

Fat chance of that happening. "Forget it, princess. I don't trust you." The nickname sprang to his lips before he could censor himself, but she didn't seem to notice, or if she did, she didn't mention it.

"You can't just leave my car here!" she protested as Kade drove out of the lot.

"No one will steal it, if that's what you're worried about."

She seemed to take that as a personal insult to her car, not that Kade cared. He was still trying to get a handle on his roiling emotions. Anger, worry, jealousy, guilt, desire. They were a tangled web in his mind.

It was silent in the car for the drive to her apartment, the atmosphere thick with tension. Kade gripped the steering wheel so tightly his knuckles were white, and as soon as he'd parked in her lot, she was up and out of the car.

That sparked another flame of fury and Kade was on her before she'd made it halfway up the flight of stairs, snagging her around the waist and tossing her over his shoulder. Just what he'd thought. About a buck ten.

She squeaked in surprise. "What the hell?" she yelled, grabbing his jacket as he finished climbing the stairs.

"If you're not going to wait for me to play bodyguard, then I'll have to keep doing things my way," he said.

"I don't want a bodyguard," she fumed.

Kade swung her back down onto her feet, keeping his hands on her waist until he was sure she was steady. "Then we're in agreement," he snarled, "because I don't want to be one. Now give me your keys."

Kathleen stared daggers at him, but dug out her keys, shoving them into his waiting palm with enough spunk to make his lips tip up at the corner. Shit, she was even more beautiful when utterly pissed off, her blue eyes flashing sparks.

Pulling his gun from its holster, Kade unlocked the door and stepped inside, carefully sweeping the place before going back to the door. Kathleen very obviously made certain she didn't touch him as she hurried past him. A moment later, she was slamming her bedroom door shut.

Kade glanced at the dog and cat snuggled together on the obnoxiously pink pet bed.

"She might be pissed," he deadpanned. "It's hard to tell."

The animals didn't react to the joke, the dog's tongue lolling as the cat blinked lazily at him.

With a sigh, Kade tugged off his shirt and took some clothes from his suitcase. A shower would be good, and a shave. Kathleen hadn't given him the grand welcoming tour, so he made himself at home in her bathroom, stripping off his clothes and stepping under the steaming spray.

Water was running in a warm cascade down his back when he heard the screaming.

He was out of the shower and yanking on his pants in the next breath, not bothering to fasten them, then out the door with gun in hand. Kathleen was still screaming.

Adrenaline flooded through him as he flung Kathleen's bedroom door open. She was standing with her back to the wall and as far away from the bed as she could get, wearing nothing but her shirt . . . which had blood smeared on it. Kade was in front of her in two strides and she stopped screaming.

"Kathleen, what happened? Where are you hurt?" He couldn't see any visible marks, and yet the blood was fresh. Frantically, he searched her skin, but her arms, legs, head were all unscathed.

She glanced down, seemingly unaware of what he was talking about.

"Get it off! Get it off me!" She was crying now, and yanking at her shirt until it was off, then flinging it away. Her knees suddenly gave out and she slid down the wall to the floor.

Kade dropped down in front of her, focusing his eyes on hers. She was hysterical, sobbing and shaking like a leaf.

"Kathleen, talk to me! Are you hurt?"

She gave a shake of her head. "The blood's not mine. It's from the eyeball."

What the fuck? The eyeball? "From the what?" he asked, but she only pointed.

Turning, Kade got up and saw a box on the bed and something on the floor where Kathleen had indicated. Crouching down, Kade saw a human eye, still bloody and intact. Grabbing the box, he used it to get the eye off the floor, then saw the packaging it had come in. There was no return address, but a scrap of paper was still inside. Taking it out, Kade read:

Kirk—your girl's baby blues are next. I'm always watching.

Blane had been right. There really was a sick fuck targeting Kathleen.

He returned to Kathleen, who asked, "What did it say?" Kade handed it to her. She read it without comment, though what little color remained in her face drained away.

There weren't many women who could've handled something like that, and yet Kathleen had. She'd stopped crying. The only indication she was upset was the terror in her eyes and the tremors wracking her body. Her knees were pulled tight to her chest, as though to make herself as small as possible.

Kade sat down next to her, taking the paper from her hands and setting aside the box and his gun. He pulled her into his arms, wishing there wasn't a sick part of him that enjoyed the feel of her skin against his despite the gruesome circumstances.

"You all right?" he asked. He couldn't help sliding his hand down her naked back. It was a gesture meant to be soothing, though he found it was far from that for him.

She nodded. "I'm fine," she said in a small voice.

Somehow Kade thought that would be her response no matter how badly she was hurting, upset, or afraid. But she wasn't fine. Her whole body trembled as she curled into him.

"Sorry for the screaming," she said, her voice slightly hoarse.

The fact that she felt she needed to apologize to him because he might be angry with her for losing it made him wince. "You're entitled," he said. An understatement.

Kade thought he should probably move, should probably stop touching her, but he didn't. Her skin was like silk beneath his fingertips as they trailed lightly up and down her spine, brushing over the thin strap of her bra. He tried not to think of how easily he could undo the clasp, a skill he'd honed way back in high school, or how her naked breasts would feel pressed against his chest.

Kathleen tipped her head back and Kade automatically looked down at her. As soon as his eyes met hers, he knew he was in trouble.

"Thanks for being here," she said, her blue gaze so trusting, it made his gut ache.

"No problem," he replied. Though it was a problem. A big one. And if he gauged the tension between them in any kind of accurate way, it wasn't just *his* problem. She had to feel it, too, the attraction and energy.

He couldn't help lifting his hand to brush her hair back from her face, the clear blue of her eyes steady on him as the strands sifted through his fingers. Kade couldn't look away from her, only too aware now of the lack of adequate separation between his hands and the parts of her body most off-limits to him.

Who the fuck was he kidding? *All* of her was off-limits, but that didn't stop him from touching her. Her hands rested lightly on his chest and his dick was hard as a rock inside his jeans.

Her gaze drifted down his neck and chest, and suddenly Kade was glad for the hours he spent staying in shape. The line of her throat moved as she swallowed and her eyes again lifted to his. Kade's self-control was slipping, the pull she had on him strong enough to make him forget all the reasons he had for keeping his distance. He didn't have it in him to push her away, not when every muscle was screaming at him to pull her closer. She'd have to do it.

He slipped his hand further down her back to where the thin satin covered her incredible ass. "You know, if I didn't know what a shitload of trouble you were, I might be persuaded to get the wrong idea," he murmured, forcing his lips into a smirk.

Kade's thinly veiled insinuation had the desired effect. She was on her feet and running for her closet in two seconds flat while Kade admired the view.

"You're vile and repulsive," she spat at him, pulling on a robe and belting it tightly.

Check and check.

"I'm not the one throwing themselves at me," he said, insolently shrugging.

As expected, that sent her off the deep end.

"*Throwing* themselves?" she spluttered. "You bastard! And to think I *thanked* you for being here!"

Kade got to his feet, then ducked as she launched a heavy scented candle at him. She'd already sent another projectile his way and was looking for more when the candle hit the wall.

Yeah, he'd guessed he wouldn't be touching her naked back again anytime soon. But seeing her mad was better than seeing her terrified, and after she'd gotten some of it out of her system, Kade dodged the barrage and grabbed her.

Pressing her body against the wall, he pinned her arm over her head. Her wrist felt way too fragile in his grip.

"Enough," he ordered.

"Fuck you."

Okay, that was hot.

Her snarled insult was a pleasant surprise, and a turn-on. God, he loved a woman who could go toe-to-toe with him. He shoved the thought aside.

"You feel that?" he said, getting close enough to smell her lingering perfume. "You feel that rage inside? Burning hot in the pit of your stomach?" He'd felt it from the time he was six years old.

She nodded, her brow furrowed in confusion.

"That's what's going to keep you alive. Hold on to it. Fear will only sign your death warrant. Stay mad, princess."

In the end, he couldn't resist pressing his lips to her forehead, the satin of her skin as intoxicating as the scent of her hair. She didn't move and he made himself grab the box and walk out of the bedroom.

Time for a cold shower.

Kade made quick work of it, bypassing shaving for now. The five-o'clock shadow was more than a shadow, but it'd have to wait. After dressing, he dialed a number on his cell.

"Donovan, hey, it's Dennon," he said. "Listen, I have a . . . bit of a situation. Was hoping you could help me out."

In a few minutes, he'd explained what was going on.

"I got a handle on it," he said, "but I could use some forensics on the eyeball."

Grabbing a pen, Kade scrawled an address on a notepad left on the kitchen counter.

"Got it. I'll be there shortly," he said, his cell beeping to inform him of another call. He switched over. It was Blane.

"What a shitty fucking day," Blane said by way of greeting. "Tell me everything's okay with Kat."

"Everything's okay with Kat," Kade echoed. He decided to hold off on telling Blane about the eye.

Blane sighed heavily. "Good. One less thing to worry about. I had an idea to throw off whoever's watching."

"What's that?"

"No time to explain. I'll show up at the bar tonight. Just tell Kat to play along, okay?"

"Will do." *Play along.* That sounded like something Kathleen wasn't going to like very much.

"Thanks. Gotta go."

Kade ended the call just as Kathleen emerged from her bedroom.

She was in her usual work garb of black pants and a black shirt, the neckline low enough to make his mouth water. Her skin was the color of pearls against the dark material, the color making her hair shine in the ponytail she'd put it in. But the set of her lips was grim and the circles under her eyes couldn't be fully concealed with makeup.

"I called a buddy of mine who works for the FBI," Kade explained. "He's going to get the eye and note examined, see if there's anything we can find out about where it came from."

She nodded, then hesitated before saying, "The person . . . the eye . . . they're dead, aren't they."

Ah, the bleeding heart. He should've known that she wouldn't be thinking about herself and the danger she was in, but about the person who'd likely died at the hands of the sick fuck who'd sent the package.

Kade's fingers itched to touch her again and he didn't resist the compulsion to step closer to her. She swallowed, her gaze lifting to his.

"I'd say so, yeah."

Another nod, and he saw her hands clench into little fists. Time to change the subject.

"I talked with Blane. He's had a bad day."

"That makes two of us," she said.

Her wry wit, even in the face of what had happened tonight, amused Kade.

"He said he'd come by the bar tonight and that I'm to tell you to 'play along.'"

"Play along? What does that mean?"

Kade shrugged. "I have an idea but I'm sure we'll find out soon enough."

Kathleen chewed her lip, seemingly lost in thought, and it occurred to Kade that it would be just like her to keep things from Blane—information that could be beneficial to keeping her alive.

"Is there anything else that's happened?" he asked. "Anything that you haven't told Blane?"

Kade could tell immediately that he'd guessed right. Everything she was thinking showed on her face. She didn't have a deceitful bone in her body and he had a brief flash of regret for ever believing she'd been in on a plot against Blane.

"Tell me," he ordered, before she could gather her wits.

She hesitated, then spoke. "It was yesterday in the morning. I went out to my car to go to work."

"And?" Kade prompted.

"And there was a dead possum," she blurted. "Someone had slit its little throat and they'd used its blood to write in the snow on my car."

Kade inhaled sharply, his jaw clenching. Mutilation of animals was never a good sign.

"And it said?" he asked.

"It said *Kirk's whore*." She raised an eyebrow. "Maybe a friend of yours?" Ouch.

She ducked past him, but Kade reached and snagged her arm, jerking her back.

"You didn't think that was something you should've told Blane?" he asked. *Who would've gone apeshit*, he thought but didn't say. God knows how close this guy had been to her while she'd been looking at the dead animal. He could've been watching, just waiting for the right moment. The thought chilled Kade, which just pissed him off.

"Since you haven't been around to notice, Blane's been a little busy. The last thing he needs is for me to be laying more crap at his doorstep." Her sneering said she wasn't backing down no matter how hard he was gripping her arm.

And it wasn't like he could tell her that he'd have the image of her with *her* throat cut in his head to add to the nightmares he already fought on a nightly basis, so he lashed out.

"Usually, I would agree," he snarled. "But he's been shot at twice now, and I'm not willing to let him get hurt if you're the target."

"Gee, thanks for the support," she said, her sarcasm thick. "With a bodyguard like you, I might as well just slit my wrists." With that, she snatched her arm away and stalked to the door, angrily jerking on her coat.

Kade had to stifle a full-out grin at that, Kathleen again taking him by surprise. It was rare that someone made him laugh, so he had a great appreciation for it when it happened.

He was by her side by the time she'd opened the door, gun in hand and shielding her from the direct line of sight of anyone who might be watching. He scanned the lot while she locked the door, then didn't bother asking before wrapping an arm around her and tucking her against his side. She stiffened immediately.

"Is this really necessary?" she asked, trying fruitlessly to push away from him.

Her squirming only served to press her breasts and hips more closely to his side. As if he needed reminding.

"Shut up and walk."

Silence again reigned in the car on the way to the bar and Kade took her inside the same way he'd gotten her to the car—by using his body as a shield and keeping every sense on high alert for a possible ambush. The irony that he was putting himself in harm's way for this chick was not lost on him.

And he didn't like it.

"I have to leave for a while," he told her once they were inside. "Meet my friend and give him the package. What time do you get off?"

"I work until close tonight."

Good. "I'll be back before then."

"That's just great. I'll be counting the minutes." Her snide comment coupled with a fake smile ignited his temper. Here he was ready to take a fucking bullet for her and she was being a little snot. Somehow he bet Blane had never seen *this* particular side of Kathleen.

"Try to lose the bitchy before I get back," he retorted, then he was out the door before she could come up with some other wiseass remark to piss him off, which would be bad—or make him laugh, which would be worse.

He was already attracted to her. He didn't want to *like* her, too.

It took over an hour to drive to the FBI forensic lab and drop off the eye. Kade called Donovan again on his way back to the bar.

"It's in," he said. "Have them run handwriting analysis, too, along with prints. The girl's prints and mine will be on there, but maybe he left behind some of his own."

Donovan confirmed the orders, then said, "I opened a case on this. I'm having an agent go through missing persons now to see if we can find a possible match for the eye. I can't put any agents on the girl right now, though. Local PD might help."

"That's fine. I'm on protective detail for the foreseeable future."

"All right then. I'll be in touch."

"Thanks, man." Kade ended the call as he pulled into the lot for The Drop. When he walked in, he saw that once again, Kathleen had a talent for being a shitload of trouble.

She was standing by a table of guys, one of them with his arm locked around her waist. As Kade watched, the biggest asshole pulled at the neckline of her top to peer down inside. Kathleen grabbed a mug of beer and tossed it in his face. Kade's lips lifted in admiration as the man let her go, but she didn't get away quick enough. In the next moment, he'd jerked her back by her hair and had his hand squeezing the back of her neck.

And Kade went from amused to enraged in the span of a split second.

People took one look at him and scurried out of his way as he stalked toward the table. Kade didn't notice, his eyes locked on the asshole who was going to regret laying a finger on Kathleen.

"—already got a beer dumped on me, I should at least get to cop a feel, right, sugar?" the guy was saying.

"Let her go and I might consider not breaking your arm," Kade said. Which was a lie. He'd be lucky if that was all Kade did to him.

The guy glanced at Kade, assessing him. Deciding he wasn't a threat—big mistake—he dismissed him with a "Fuck off."

Perfect.

Kade had a hand on the guy's arm and another on the back of his neck. A twist of the wrist and Kathleen was free, then a hard kick to the guy's chair dislodged him enough for Kade to slam his face into the wooden table. He missed a mug by a hair. Damn. That would've left a nice mark.

The mugs toppled to the floor and shattered as the other men jumped to their feet, their eyes wide at Kade's assault. A hard jerk and Kade heard the satisfying crack of a broken bone and a dislocated shoulder.

The asshole was grimacing in pain, his face white, and Kade leaned down to whisper in his ear.

"Apologize to the girl, fucktard."

"I . . . I'm sorry," he babbled.

"Tell her you're a fucking asshole and that you won't bother her anymore."

"I'm a . . ."

"Fucking asshole," Kade repeated.

"I'm a fucking asshole and . . ."

"And you won't bother her anymore," Kade prompted.

" . . . and I won't bother you anymore. I swear."

Kade jerked his injured arm up higher, satisfied when the guy howled in pain. He whispered again. "I see you in here again, your friends will have to carry you out because I'll break both your fucking legs."

He let him go and the group of them hustled fucktard out the door. Just then, another waitress and a guy—probably the cook, judging from his stained apron—appeared.

"What happened?" the girl asked. Her name tag read *Jill*. "Are they gone?"

"Yeah," Kathleen answered. "They're gone. Thanks anyway, though." Her voice wasn't all that steady. She redid her ponytail in what seemed more of a nervous reaction than an actual attempt to fix her hair. Looked like those dicks had shaken her more than she was letting on.

Kathleen dropped to her knees and began cleaning up the mess while the other waitress went to get a mop. Kade watched for a moment as she picked up glass. Her knees were in a puddle of beer, but she didn't seem to notice. He crouched down.

"You all right?" he asked.

She glanced at him. "I'm fine." Her lips stretched in a fake smile that was more of a grimace.

Kade raised an eyebrow, but Kathleen just cleared her throat and dropped her gaze, resuming her task with shaking fingers. It would seem pretty asshole-ish if he didn't help, so Kade picked up some glass, too, standing back when Jill returned with a mop.

Finding an empty seat at the far end of the bar, Kade settled in. After a while, Kathleen asked him if he wanted anything to drink. She returned with a mug of fresh black coffee and slid it in front of him, which was the extent of their interaction for a couple of hours.

It was busy at first, then it slowed down, and Kade kept a close eye on her, which wasn't a hardship. She was graceful in her movements, efficient as she worked. Occasionally, she'd laugh at something one of the waitresses or customers said, and soon Kade was watching for when those moments occurred.

Her whole face would light up, her lips spreading wide in a smile as she laughed, a feminine sound that didn't grate on his nerves, but made

Kade want to smile, too. It was a carefree sound, evoking feelings and memories he could only recall having at a very young age. It simultaneously made him want to hear more . . . and made his chest ache with a feeling too close to loneliness.

She was singing softly to herself—some ridiculous Christmas carol—when Blane walked in. The blonde on his arm made Kade's eyebrows climb, but it damn near made Kathleen gasp, judging by her reaction. The glass she'd been washing slid back into the water as she watched them walk to a booth and sit down. And Kade abruptly realized what Blane's ploy was.

Dick. He could've at least warned her.

"Excuse me, bartender, can I get a refill?"

Kathleen turned, her face blank, then seemed to realize it had been Kade who'd spoken. She grabbed the coffee pot and walked to his end of the bar, stiffly pouring more coffee in his mug.

"Play along, remember?" he said in an undertone.

She blanched and Kade tipped his head ever so slightly toward Blane. Understanding dawned in her eyes and her entire body relaxed. Interesting. So she felt enough for Blane to be upset that he'd bring another woman here.

Kade nipped that thought in the bud. It wasn't like she was in love with him. Any woman would be pissed. Their pride demanded it. It had nothing to do with what feelings she may or may not have for him.

"Oh my God!"

They both turned to see another waitress standing by the bar, her eyes glued to Blane and the blonde.

"Isn't that your boyfriend?" she asked Kathleen, appalled.

Kade winced at the designation. If some woman called him her "boyfriend," he'd slit his fucking throat. Or hers.

Kathleen and the waitress started talking, their heads together, and Kade watched as the waitress approached Blane's table a few moments later, then hurried back to report to Kathleen. Throwing her shoulders back, she walked to the table.

The three of them talked for a minute and Kade couldn't hear them, but he could see perfectly well when Kathleen dumped an entire glass of ice water right in Blane's lap. Kade had just taken a sip of coffee and damn near spit the whole thing out.

Kathleen was making tracks back to the bar, high-fiving the waitress when she got there, and sent a quick glance Kade's way. What else could he do but raise his mug in silent toast to the size of the balls she had to possess to pull off a stunt like that. Blane was never going to hear the end of it, courtesy of Kade.

Kade watched in silent amusement as Blane hustled the blonde and his soaked slacks out the door. Yeah, it was below freezing out there. Have fun with that.

By the time closing rolled around, Kade'd had enough coffee to keep him awake for half the night. Kathleen hadn't said a word beyond refilling his cup and she headed to the back for what he assumed were more supplies. But after several minutes, she hadn't returned. Uneasy, Kade was just getting ready to head back there when she reappeared carrying several bottles.

Her face and neck were flushed and she wouldn't look at him. Her lips were pink and swollen and he could read the signs of arousal on her as though she held a flashing neon sign.

"Christ," he groused. "Blane couldn't stay away, could he?" Not that Kade could blame him. Knowing Kathleen had just been making out with Blane in the back room was enough to give him an uncomfortable niggle of jealousy. "Blane doesn't usually do something so stupid," he continued, irritated at her, at Blane, and now at himself.

"He made sure he wasn't seen," she said.

Her defense of Blane only pissed him off more. "You don't know that. And neither does he. It was a dumb move."

She didn't reply, just grabbed a rag and started wiping down the bar.

"We're going to have to fix it," he continued, an idea forming in his head. An idea she wasn't going to like and one Blane would hate, but hey, what he didn't know . . .

"How?" she asked.

Kade's lips twisted. "Ever pick up a customer, princess?" Of course she hadn't. Little Miss Innocent would be shocked at the idea of a one-night stand. But she got the message, judging by the appalled look on her face.

Yeah, that wasn't a blow to his pride or anything.

He held her coat for her and she obediently slid her arms into the sleeves, hurrying to retrieve her purse from under the bar. The waitress caught up with her and they started talking in an undertone, both of them shooting glances his way. Kade's lips lifted in a one-sided smile.

The waitress headed out the front and Kade herded Kathleen toward the back. Just before she reached for the door, he grabbed her arm.

"Try to make it look good," he said, "or at least believable."

Confusion was written in her eyes as she looked at him, but she nodded, heading outside and locking the door behind them. And maybe Kade could be honest enough with himself that his pulse was racing in anticipation of what was coming.

He scanned the alley. Not only was no one around, but there wasn't even a place someone could hide and watch. Which made what he was about to do damn near inexcusable, but that didn't stop him from doing it.

Grasping her shoulder, Kade spun Kathleen around, his hands pressed to the wall on either side of her head as his body closed in on hers.

"What are you doing?" she squeaked.

"Making it look good," he said. "Pretend you like me and I'll do the same."

He couldn't resist her. Even here in the back alley, her elusive scent teased him. Leaning into her, he nuzzled her neck where the scent was potent. Kade's eyes slid shut. This was what he remembered. The last time he'd smelled that was when he'd been in her apartment the morning after Blane had disappeared. She'd been sleepy and rumpled from bed and he'd had her pinned to the wall just like this.

"Put your arms around my neck." He wanted her to touch him. Her hands tentatively rested on his shoulders. The slim fingers clutching at the leather of his jacket made him wish he had on fewer layers.

"Blane's not going to like you doing this," she said in his ear.

No fucking kidding. "Blane told me to keep you alive. This nut job needs to think you and Blane are through, that you have no influence over him. So I'll do what I have to do."

He slipped his hands inside her coat, already knowing how well she fit in his palms. The curve of her waist, flare of her hip—all of it had been committed to memory. But memory hadn't done justice to the feel of her, the softness of her skin, the sweet brush of her breath against his ear.

Tasting her was imperative and he no more could have resisted than if someone had pulled a gun on him and ordered him to step away. He pressed his lips against her neck. Once, twice, a third time.

"Close your eyes," he whispered.

Kade forgot everything—where they were, why he was doing this. He was blind and deaf to all but the woman in his arms.

He pressed closer, working a leg between her thighs. Desire coursed through his veins as he nipped at her delicate collar bone, moving toward the tantalizing swell of her breasts bared by the deep V of her shirt.

His tongue traced the line of skin at the edge of the fabric, dipping between her breasts as his hands moved to cup her ass. His dick ached inside the confines of his jeans. Kade pulled her hips closer and heard the soft gasp from her lips as his thigh connected with her pussy. He could almost pretend he could feel the heat of her through the fabric separating his skin from hers.

Kathleen was breathing hard now, her fingers threading through his hair in a way that made him have to swallow a groan.

He didn't even think. He just spoke. "You taste like cotton candy and smell like spring after a storm," he murmured against her skin.

And those must have been the magic words because, while she hadn't been pushing him away, now she melted into him like warm caramel. It was amazing, exquisite, and left him wanting more.

Which was precisely when reality hit like a ton of fucking bricks. What the fuck was he doing? Judging by how things were going, in another two minutes he'd have her pants off and he'd be fucking his brother's girlfriend in a goddamn alley. He was supposed to make sure she hated him. She was pretty far from hating him right now. Instead, she was clinging to him like a vine while he licked her neck and tried to see if he could keep one hand on her ass and pull her neckline down with the other hand so he could suck her nipple into his mouth.

He said the first hateful thing that popped into his head. "Do you always melt for a man who'll fuck you up against a wall?"

Kathleen stiffened immediately, a sharp gasp issuing from her lips, and this time it wasn't one of pleasure. Her fingers were still threaded through his hair and she fisted a handful, causing a sharp pain in Kade's scalp. He welcomed the pain. She should knee him in the balls for that one.

She pulled on his hair until he lifted his head from her breasts to look her in the eye.

"I just closed my eyes and pretended you were Blane."

And there it was. Maybe not an *actual* kick in the nuts, but it hit somewhere just as sensitive. Kade clenched his jaw. The sugar-coated venom in her voice had the same fire it'd had earlier. But the thought of Blane's hands and mouth on her, of Kathleen lying spread beneath him, sent a jolt of burning jealousy through Kade. Guilt was close on its heels.

"And who do you pretend it is when it's Blane?"

Kade's vicious insult smothered the fire in her gaze and he watched in dismay as her face visibly paled. Hurt and betrayal echoed in her eyes and now the guilt Kade felt was twofold.

He cursed and stepped back, his arms immediately feeling her loss. "Let's go." Taking her hand was necessary for his sanity, an unspoken apology he couldn't utter. She hated him all right. And that was good. Because *that*—kissing her, touching her—could not *ever* happen again. If it did, Kade didn't think even the threat of overwhelming guilt and regret would make him stop.

CHAPTER THREE

Kathleen's silence as he drove seemed to accuse Kade. He'd hurt her, which she didn't deserve, but he couldn't make himself stop. He felt like he was sliding down a slickened, ice-covered hill toward a cliff, desperately trying anything to stop the destruction waiting for him at the bottom. Because that's all this would be—it's all it *could* be. Obsessing over his brother's girl was about as clichéd as he could get and one helluva way to fuck up his relationship with Blane.

But then again, it wasn't like Kade had ever chosen the easy way.

"Where were you really today?" he asked her. There was a sicko out there, that much was certain. It would be wise for Kade to get back on track. Blane hadn't called him here to fuck with his girl, but to keep her safe.

"What are you talking about?" she replied.

As if she could lie to him. Kade was a master at lying, and as such, he knew how to spot 'em. "Don't give me that crap about errands again. I'm not an idiot, princess, and I want to know where you were."

But she refused to answer. Turning away from Kade, she stared silently out the window.

Kade was cussing a blue streak inside his head, his hands clenched on the steering wheel. *Way to go, dick.* She'd trusted him earlier today, but that little stunt outside the bar had set things back a whole fucking lot, and he had only himself to blame.

Kathleen didn't speak until they were pulling in to her building's parking lot.

"You can't stay," she blurted, still not looking at him. "Not with me."

Alarm shot through Kade, but he carefully disguised it when he replied. "You don't get a say in this, princess." Hoping to end her little rebellion, Kade got out and shut the door behind him, but he'd been wrong. She was out of the car and met him on his way around to her side.

"I absolutely have a say!" She was furious, angrily poking her finger into his chest. Ouch. "And I don't want you here. Tell Blane whatever you have to, I don't care, but you have to leave. I know that you couldn't give a shit what happens to me, and I know you don't want to be here. So just go already!"

Her eyes were bright with unshed tears, though Kade didn't think she realized it. Every word had been like sinking a claw into his skin. She believed he didn't care, that he didn't want to be here, and while she was right on that last part, it was for an entirely different reason than what she thought.

Kade pressed his lips firmly together so he wouldn't speak the words to contradict her, to tell her he was sorry, that he didn't know what the fuck he was doing, and that he felt like he was drowning.

Turning on her heel, Kathleen hurried away, not looking back until she'd unlocked the door to her apartment. Kade stared at her, willing her to come back, beckon him in, anything. But she just went inside and closed the door behind her.

Kade's breath let out in a rush. He hadn't realized he'd been holding it. Bracing his palms on the hood of his car, he bent and took a deep breath. He had to get a fucking grip. Blane was going to kick his ass just for being a little bitch.

Straightening, Kade headed for the stairs, taking them two at a time. A moment later, he was letting himself into Kathleen's apartment. She'd be pissed if she knew he could break in inside of thirty seconds, but it wasn't like he planned on telling her anytime soon.

Tigger and the dog ran to greet him and Kade absently crouched down to pet them, the sound of running water meeting his ears. Kathleen was taking a shower. *That* was an image he didn't need inside his head.

Then he heard another sound. Getting to his feet, he moved toward the bathroom, pausing outside the door to listen.

Kathleen was crying.

Fuck.

Kade could hear her sobs over the spraying water and it felt like someone had sucker punched him in the gut. His hand was turning the doorknob before he even realized what he was doing.

What was he going to do? Bust into the bathroom while she was taking a shower just because she was bawling? Really?

Kade jerked his hand off the knob as though it burned and took a step back. Christ. He scrubbed both palms over his face. He had to get out of here.

He called Donovan on his way to his car.

"Do me a favor," he said. "Send a couple uniforms to watch the girl for a few hours. I need to . . ." he faltered, " . . . be somewhere." He winced. Yeah, that was lame.

"No problem," Donovan said. "They'll be there in ten."

"Thanks, man."

Kade waited until he saw the cop car pull up and park on the street. He flashed his lights and waited for the return flash before he drove out of the lot, then he headed for Blane's.

He fully expected Blane to be pissed when he arrived. What he didn't expect was to meet Kandi leaving his house.

"What an unpleasant surprise," she sneered as they met on the sidewalk. "Blane's favorite charity case."

Kade took note of the shirt she was wearing—Blane's—and his eyes narrowed. "Hey look, it's Blane's *easiest* lay, though not his best. It's still early so I'm guessing that was a wham-bam-don't-let-the-door-smack-you-in-the-ass."

Even in the low light, Kade saw a flush creep up her neck and her eyes flashed.

"At least Blane doesn't have to pay for it," she retorted.

"Oh, he pays," Kade shot back. "Trust me on that one." His lips twisted in a smirk as his gaze ran over her. "Don't let me keep you. I'm sure you need your—well, not beauty sleep, that's for sure. Let's say not-look-like-a-middle-aged-hag sleep, shall we?"

He brushed past her as she sputtered in anger.

"Fuck you, Kade!" she called after him.

"Not on my worst day, sunshine."

Kade closed the door behind him and walked through the darkened foyer. God, he'd never know what the hell Blane saw in that bitch. His cell buzzed in his pocket and he glanced at the caller ID before stepping into Blane's study.

"Looking for me?" he asked.

Blane turned, grimacing as he ended the call and tossed his phone onto his desk. "I just got a voice mail from Kathleen. She said you staying there, protecting her, 'isn't going to work out.' What the fuck does that mean? Did you piss her off? Can't you *not* be an asshole for a couple goddamn weeks? For me?"

Yep. Blane was pissed. Shit.

Too bad Kade was, too.

"Maybe *you* could be over there watching her back if you didn't need time off from your girlfriend to screw Kandi."

Blane's jaw clenched. "I'm not screwing Kandi. Not that it's any of your business."

"So she just *happens* to be at your house, wearing your clothes, at nearly one o'clock in the morning, and you're not sleeping with her?" Kade snorted in derision.

"That's right," Blane said.

Kade just shook his head. "I've seen you bounce from woman to woman and back to Kandi too many times to believe that."

"Can we get back to Kat now?" Blane said impatiently. "Why are you here and not there?"

Kade bypassed Blane to pour himself a drink. "I've got someone watching the place. She's fine. Just taking a break, that's all."

"Bullshit. What'd you do?"

"You know what?" Kade slouched onto the leather sofa, stretching one arm along the back while he took a sip of the aged scotch. "Let's talk about all the things your 'girlfriend' isn't telling you." He used quotey fingers for *girlfriend*.

"What are you talking about?"

"Like the dead animal someone left for her yesterday morning, complete with creepy message written in blood on her car. Or the package she got today. A human eye, lovingly wrapped and left on her doorstep." His lips twisted. "Someone's been watching too many movies," he singsonged, waggling his eyebrows. He took another drink of the scotch.

Blane stared at him. "Are you shitting me right now? I asked her if anything had happened yesterday. She said no."

Kade shrugged. "She lies."

"No, she doesn't. I know her and she's not the lying type."

Kade snorted. Blane could usually spot a liar, and Kathleen was awful at it. Maybe he had a blind spot when it came to her. "Maybe you don't know her as well as you think you do," he said.

Blane cursed, turning away and shoving his hand through his hair. He walked behind his desk and started searching through drawers.

Kade frowned. "What are you looking for?"

"A fucking cigarette."

Digging into his inside jacket pocket, he tossed a pack at Blane, who caught it. "Better use air freshener afterward," Kade cautioned as Blane lit up. "Mona's like a bloodhound."

Blane took a deep drag before replying. "I can handle Mona," he said on an exhale, smoke writhing in the air.

"Yeah, but not as well as me."

Blane glanced sideways at him. "True."

"Any idea who'd pull a stunt like this?" Kade asked, watching as Blane grabbed a file off his desk. He dropped it in Kade's lap, then sat opposite him in one of the two matching wingback chairs.

"No clue." He gestured to the file. "There's info on the case. You can take a look. See if anything jumps out at you."

Kade started flipping through the file. "So what happened today?"

"One of my witnesses disappeared. Brian Bowers. A SEAL who was on the same mission. He was going to testify in my client's defense. Now he's in the wind."

Kade glanced up. "That doesn't sound good."

"No, it doesn't," Blane replied, taking another drag. "And between that and another one doing a one-eighty on his testimony, things don't look real great for my guy."

"That sucks."

"Yep."

They sat in companionable silence for a few minutes, Kade polishing off the scotch while Blane finished his cigarette.

"How's Kat holding up?" Blane asked.

"Better than most," Kade said. "I dropped the eye with a buddy at the FBI, asked them to run forensics on it."

"Someone sent her a fucking *eye*?" Blane asked, shaking his head. "Really? Fuck me."

"No shit. This is one serious motherfucker. Think it'd be a good idea for Kathleen to have a sick day. Or three."

Blane nodded. "Agreed. I'm at court first thing in the morning, so call it in to Diane, would you?"

"You bet."

There was a pause before Blane asked, "So. You and Kathleen. How much sucking up do you have to do before she'll let you back into her apartment?"

"I'll use my charm," Kade joked.

Blane rolled his eyes. "God forbid."

An image of Kathleen in his arms, Kade's tongue in her cleavage, flashed behind Kade's eyes. He squirmed uncomfortably, then got to his feet.

"I'm headed back then. She ought to be in bed by now. She can't throw me out if she's asleep," he reasoned, avoiding Blane's eyes.

Blane heaved a sigh. "Try not to piss her off, will you? She's sweet and nice. Too nice."

Sweet and *nice* weren't what Kade thought of when he pictured Kathleen snarling a *Fuck you* at him or when she'd been hurling heavy objects at his head. But he didn't mention that to Blane.

"Got it." Setting aside his glass, he caught Blane's eye. "I'll keep her safe," he promised. "You do the same. If somebody kills you while I'm playing bodyguard for your flavor of the month, I'm gonna be pissed."

Blane just nodded, a small smile playing about his lips. "You worry like an old woman. Get the hell out."

Kathleen was asleep by the time Kade got back, which was a relief. She seemed zonked but looked like she'd tossed and turned, the covers now all twisted around her bare legs. She was just wearing that damn T-shirt to bed again. He was going to buy her a pair of those footy pajamas for Christmas just so he wouldn't be tempted to stand here and stare at her satin- and lace-covered ass all night.

Carefully, Kade tugged the blankets free and pulled them up over her, not wanting to wake her. But she didn't move, her breaths even and deep. Both the dog and cat were snuggled in the bed with her, the lucky little bastards.

Kade grabbed Kathleen's purse on the way to the living room, flicking on a light before dumping its contents on the couch. He discarded his jacket, then tugged off his shirt, tossing it in the general direction of his suitcase.

Grabbing her cell, he popped open the battery cover. From his pocket, he pulled out a tiny GPS he'd put together himself and stuck it inside.

"No more pulling that disappearing shit on me again," he muttered to himself as he replaced the cover.

Digging through the pile of stuff, he found some lip gloss, a small hair brush, two pens emblazoned with the firm's *Gage, Kirk, and Trent* logo, a dog-eared book that looked like it had been read several times—*Vampires? Really?* Kade thought—a few receipts, a checkbook with about three hundred dollars and change in the account, a set of keys, and several scraps of paper. Looking through these, one caught his eye.

"Jackpot," Kade murmured, scanning the list of names and addresses. They were all in the file Blane had given him. Looks like Little Miss I-Ran-Errands had been doing some investigating of her own. Interesting.

Shoving the paper in his pocket, Kade replaced the stuff in the purse and set it back on the kitchen table. Unsurprisingly, Kathleen hadn't made up the couch for him, but that was okay. A homemade quilt was thrown over the back and that suited him just fine.

~

Kade was awakened shortly after dawn by a weight on top of him. Cracking open his eyes, he saw Tigger had made himself at home on his chest and was staring at him, purring.

A noise made Kade turn his head and he saw the dog sitting next to the couch, its tongue lolling out. He immediately regretted making eye contact because the dog began wagging his tail, stood, and turned in a circle. Twice.

"This is why I don't have animals," Kade groused. He dislodged the cat, who was not pleased. "Talk to your buddy," Kade said. "He's the one who wants to go outside."

Throwing his jacket on over his bare chest, he shoved his gun in the back of his jeans, grabbed the leash, and took the dog out. It was bitterly cold and the dog took its sweet time. When they were finally back inside, Kade was wide awake. He started a pot of coffee, then headed for the shower. By the time he was done shaving, the coffee was brewed and he felt more human.

The paper had been delivered to a neighbor downstairs and Kade had snatched it off the sidewalk on his way in. Sitting down at the kitchen table, he read the sports section while he drank his coffee. He called the office and reached a paralegal who said Diane wasn't in yet.

"When she does get in, tell her Kathleen's ill today and won't be at work," Kade said.

"Will do."

Two cups of coffee and an hour later, he heard Kathleen.

"Holy crap!"

She flew out of the bedroom into the bathroom so fast, she didn't even see him. Kade turned a page and waited, though his attention was no longer on the newspaper in his hand. Exactly how pissed was she going to be? Guess he'd find out.

After a faster shower than he would have thought a woman capable of, she emerged, dripping wet and wearing nothing but a tiny bath towel.

Fuck.

It seemed she had the same thought because she stopped short at the sight of him.

Kade could no more stop his eyes from wandering over her than if someone had asked him to stop the sun from rising. Her long hair was plastered to her naked shoulders, water streaming in rivulets over her breasts. The thin, white towel was nearly transparent and ended right at the tops of her thighs.

"What are you doing here?"

She pulled the towel tighter and higher and Kade clenched the paper in his hands. His dick was hard as a rock—apparently a perpetual state of being around her. He swallowed down a groan.

"You didn't think you could get rid of me that easily, did you?" He managed a smirk, simultaneously hoping she'd pull that towel an inch higher and that she'd hightail it back to her bedroom.

"Actually, I thought I had," she shot back.

"Doesn't work that way, princess," Kade said, "especially since you have my clothes." A pathetic excuse, seeing as how he had an apartment in Indy, but she didn't know that.

Kathleen glanced where he indicated, at the couch where his suitcase stood.

"I'm late for work," she said.

"Don't worry about that. I called in sick for you."

Her mouth dropped open. "You called in for me?" she repeated. "You . . . you can't do that!"

"Already done. Blane thought it was a good idea, if that helps at all," Kade replied. "Though if prior experience has taught me anything, it's that you have a mind of your own."

The words came out automatically, but part of his brain was busy drinking in the fact that she still stood in next to nothing. A drop of water trailed down her jaw and throat, disappearing into the shadow of cleavage.

Kade cleared his throat, jerking the paper up in front of him.

"Get dressed. Then we'll talk." Or fuck, which sounded way more fun.

He tried to focus on the words on the page, but all he could see was her. The blow dryer started up in her room and Kade tossed the paper down in disgust. It looked like he was going to spend his day working on this case of Blane's because the sooner he could get out of town, the better off he'd be.

When she finally came back, Kade's lips twisted at what she was wearing—dark jeans and a navy turtleneck. She'd pinned her hair up and Kade couldn't tell if she wore makeup, not that she needed it. Her skin was flawless, the color of her eyes made even more prominent by the blue shirt. She poured herself a cup of coffee and sat down at the table, her eyes glancing down to the paper Kade had casually placed in the middle.

"How did you get that?" She made a grab for it, but Kade was quicker, snatching it away.

"Since you weren't being very . . . cooperative," which was an understatement, "I thought I'd see for myself where you'd been yesterday." He held it up so she could see it. "Who are these people?" Of course, he already knew who they were, but he wanted to see if she'd tell him, if she'd trust him again.

She hesitated, seeming to consider her words—consider him—before she spoke. "They're people I thought might know something about who is behind these threats to Blane."

Something like relief melted through Kade. She'd told him the truth.

"And how would you know that?"

"I read through the case. Ryan Sheffield is the JAG officer who testified the other day for the prosecution. Stacey Willows is the fiancée of the man who commanded the mission. Ron Freeman and Brian Bowers were SEALs on that same mission with Blane's client, Kyle Waters."

Not only had she read the file, she remembered it without even glancing at the list in his hand. Nice.

"I figured whoever was doing this might be someone they knew," she continued. "Someone who disagreed with what they'd done and had the know-how and skills to fire that sniper shot at me."

Beauty and brains? In a girl of Blane's? Unheard of.

"How unexpectedly intelligent of you," he said, hiding the tinge of admiration he was feeling. "Color me shocked."

Color crept up her cheeks, but she didn't respond to his light jab.

"You went to see these people yesterday?" Kade asked, hoping the answer was no. If she was right and one of them had someone stalking them, they could have easily taken her out, too.

"Two of them," she answered. "Stacey Willows and Ryan Sheffield. I was planning on going to see Ron Freeman and Brian Bowers today."

The name *Bowers* struck a memory. "Well, you can mark Bowers off the list."

"Why?"

"Blane told me he's disappeared. No one can find him. That makes him look guilty, makes Kyle look guilty, and makes things a hell of a lot harder for Blane. But that just leaves us Freeman to visit." Standing, Kade again pocketed the paper, but Kathleen just sat there, staring up at him.

"Really?" she asked.

"Really." He bent over her, bracing his hands on the arms of her chair. "See how easy that was? If you'd just told me this yesterday, you wouldn't have pissed me off, resulting in that rather . . . unpleasant scene when you got back."

She didn't speak, just stared up at him with those wide blue eyes. Kade caught a whiff of her scent and wished he hadn't. Getting close had been a bad idea, and suddenly he was reliving last night inside his head. His hands tightened on the chair so he wouldn't touch her and the moment stretched longer than it should have. Her pulse beat under the delicate skin of her jaw, speeding up noticeably.

"I'm hungry," he blurted. "Let's eat first." He put some much needed distance between them, going to the refrigerator to look inside. Actually, it was to cool off—Kade already knew there was nothing to eat in there—but the frigid air on his face helped.

"Don't you eat?" he asked her over his shoulder.

"Of course I eat!" she quickly replied. "I just haven't been to the store lately, that's all."

Right. And the three hundred dollars in the bank account had to last until her next paycheck, which wasn't for two weeks. Why exactly hadn't Blane given her a raise or something? She obviously wouldn't take money from him, but Blane could've put through a jump in her salary. It's the least she deserved for putting up with all this shit.

Of course, Blane had never had to worry about money, had never lived paycheck to paycheck where you had to decide whether you wanted to eat or put gas in your car. It was fortunate for him, but meant money wasn't something he really thought about, which was *un*fortunate for Kathleen.

"Come on," he said, grabbing his jacket. "I know a great breakfast place."

Kathleen seemed good with that, getting her coat from the closet and shrugging it on when the phone rang. She picked it up.

"Hello?"

Whoever it was must've been someone she knew because rather than saying she was on her way out, she sat down on the couch.

"It's good to hear from you! How are you doing?"

Shit. Looked like breakfast would be delayed. Kathleen glanced his way and he rolled his eyes to let her know what he thought of having to wait for her to chat on the phone. She looked away as she listened so Kade sauntered over to the Christmas tree. Damn, she had a shit-ton of those ornaments.

One caught his eye while he listened with half an ear to the conversation. A gold locket. Taking it off the branch, Kade popped it open to reveal a picture of a man and woman standing in front of a fireplace. The woman looked too much like Kathleen to be anyone other than her mother, and Kade remembered his file on her. Both parents deceased.

"Five thousand dollars! For what?"

That caught his attention and Kade listened more closely.

"Why so much? Why now? It's been weeks." She was quiet again, then let loose a high-pitched "What?" that made Kade wince.

"That's a 'good offer'?" she asked.

Kade abandoned any pretense that he wasn't listening, now watching Kathleen closely as she talked.

"Um, okay . . . Yeah, sure . . . Thanks for letting me know, Gracie. I'll talk to you later."

Gracie. The prostitute Kathleen had shacked up with that night she'd run away from Blane's. What the hell did she want?

"Who was that?" he asked once she'd hung up.

"Gracie. She said that I . . . owe . . . Simone five thousand dollars and if I don't pay, she'll send someone to collect it. Simone said I could work it off by meeting some guy at the Crowne Plaza Saturday night."

How cute. She was too embarrassed to even meet his eye when she said *work it off*.

Simone was a practical businesswoman, so the phone call and attempt to collect wasn't that far out of the realm of possibility.

"I fail to see the problem," Kade said, which was obviously the wrong thing to say because Kathleen got pissed pretty damn fast.

"Of course you wouldn't. Just another day in the life, right? You think I sleep around already, so why not get paid for it?"

If only she *was* the kind who slept around and not one of those women who thought sex should mean something. But the fact that she was certain Kade thought she was a slut made him feel like shit, so he lashed out.

"I meant that I'm sure Blane will pay whatever the cost to make sure you don't have to fuck somebody on Simone's orders."

She winced and Kade wanted to kick himself. Blane was right. Was it impossible for him to go for a week without being a total dick to her? She didn't deserve it. It wasn't *her* fault Kade couldn't get her out of his head.

"I'm not asking Blane for that kind of money," she said with a firm shake of her head.

Kade snorted. "Don't be ridiculous. It's not like he doesn't have it." But she only shook her head again. Her pride, Kade was sure, was getting the best of her common sense at the moment. He could relate to that. But come Saturday and the threat of becoming a prostitute in actuality, she'd see sense.

"I thought you were hungry," she said, getting to her feet and obviously changing the subject. "Let's go."

But Kade still held the ornament.

"Your parents?" he asked.

"Yes." She took it from him and carefully replaced it on the tree.

Kade knew more about Kathleen than she realized or would no doubt want him to know. Thinking he might let something slip if he didn't ask her to tell him something about her history, Kade asked, "Where are they? Where are you from, anyway?"

"I'm from Rushville, Indiana," she said. "And they're no longer with me."

The note of sadness in her voice and longing in her eyes as she looked at the picture struck Kade. Why would she let herself show such vulnerability? Didn't she know that if you showed a weakness, it could hurt you? Caring was like painting a target on your back.

She gave him a tight smile that didn't reach her eyes. "Ready?"

Ready for an entire day in her presence? Only if *ready* meant equal parts anticipation and dread—anticipation because being with Kathleen for such a long period of time made him feel like it was Christmas morning; dread because despite his best intentions, Kade knew he'd fuck it up somehow.

CHAPTER FOUR

It was cold outside but clear, the sun promising to be blinding later as it reflected off the snow. Kade took Kathleen to his favorite breakfast joint off Meridian. Ushering her inside, they sat at the counter and a waitress handed them menus.

One of everything sounded good, but Kade settled on the house omelet. Peering at Kathleen as the waitress waited for her order, he saw her face crease in a frown.

"Um, I'll have coffee and a plain bagel, toasted."

Bullshit. Kade grabbed the menu from her. "You can't live on that," he said. He couldn't remember seeing her eat last night. Had she eaten while he'd been gone? "She'll have . . ." something sweet and full of carbs . . . "the croissant French toast. That looks good." He handed the menu over. "And you know what? Skip the coffee for both of us. We'll have two Bloody Marys instead."

The waitress left and Kathleen turned to him.

"Why did you do that?" she asked, sounding exasperated.

"Relax. You don't come to a place like this and just order a bagel. And I think if we're going to be spending the day together, some booze would help." Lots of booze would help more, but he was driving, so . . .

The waitress brought their drinks and Kade discarded the straw before taking a long swallow. He eyed Kathleen primly taking a sip beside him. He wanted to talk to her, ask her more about her past, why she'd come to Indianapolis, what she wanted today, tomorrow, ten years from now—but he made himself look away from her and stay quiet.

Her presence at his side felt easy. It felt . . . right. Kade had been alone for so long through the day-to-day acts of living and working and being—it was almost a comfort to be with someone. He wondered if he was just tired of being alone . . . or if it was because it was her. She seemed to sense his mood, not trying to fill the silence with idle chatter that would drive him nuts. Seemingly content, she sipped her drink and people-watched.

The food arrived quickly and Kade dug in. He watched Kathleen surreptitiously as she poured way too much syrup on the French toast and took a bite. Her eyes slid shut.

"Good choice?" he asked, absurdly glad he'd changed her order from a bagel.

She nodded as she chewed, a small smile curving her lips.

Ridiculous, how pleased her happiness made him. God, he must be going soft.

"Want to try?" she asked, piercing another bite with her fork and holding it out to him.

Obediently, Kade leaned forward and ate it, then grimaced. Yeah, he'd been right. "Too much syrup," he said.

Kathleen laughed, a sound Kade instinctively knew he'd never tire of hearing. "There's no such thing," she said, her blue eyes twinkling.

She ate the whole thing, though Kade finished before her. Returning to sip at what remained of the Bloody Mary, she surprised him.

"Why didn't you come home for Thanksgiving?" she asked.

She wasn't looking at him, not even when Kade glanced her way, and he wondered at the question. What did she care why he'd stayed away? And how was he supposed to answer that?

I've been obsessed with you for months and sitting across a table eating turkey and watching you and Blane be all lovey-dovey and shit was not my idea of a holiday.

"I was working," he answered. Vague usually did the trick—at least it did with Mona and Blane. The minute he mentioned work, they stopped asking questions.

"Well, you're going to stick around for Christmas, aren't you?"

Fuck. He shrugged, but who the hell was he kidding? If Kathleen wanted him there for Christmas, there was no way he was going to disappoint her. Especially when she turned to him, those blue eyes wide and pleading.

"You have to. I know Mona and Gerard want you there and I'm sure Blane does, too."

Not if he'd known why I bailed on Thanksgiving, Kade thought. He gave a short huff of laughter, then met her gaze. "And what about you?" he asked, despite the fact that he shouldn't want to know.

She was so close . . . Kade's eyes dropped to her mouth. Shit. She had a tiny drop of syrup on her upper lip, right at the corner. He was struck with an insane impulse to lean forward and lick it from her skin. He doubted she'd appreciate that.

"You have some syrup . . ." he murmured, reaching out and gently swiping the drop away. Her skin was so soft, he couldn't help touching her lips. Were they still as smooth and silky as he remembered?

The satin texture of her skin sent Kade's pulse into overdrive. Her lips parted slightly and he could just see the pearl of her teeth and feel the heat of her breath.

Dropping his hand, Kade's gaze met hers. Her eyes were wide and surprised as they stared into his, then she seemed to recollect herself, turning away and taking a deep swallow of her drink.

Kade hid a grin. So she wasn't unaffected by him. Why that gave him such satisfaction, he didn't want to dwell on.

"It doesn't matter what I want," she said, and it took him a second to remember what question she was answering. "I'm not family. You are."

Kade went still, utterly taken aback at her matter-of-fact statement. He frowned. He'd told her about his past, sort of, that Blane was his half-brother and Kade the bastard he'd taken in when their father had died. He was blood, true, but . . . family . . . that had a whole different connotation. And she'd said it automatically, like it just . . . was. He and Blane were family.

This was still turning over inside his head when the waitress came with the bill. Kade saw Kathleen reach for her purse, but he preempted her, tossing down some cash to cover it. Not only could she not afford it, but if he paid, then technically it was a date.

"Thanks for breakfast," she said, buttoning her coat as they walked outside.

"Thank Blane. I'm sending him the bill." Not. He'd taken Kathleen on a date. It was like his own personal secret, a guilty pleasure.

Kade turned toward where he'd parked the car, but Kathleen stopped, her eyes on a store across the street.

"Can you give me a minute?" she asked.

"What for?"

"I just need to go in there"—she pointed to the store—"to do some Christmas shopping. Please?"

Ugh. Shopping. Like being tortured, only you paid to do it. But her eyes pleaded with him, so that was pretty much that.

"All right, but ten minutes, tops."

Kade had no idea what she could possibly be shopping for in an art studio, but she disappeared into the recesses of the store in search of someone who actually worked there. The front of the store was deserted so he killed time by looking around.

Paintings on canvas and prints hung on the walls and he browsed. One caught his eye and he stopped.

Picasso. He hated Picasso. But he'd never seen this one before. Entitled *Maternity*, it depicted a woman breast-feeding a baby. She had long, dark hair and her shoulders were wrapped in fabric. She gazed down at her child while he fed. You'd expect her to be smiling, but she wasn't, not really. Instead, her face was solemn with only a small tilt to her lip, as though she was sad but couldn't help feeling the bit of happiness brought about by being so close to her child.

Her expression was so similar to his memory of his mother's, it rendered Kade immobile.

She'd always seemed just a bit sad, always worrying, but trying not to show it. He remembered dinners of canned soup that they'd split, or baked potatoes. He'd been five when she'd had to leave him alone at night to go to work. She'd put him to bed, kiss his cheek, and tell him she'd be home by the time he woke up.

And she had been.

Exhausted but always wearing a smile, she'd get him ready for school and put him on the bus. Her day job was from nine to three and Kade had no idea now when she'd slept or how she'd kept going. But she'd been determined to keep them off welfare, and she had.

Then she'd gotten sick.

In retrospect, she'd gone awfully fast and Kade wondered if they'd have been able to do anything for her even if she had gone to the doctor. But they couldn't afford doctor bills or the necessary tests, and a month after she'd gotten sick, she'd been too ill to go in for her night job. That night, she'd died.

Had it been worth it? Kade often wondered if his mother had thought having him had been worth the price she'd paid. She'd sacrificed her youth—her life—for him. Had she regretted it? Would she regret it if she knew what he had become?

"It's lovely, isn't it?"

Kathleen's words broke through Kade's thoughts and he turned to see her standing next to him.

No, *lovely* wouldn't be the word he'd choose. His mother's sacrifice for him had been stupid. He wasn't worth it. If not for him, she'd still be alive today.

"Are you done?" he asked, forcing his thoughts back to the present.

She nodded, searching his eyes as though aware he'd been lost in a dark place.

Kade slipped his sunglasses back on once they were outside. He'd been right. The glare was blinding. They walked in silence for a minute, then she spoke.

"So, can you tell me what it is exactly that you do?" she asked once they'd reached the car.

So she'd look at him like the monster he was? No, thanks. "I could tell you, but then I'd have to kill you," he said instead.

She rolled her eyes. "Isn't that line a little overused? Even for you?"

Kade unlocked the doors and opened the passenger side for her. He didn't know when he'd decided to brush up on the manners for her—opening doors and shit—it had just happened.

"Ouch," he said. "I must be losing my touch if you think that was a line."

"You don't scare me, Kade." She crossed her arms over her chest, gazing at him as if daring him to contradict her.

Damn, but she was brave. Stupidly so. How many times was he going to have to prove to her what a dick he was?

Kade got in her space, bracing his hands against the car on either side and caging her. She jumped, startled, and he bent down until their faces were only inches apart.

"You sure about that, princess?" He spoke in a voice meant to frighten, all hard chips and nails and threat.

Her throat moved as she swallowed. "Do you want me to be?"

Kathleen's question took him by surprise, the stark simplicity of it rendering him speechless.

Did he want her to be? He should. She should be terrified of him. Kade was a man with no conscience and no soul. To someone as pure and good as Kathleen, he was a tainted parasite who would do nothing but destroy her.

But he didn't want her to hate him. Didn't want her afraid.

The easiness of her company was like a balm for the darkness inside him, a warm ray of sunshine after a harsh, bleak winter. Despite the vicious way he'd spoken to her, the disdain and contempt he'd shoveled her way, she seemed to forgive so easily, to *want* to see something good in him that she could trust.

It defied logic, and yet . . .

She reached up, slowly removing his sunglasses, her brow creasing in a frown as she gazed into his eyes.

For the first time, Kade felt like someone was looking into his soul—someone who understood and didn't judge him.

It terrified him.

Snatching his glasses back, he jerked away from her. "Get in." He didn't look to see if she obeyed. He was too busy trying to pull his shit together.

Kade didn't want to talk, and he didn't want her to talk either. He felt as though the ground was shifting under his feet and that slope he was on was getting steeper by the minute.

Kathleen was blessedly silent. But she fidgeted, her hands twisting in her lap, obviously nervous and maybe even afraid. He should be glad of that, but he wasn't.

It was a good twenty minutes before he couldn't take it anymore.

"Stop it," he ordered.

"Stop what?"

He glanced at her, then back at the road. "You're acting like I'm going to hurt you," he said.

She laughed, but it wasn't quite right. "And that would be a surprise how?"

Ouch. He had to hand it to her, she seemed to know just the thing to say that would get under his skin.

"I've never laid a hand on you and you know it." As if he'd deliberately cause her physical harm. He'd sooner eat a bullet.

"You don't have to."

And she goes in for the kill.

Their eyes met for a moment, but Kade couldn't handle the hurt and accusation in hers, so he quickly looked away.

"Why do you do . . . what you do?" she asked.

She couldn't even say it, that's how offensive it was.

"You mean kill people for a living?" Might as well call a spade a spade. "Is that what you do?"

The urge to make himself not look like such a sorry excuse for a human being was strong, so he told her the truth.

"I do what needs to be done. Last week I stopped a man from raping and murdering a fifteen-year-old girl. He'd done it before and gotten away with it. I just made sure he wouldn't be doing it again."

She was quiet for a moment, seeming to digest this, before saying, "But you can't be judge and jury."

"Why not? Who else was going to save that girl? Or the one after that?"

"I don't have an answer. I just know that it can't be good . . . for you . . . for your soul . . . to do that."

What the fuck did she know about his soul? Kade had lost whatever innocence he'd been born with by the time he turned seven. Anything good in him had long since been eaten up by the bad. Kade could look in a man's eyes as he begged for mercy and not feel a fucking thing before he pulled the trigger, or after. He didn't lose sleep at night over the things he'd done. The fact that she thought there was something to be redeemed in his soul was a fucking joke.

Parking the car in Freeman's driveway, he turned off the engine and turned her way.

"Don't try to rescue me, Kathleen. I'm beyond saving."

With that warning, he got out, leaving her to follow along to the front door. Or not. At this point, he didn't particularly care if she came with him or stayed in the car.

But she did get out and in a moment, stood by his side on the porch. Kade pressed the doorbell and waited. Nothing. He tried again. Still nothing.

"I guess he's not home," Kathleen said with a shrug.

Which would be a perfect time to break in and take a look around, not that Kade told her that.

"I'll check out the back," he said instead. "You stay here."

Kade left without waiting for her reply and headed around to the back of the house. They had a chain-link fence, but the latch was frozen solid, ice encasing the metal. Grasping the top of the fence, Kade vaulted over, landing on his feet in the snow.

The back patio had a charcoal grill next to a table and four chairs that had seen better days. A flower pot with a dead plant stood in the corner. The sliding glass doors had a lock that was also frozen, so it took Kade longer than usual to get inside.

The patio led into a dim living room and Kade silently stepped through the doorway. No one was around and the house was completely still. He explored until he came across the kitchen . . . and Kathleen, doing exactly what he'd told her *not* to do. He'd said to stay put and here she fucking was, her back to him and gazing at—

—the dead body on the floor.

She stumbled backward, right into Kade, and let loose a blood-curdling scream. She shoved away from him, but Kade instantly had his arm locked around her, spinning her around to press her body against his, and putting his hand over her mouth to shut her up. As soon as she saw who held her, she sagged against him in relief.

Kade took in the blood underneath the body of the man and knew he'd been dead a while, which meant whoever had done it was long gone. But Kathleen was shaking all over. It had scared her, and who could blame her? She'd probably never seen anything like this before.

"Are you all right?" he asked.

She gave a jerky nod, her chest still heaving.

Kade didn't want to let her go, but the sooner he took a look, the quicker he could get her out of there.

Carefully setting her aside, he stepped to the body—it had to be Freeman—carefully skirting the pool of blood.

The cause of death was easy to see—a gunshot to the head. Considering the nearly pristine skull and splatter of brain matter from the exit wound, most likely a professional hit, maybe an attempt to make it look like suicide. Getting to his feet, he returned to Kathleen, who'd stayed where he'd left her for once.

"Gunshot wound to the head," he said. "Possibly self-inflicted, but I doubt it."

"Why? Why would someone kill him?" Kathleen's distraught question tugged at Kade. She felt something for the guy—horror and pain at what had happened. He didn't feel a thing besides irritation that another of Blane's witnesses was gone.

"No idea," he answered. "But we have to call in the cops, and get out of here before we contaminate the scene any further."

Taking her back to the car, Kade turned it on and pushed the heat to full blast, hoping that would ease the tremors that still shook her. Kade called the cops and reported the shooting.

Talking to the cops was always a time-sucking pain in the ass and today was no different. If not for Kathleen being there, Kade wouldn't have bothered calling the cops at all, but her fingerprints were inside and he didn't want them breathing down her neck.

"And why were you here, Dennon?" one of the homicide detectives asked, suspicion in his eyes.

"None of your fucking business," Kade said, glancing over the man's head. Where was Kathleen?

"Always the asshole, Dennon," the detective sneered. "Why don't I arrest *you* for murder? You can spend the next forty-eight hours in a cell."

Kade flicked his gaze to the detective. "You've got nothing on me and you know it. The gunshot wound was made by a thirty-eight and I've got nothing but nine millimeters." He glanced away, still searching. There she was, with a uniformed cop who was taking her statement. "Not to mention I'd be out in less than thirty minutes and slap you with a harassment suit."

Sometimes it really paid to have a lawyer for a brother.

Kade could practically hear the detective grinding his teeth, but he didn't give a shit. Some lady had just pulled up and lost it when she saw the EMTs carrying a stretcher out with the body. Must be the wife.

Suddenly, Kathleen was rushing over to the woman, who was now kneeling in the snow and sobbing. Sinking down beside her, Kathleen put her arms around her, comforting her, a total stranger.

Brushing past the cop, Kade approached them, still keeping his distance. The woman was leaning on Kathleen and even from this far, Kade could see tears welling in Kathleen's eyes, too.

Way too soft-hearted for her own good. Too compassionate. Too empathetic.

When the woman had regained control, Kathleen helped her to her feet. Kathleen's jeans were soaked, but she didn't seem to notice, asking the woman if she was all right. She glanced around, searching for him. When her gaze landed on Kade, he walked over.

"My friend and I found him," Kathleen was saying.

"How? Why were you here?"

"I was coming to ask your husband about Kyle Waters. The defense attorney on this case has been threatened and I thought there might be something your husband knew that could help us."

Kade noticed she didn't say a word about how *she* had been threatened.

"I can't talk about it," the woman said, taking a step back. It didn't take a rocket scientist to know they'd hit a nerve.

"Please," Kathleen implored. "Whoever killed your husband might be after me and someone I . . . I care about. If there's anything you know that could help me, please, tell me."

Someone I care about. Not hard to miss the *love* that had almost come from her lips. Was she so naive, so innocent, as to think she was in love with Blane? Or that he felt that way in return?

But the plea had the desired effect and the woman talked.

"I think Ron was being threatened," she said.

"What do you mean? Why would someone threaten him?" Kathleen asked. Kade was content to let her do the interrogation. She'd gotten the woman to trust her, despite her husband having just been murdered.

"He started getting these phone calls," the woman continued. "He'd have to go out once he got them and he'd never tell me who they were from or where he went. But then he suddenly wanted to know where I was all the time. I couldn't even go to the grocery store without telling him."

Classic case of blackmail. "How long has this been going on?" Kade asked.

"A couple of months, more or less," she said with a shrug. "I kept trying to get him to tell me, but he wouldn't. He said to just trust him. That's when he changed his testimony."

"He did what?" Kathleen sounded surprised. Kade wasn't.

"Ron had said in his deposition that all four of the SEALs agreed the man was a threat. After the phone calls started, he changed his story and said that Kyle had taken it upon himself to kill the guy."

"Which version is the truth?"

"They all agreed," the woman said. "I couldn't understand why he was doing that, why he'd lie and hang Kyle out to dry, but he refused to talk to me about it and he made me swear not to tell anyone. He told me our lives depended on it."

And considering how much she'd just told them, her life was in serious jeopardy.

"If I were you," Kade said, wondering why he cared enough to bother, "I'd leave town for a while. Go visit family, go on a vacation, whatever."

The woman nodded. "Thank you." She turned away, walking toward the police, who were waiting for her.

Kathleen shivered and Kade glanced at her. She had to be freezing.

"Let's get out of here," he said, taking her arm and helping her into the car.

CHAPTER FIVE

The inside of the car was a sauna in no time, but Kade just dealt with it. Kathleen had stopped shivering, though she still held her hands to one of the vents, letting the warm air blow on her fingers.

"Who would have had the power to make him change his story like that?" she asked. "And threaten him and his wife?"

"He was a SEAL," Kade replied. "It had to have been someone he believed would make good on the threats. SEALs aren't exactly easy to scare." If his experience with Blane's Navy buddies was any indication.

"If they called him, maybe we could get authorization to pull his phone records."

Kade smirked. "I can do that, and I won't even have to ask."

"Blane needs to know this," she said.

Making a split-second decision, Kade took the next exit, heading toward the firm. "Agreed."

"Wait, what about Diane? I can't just go walking into the firm when I called in sick today. She'll fire me."

Just let her try. "You worry too much," he said instead. "I'll take care of it." With pleasure.

It was quiet for a bit, then she cleared her throat.

"So, you have any music or . . . anything?"

Kade's lips twisted. "No, this car doesn't come equipped with something as fancy as a radio."

Her eyes narrowed at his smartass wisecrack, but there was a slight lift to her lips, too, telling him she could appreciate his response to a stupid question.

"Oh, you meant you wanted to *listen* to some music. My mistake."

This time there was a definite smile on her face, albeit small.

Reaching over, Kade pressed the button for the radio and the strains of Maroon 5 filled the car.

"Are you warm enough?" he asked, hoping she was. He was sweating over here.

"Yeah, thanks."

Thank God. He turned down the heat to something more reasonable and resisted the urge to crack a window.

"Why did you go to that woman?" he couldn't help asking. "You didn't know her."

Kathleen glanced at him. "I know, but she was devastated, and she had no one else. If it'd been me, I'd have wanted someone to put their arm around me. Wouldn't you?"

Kade just shot her a look.

"Okay, maybe you wouldn't," she said, the dryness of her tone making Kade's lips twitch.

"And I don't cry at chick flicks, either," he said.

"Me neither," she said. The vehemence of her reply struck Kade.

"No sobbing your heart out over some Nicholas Sparks movie?" he teased.

But she shook her head. "There's enough tragedy and death and sadness in real life. I don't want to watch it in a movie, too."

Her words made Kade's amusement fade. Yeah, he could relate to that. Some of the shit people found entertaining—be it some sob story or a horror flick sensationalizing a sadistic serial murderer—he found too reminiscent of the things he dealt with on a daily basis. It seemed Kathleen felt the same way.

They passed the rest of the ride in silence, listening to Adam Levine sing about another one in his bed. Once they arrived, Kathleen followed him inside. Kade stayed a bit ahead of her, hoping they'd run into Diane. Luck was with him.

"Diane!" he heard Kathleen say. He stopped, backtracking a few steps to see the two women facing off.

"I thought you were home sick today," Diane said accusingly.

"I am. I mean, I was. Then I was feeling better so—"

"She's with me," Kade interrupted.

Diane spun around, her eyes widening when she saw Kade, and she took a step back.

"Mr. Dennon, I didn't realize you were in town," she said.

"I wasn't aware I was to report my comings and goings to you," Kade said coldly.

"Of course not," Diane backtracked. "And you say Kathleen is with you?"

Why didn't Blane just fire this bitch? She was a pain-in-the-ass busybody on a power trip. The fact that she'd been mistreating Kathleen made Kade's blood pressure climb.

"It's Miss Turner," he said, "and her position here has changed. I'm promoting her and will notify you of her change in salary. Her comings and goings are no longer your concern."

"What? Promoting her to what?"

Kade's lips twisted. "Investigator. She'll report to me from now on." He didn't know where the hell that had come from, he'd just made it up on the spot, too pissed off to think it through. But it sounded good. And hell, she might even be good at it, given some training.

Grabbing Kathleen's arm, Kade propelled her into the elevator while Diane stared after them in shock. That had felt pretty damn good. It was nice to have power, especially when you could use it to put a bully in her place.

Once the elevator doors closed, Kathleen seemed to recover from her surprise, too. "What was that about?" she asked. "How can you do that? How does she know who you are?"

Okay, maybe he'd been wrong about the investigator part.

"You're a little slow on the uptake," he prodded.

Her eyes went wide. "You work for Blane?"

As if. "I bought in, actually," he said, "when Gage was indicted. Thought it would be a good investment. I'm what you'd call a silent partner."

"And you just . . ." She couldn't seem to finish the sentence, so she just stared at him as though finding it hard to comprehend.

"Promoted you," Kade finished for her. "Surprised Blane hasn't done it himself." He couldn't help saying it. She needed to have her eyes opened about Blane, this girl who comforted strangers and insisted on worrying about Kade's soul.

"Well, maybe it didn't occur to him," she said in a small voice.

Kathleen's defense of Blane wasn't unexpected, given what Kade was learning of her nature, though it was disappointing.

When they reached Blane's floor, Kade ushered her to the sofa. "You wait here," he said, giving her a little push so she sat, but she bounced right back up.

"I want to come with you," she insisted.

"You're supposed to be broken up, remember?" And Kade needed some private time with Blane. "Now wait here."

She rolled her eyes, the little snot, but didn't say anything. Kade couldn't resist adding, "Unless you want to reenact last night."

That got a reaction. Her eyes went wide and she abruptly sat, which is exactly what Kade should've wanted her to do, though that didn't stop a pang of disappointment.

"That's what I thought," he said, unable to keep a note of bitterness from his voice.

Kade went into Blane's office without knocking, closing the door behind him. Blane was working on something, a file and paper spread across his desk. He glanced up as Kade entered.

"Where's Kathleen?" were the first words out of his mouth.

"Relax," Kade said, heading for a chair. "She's fine." He sprawled in one of the leather chairs facing the desk, his legs extended in front of him and crossed at the ankles.

"What are you doing here?" Blane asked.

"Trying to figure out who's behind all this," Kade said. "Thought you should know Ron Freeman is dead. Murdered. Professional hit, by the looks of it."

Blane sat back in his chair. "You're kidding."

"Wish I were. But that's not the worst. Looks like someone was threatening him and his wife."

"That would explain his sudden change of heart on what he remembered from Iraq," Blane said. "Kyle's ex-wife is testifying tomorrow for the prosecution. I wonder if she's being threatened as well."

"I can check it out. Where is she?"

Blane read off an address and Kade memorized it. He and Kathleen could check it out later. Another woman, so Kathleen would probably have a better chance getting her to talk than he would. Of course, that depended on the woman, though. They'd have to tag-team her and decide on the fly who had the better shot.

"I got another package today," Blane said, and the tone of his voice had Kade glancing up at him. He was reaching for a large manila envelope. "Want to tell me why you were practically fucking Kathleen outside the bar last night?"

Kade leaned forward, reaching for the folder and dumping the contents into his hand. That's when he noticed a light on Blane's phone was lit. The intercom.

Kathleen was hearing every word of this conversation.

The photos were long-distance and grainy, but there was no mistaking who was in them or what they were doing. Kade had the urge to ask if he could keep them, but didn't think that would go over real well.

"Nice photos," he said.

"Kade . . ." The warning in Blane's voice said he was ready to go from irritated to seriously pissed off in about three seconds.

"It was just a decoy, a ruse," Kade lied. "Hopefully, that'll help throw off whoever's watching." He hadn't seen who had taken those pictures, and they could just as easily have had a sniper rifle on them as opposed to a camera. And he'd been too consumed with having an excuse to touch Kathleen to do a better job clearing the area. A chill went through him at what might have happened.

He thought again about Kathleen listening in. She should know the truth about Blane and how he felt about women and relationships. Better to have her eyes opened now while she still just *thought* she was falling in love with him than a month from now when she was sure she had.

"You know, judging by these photos, it looks like she was rather enjoying it. You might want to think about that before you put your life and career on the line for her."

"I could say the same to you," Blane retorted.

"Knock it off, Blane," Kade shot back. "I refuse to become some cliché, you and me fighting over some chick. It's not worth it and you know it." Which was the absolute truth and he believed it utterly. No one was worth risking Blane, not even Kathleen.

Kade shoved the photos back in the envelope and tossed them onto Blane's desk.

"Whoever said we're fighting over her?" Blane asked. "Last she told me, she hates you."

That struck Kade like a slap across the face. She'd actually said that? That she hated him? But why wouldn't she? It wasn't like he'd given her much cause to actually *like* him. Not to mention that he shouldn't give a damn one way or the other how she felt.

"Well, there you go then," he said, realizing he'd been quiet too long.

"Even if she does hate you, do it again, and you and I are going to have a problem."

Blane suddenly going all territorial about Kathleen made the jealousy Kade had been trying to ignore surge to the front, along with his temper. If Kathleen was listening, then by God she should know the truth.

"What do you care anyway?" Kade lashed out. "It's not like you're going to marry her. Isn't that role reserved for Kandi?"

Blane just looked at him for a moment, a slight frown on his face. "What's with the sudden interest in my love life, Kade? I thought I made it clear it's none of your business."

Kade scrambled for a reason other than the one he was most trying to hide: *I'm obsessed with your girlfriend.* "When your relationship starts putting expiration dates on your life, then it becomes my business."

"None of this is Kathleen's fault," Blane said. "I'd appreciate it if you'd try to remember that. She's not the enemy here."

"I'm aware of that," Kade said. His voice was calm, but anger, jealousy, and guilt teemed just below the surface. He couldn't deal with jealousy and guilt, but anger was no problem at all. "Which reminds me, since you've been too wrapped up in yourself to realize how miserable she is working for Diane, I promoted her."

"What do you mean, she's miserable working for Diane?" Blane asked. "She never said anything to me about it."

"Please. Diane knows you're sleeping with her and treats her like shit. You obviously weren't going to do anything about it, so I did."

"And you promoted her to what?" Blane asked. "Is she qualified for anything else?"

For the first time in his life, Kade lost some respect for Blane. The way Blane had been acting, Kade had thought that maybe he saw her as more than just another piece of ass. Looked like he'd been wrong. He almost felt bad for her, hearing all this, but yeah, tough love.

"I made her an investigator, reporting to me. And your faith in her is staggering." His voice was cold and now his temper had cooled, replaced by a contempt he'd never before felt toward his big brother.

"It has nothing to do with faith, it's reality," Blane said. "She's smart, but she's young, inexperienced. What is she going to do as an investigator? And how much danger will that involve?"

The veiled accusation that Kade had deliberately put Kathleen in danger just pissed him off. "No more danger than you've already put her in," Kade shot back. "How long are you going to drag this out anyway? She's lasted longer than most of your relationships, I'll give you that, but it would no doubt be better for her if you ended it. Politics won't wait forever and neither will Kandi."

And if you dumped Kathleen, I could make a move without feeling any guilt. The thought drifted right beneath the surface, tantalizing and shaming Kade at the same time. Was he really trying to make Blane break up with Kathleen just so he could have her?

"Did I miss the part where we're telling each other how to run our lives? Because if so, I certainly have some things I'd like to say to you." Blane's retort jerked Kade out of his thoughts.

This was the closest they'd come to fighting in a long time. They bickered occasionally, disagreed, but there was real anger now between them and it shook Kade. He didn't want this, didn't want Blane mad at him, didn't want to feel confused and jealous and angry.

Kade struggled to put a lid on all the emotions and get back to common ground with his brother. "Speaking of changing the subject," he said, "did you check out Junior? It wouldn't surprise me in the least if that little prick was behind this."

Blane's body relaxed slightly. "He's got an alibi for where he was the other night, so if it is him, he's working with someone."

Suddenly a voice erupted from Blane's phone.

"Thanks so much for watching the phones for me, Kathleen." Clarice's voice was tinny over the speaker.

Shit. Busted.

Blane's eyes slid shut and he rubbed a hand across his forehead, muttering a "Fuck" under his breath.

"Kathleen, please come in here," he said more loudly, then hit the button on the phone.

Kade was up and at the door a second later, sure he'd see Kathleen racing for the elevator, and he was right. Their eyes met and his lips twitched. He crooked his finger, beckoning her. With a sigh of resignation, she headed toward him.

"You should learn what a mute button is if you're going to eavesdrop," he whispered in her ear as she passed by.

"Thanks for the advice," she hissed back, but he could tell she wasn't really angry, just embarrassed at having been caught.

Kade left the office, closing the door behind him, but then stood right there listening. Clarice cleared her throat, giving him a look, but Kade just winked and put a finger to his lips. She rolled her eyes.

But damn if Blane didn't have a thick door. Kade could hear them talking, but couldn't make out the words, at least, not until the yelling started.

"Because I need the money, Blane! And it's great and it's nice that you want to help me, but that won't do me any good when this is over!"

Looked like Kade hadn't needed to show her how temporary she and Blane were. She already knew.

"I'm trying to tell you that I'm not going anywhere and you already have me halfway out the door," Kade heard Blane say, and he was angry, angrier than he'd been at Kade earlier.

"Isn't that how you roll, Blane? You think I don't know I'm just the latest in a very long line of women?" Kathleen's bitter retort even made Kade wince.

"You're throwing my past up in my face?" Blane sounded enraged now. "I didn't know you then, Kathleen. What do you want from me?"

Kade couldn't hear what Kathleen said, but he was not okay with this. He'd never seen Blane hurt a woman and didn't think he ever would, but sometimes shit happened.

He hesitated just a fraction before pushing open the door, and when he saw how Blane had a tight hold of Kathleen's arm, forcibly keeping her still, his eyes narrowed and cold anger filled him.

"Lover's spat?" he asked, keeping his voice light, but if Blane didn't get his fucking hand *off* her right goddamn *now*—

"I was just leaving," Kathleen bit out, jerking her arm out of Blane's grasp. She headed out the door and Kade followed her, but not before he sent one long look Blane's way.

By the time they'd reached his car, Kade had made a decision. Reaching in his pocket, he tossed Kathleen's car keys to her. She caught them, glancing at him with a question in her eyes.

"I think it's best if you have your own mode of transportation, just in case."

She'd stood up to Blane, held her own with a stalker and dead bodies. Kade was through treating her like a child.

He followed her to her apartment, then up the stairs, at which point, he couldn't take the silence any longer.

"Trouble in paradise?" he asked.

"Like you care," she muttered.

If only Kathleen knew exactly how *much* Kade cared, maybe she wouldn't have picked a fight with Blane. As much as he wanted her, Kade was under no delusions that between the two of them, he was the safer choice.

She took the dog back to the neighbor, who'd apparently just returned home, then returned to get ready for work. When Kade saw her dressed and searching for her boots, he frowned.

"Don't you want to eat first?" She had to be hungry. *He* was hungry. It had been hours since breakfast.

"I'll grab something at the bar," she said, picking up her boots. Sitting down to put them on, she didn't look at him as she asked, "So what's the story with Kandi?"

Satisfaction and guilt. That's what Kade felt at the question. But she deserved to know. An eyeball left on her doorstep gave her the right to know the truth. Blane wasn't going to tell her, so it was up to Kade to do his dirty work.

"Her dad and Blane's dad were buddies," he said. "Two strong political families, wealthy, connected. They raised Blane and Kandi side by side. She's a few years younger, but they always planned for them to get married. They've been on again and off again for years." Kathleen finally looked up from fastening her boots. "But then I guess he met you."

"Blane and Kandi broke up before he met me," she said. "I had nothing to do with it."

Kade just looked at her, wondering if that was true.

"She's quite intent on getting him back," she said when he didn't reply.

"Kandi usually gets what she wants, yes," he said. "Whether or not that's Blane remains to be seen." Though he'd put money on it.

"You don't like her," Kathleen guessed, her eyes studying him.

As if that was a secret. He shrugged. "She's a selfish, narcissistic bitch. What's not to like?"

A burst of laughter escaped Kathleen, surprising Kade and making him smile a bit, too. That had been twice he'd made her laugh today, just because she got his sense of humor, such as it was.

He followed her in his car to the bar, but didn't park. When she got out of her Honda and came to his window, he rolled it down.

"I need to check something out," he said. "I'll be back later. You good from here?"

She nodded. "I'll be fine. Where are you going?"

Kade considered it a small victory that she cared enough to ask rather than just be glad of his absence.

"Thought I'd check on those phone records and swing by where Bowers was staying."

"Be careful," she said.

And *that* was definitely a step in the right direction, or the wrong one, depending on your point of view. He decided he liked it.

Bowers's place was empty, cleaned out, and it looked like he had indeed run. If so, they'd never find him, at least not in time to do any good. Kade pulled out his laptop while he sat parked in his Mercedes three doors down. Might as well stick around for a while, see if anyone turned up, which also gave him time to hack into the phone records of the Freemans.

After downloading them, he started a cross-check running on his remote server and closed the laptop. That would take a few hours to process and come up with the names and addresses of everyone who had called the Freemans or who they had called themselves.

Reaching over to his glove compartment, he opened it, pulling out a small box. Kade sat back in his seat, looking at it for a moment before lifting the lid. Inside lay a shining gold locket.

It had been his mother's, and he'd had no idea why she kept it, but it contained a tiny picture of himself as a toddler in her arms. She could've sold it at some point, but obviously hadn't wanted to part with it, no matter what. Maybe her parents had given it to her, Kade didn't know. They'd both died in a car accident when she'd been in her early twenties, several years before he'd been born.

The chain had long since been lost, but Kade had managed to hang on to the locket, no matter how many foster homes he'd gone through, had run away from, or the years that had passed since he'd taken it off her. If he was on a job, the locket was in his pocket. If he couldn't have it on his person for some reason, it was nearby. In his car, in his hotel room, or in his apartment, but somewhere close. If he believed in good-luck charms—which he didn't—this was as close to one as he'd ever get.

Taking the locket from the box, he slid it into the pocket of his jeans, then headed back toward The Drop.

It was late, the bar would be closing soon, and Kade glanced at the nearly empty lot before parking his car in an alley two streets over. Last night he'd done a shitty job of clearing the area of threats. Tonight he'd make up for that.

Kade cased the streets two blocks in each direction of The Drop, melting from shadow to shadow and watching for any movement that would betray someone's presence. It was cold, bitterly so, with snow and ice clogging up the asphalt. Cars drove by, their lights glancing off the wet pavement, the drivers anxious to get home.

The sidewalks were empty of all but a handful of people, but no one fit the profile of the person who'd been stalking Kathleen.

It was clear.

Stopping while still across the street, Kade rested his back against the frigid brick wall of the building behind him. He stared at the warm glow of lights shining through the slats of the blinds in the bar's windows.

She was in there.

He should go in. It was freezing out here. But if he did, he'd watch her, probably talk to her. He already couldn't get her out of his head. If this bodyguard duty lasted much longer, it would drive him insane. It was bad enough he could still smell the scent of her perfume in his car.

Fuck.

Reaching in his back pocket, he took out a half-empty pack of cigarettes. Lighting one despite the chill breeze, he took a deep drag.

His hands were cold. Gloves would be useful, but they could slow you down if you had to reach for your gun, so Kade never had them.

He shoved his free hand in his pocket, his fingers brushing the metal of the locket.

Kade thought about Kathleen and her dead parents, how she was all alone, without even a half-sibling like he had. It was hard, being alone. There was no one to count on but yourself. In a way, Kathleen was tougher than either he or Blane. They at least had each other.

Who did she turn to when she needed someone? Who took care of her when she was sick? Who made sure she took proper care of herself? When money was tight and she needed something to tide her over until payday, who did she ask for a loan?

The burning feeling in Kade's gut was new to him, an overwhelming desire to be there for someone. To be there . . . for her. It was a revelation. And a goddamn tragedy. Because she wasn't his. And if she'd been with anyone else, any other fucking Joe Blow on the planet, he'd have no qualms about stealing her away. But she wasn't with just anyone.

She was with Blane.

So consumed was he by his thoughts that, though Kade noticed the three guys heading toward him, he didn't see how closely they looked at him, how their steps slowed, or how they conversed quietly. He did notice when they suddenly surrounded him, but by then it was too late.

CHAPTER SIX

Two attacked at once, one going for the face while the other went for his gut, both connecting with their respective targets.

Kade reeled back, pain exploding in his jaw and ribs. One came back for another shot and Kade grabbed his fist, giving it a hard twist, but before it could break, his buddy was slamming a blow into his side.

Grimacing, Kade lashed out, his knuckles connecting with the man's mouth. Blood spurted from his lip and Kade felt teeth scrape his hand. Slamming his elbow back, he caught the second guy in the solar plexus and he bent over. But the first guy had pulled a knife.

He slashed at Kade, who sacrificed getting close enough to be sliced so he could grab the man's wrist. This time, he didn't pull back quick enough and Kade snapped the wrist back. The sickening crack was loud, but not as loud as the guy yelling. The bloody knife dropped to the ground.

The third was behind him now, grabbing his arms and trying to pin them behind his back. Kade fought like the devil, pissed off beyond belief that they'd gotten the drop on him. It was going too fast for him to try to pull his gun from its holster and the blows started to take a toll, though he landed a few nasty ones himself. Blood dripped into his eye and he tasted more.

As good as he was, he couldn't hold them off forever and soon they had him pinned, one on each side.

"Payback's a bitch, isn't it, you fucker."

Kade focused, wincing as he panted for air, and recognized the face as belonging to the guy whose arm he'd broken last night. Guess he should've gone for the right arm rather than the left.

"Hey, buddy! Long time, no see," Kade said with a fake smile, the movement splitting the cut on his lip further. He frowned in mock concern. "How's the arm?"

"Motherfucker." Another slam in the gut from an apparently real sore-loser.

Fuck. Shit, this sucked. It'd been a while since Kade had been beaten up, and now he remembered how much it fucking *hurt*.

"Let him go, assholes!"

"Ah, shit," Kade muttered, recognizing that voice. If they went after her, he was going to have to kill them, then he was going to kill *her* for sticking her nose in.

"Well, look who's come to join us," Sore Loser yelled back to where Kathleen stood outside the bar. Blood in Kade's eyes made it hard to see. "If it isn't Miss High-and-Mighty herself. How you doing, bitch?"

"I said, let him go!"

"How about we trade him for you?" Sore Loser flung another punch to Kade's face and he felt the skin on his cheekbone split.

The sound of a gunshot was unexpected, as was Sore Loser's yelp.

"You fucking bitch! You nearly shot my dick off!"

Kade would've laughed if he'd had the energy. Gotta love her style. Or maybe she just had real shitty aim.

"You've got until three to let him go and get out of here!" Kathleen yelled. "One!"

The little bitches holding him let go and Kade dropped to the ground. The asphalt was ice-cold, bits of rock and grit rough against his palms.

"Two!"

Sore Loser slammed his booted foot into Kade's side, making him grunt in pain, then Kade heard them take off.

Once they were gone, staying on the ground for a minute seemed like a really good idea. Every part of him hurt, from his hands and knuckles to his ribs and gut, which ached whenever he took a breath, to the burn of the cuts and scrapes on his face. The slice on his chest burned, too, and he felt the warm wetness of blood. The motherfucker better not have cut his leather jacket or so help him—

"Kade, are you all right?"

He felt Kathleen's hand on his shoulder. Damn. No better way to ruin your image than let a girl watch while your ass got handed to you, except maybe that she be the one to save said ass. Nice. He'd have to give up his fucking man card.

"I've had better nights, princess," Kade managed, turning and pushing his sorry ass up to sit. His ribs sent a sharp pain through him. Cracked. Fuck. That always hurt like a motherfucker.

Blinking the blood out of his eyes, Kade was finally able to focus on Kathleen, who knelt beside him on the concrete. He frowned and blinked again.

"What the fuck are you wearing?"

She had on some kind of Santa outfit—red velvet with white fur trim—that looked like it had come straight out of one of Kade's fantasies. It fit her like a second skin, the skirt barely brushing the tops of her thighs, and the thing was sleeveless, her breasts nearly falling out of the top. The sight made her naughty schoolgirl Halloween costume look downright tame.

"What?" she asked, staring at him like he'd lost his mind.

"What are you doing in that getup? You do know it's about fifteen fucking degrees out here, don't you? You trying to freeze to death?" Or drive him absolutely fucking insane.

"Last I looked, I was saving your ass," she retorted. "I wasn't aware that you required a dress code."

That was funny. Kade grinned before he could help it, which caused his face to start hurting again. Fuck.

Kathleen must've seen his grimace of pain because she jumped up and reached down to help him, which gave him a fabulous view of her breasts. Once he was on his feet, Kade grabbed the gun Kathleen had left on the ground, tucking it in the back of his jeans.

He could make it under his own power—he'd been hurt worse—but Kathleen draped his arm across her naked shoulders to help him. Since that gave him an excuse to touch her, not to mention another amazing view of her cleavage, Kade allowed it. Careful not to lean too heavily on her—little thing might topple over—he let her lead him back to the bar.

Once inside, Kade shrugged out of his jacket. Good. It looked like the little prick hadn't cut it. Not that he couldn't get another, but this was Armani and he liked it.

Kathleen took it from him, carelessly tossing it over a barstool—*she* didn't know it was Armani—her eyes going immediately to where he'd been cut.

"Kade, you're hurt," she said, as though surprised.

Yeah, he was shocked, too.

"No shit," Kade said, tugging his shirt over his head. There went a Tom Ford. Glancing down just as Kathleen gasped, he saw the slice on his side underneath his arm.

"We need to get you to the hospital," Kathleen said.

Not. Kade just huffed a laugh. "For this? Please. Just get me some water and something to cover it. You have Band-Aids here?"

"You can't be serious?" She gaped at the wound. "That cut needs stitches."

Needles. Don't think so. "You going to get me some water or should I do it myself? And I wouldn't mind a shot or two of bourbon." Or three. Maybe four, if he was going to have to keep looking at her in that cock-tease outfit.

"Fine," she snapped, getting all pissy. Going behind the bar, she returned quickly with a bowl of hot water, a clean towel, and a glass of bourbon. Kade reached for the towel, but she pulled it back.

"I'll do it," she insisted. "You can't even see what you're doing."

Everything in his head screamed that this was a bad idea, but Kade could no more refuse her than he could stop looking at her. He didn't speak, just waited as she tentatively stepped closer, dipping the towel in water before starting on his face.

Maybe it hurt, it might've been excruciating, but Kade didn't feel it or care. She was so close he could smell her perfume, feel the brush of her breath on his skin as she worked. He should find those assholes and thank them.

Her hands were soft and gentle, carefully cleaning the blood from his face. She chewed her bottom lip, drawing Kade's eyes to the plump bit of flesh. Her brow was drawn in a slight frown, worry in her eyes, as she swiped at the cut on his cheek.

It had been a long time since Kade had allowed a woman to care for him in this way, to touch him so intimately. Sex was different. They used him as much as he was using them. But this, this was more. It involved actual feelings—trust in her, and if she bothered to take care of him, that meant she must have some softer feelings for him, right? But that was too much to hope for, and hope did nothing but destroy the soul.

He stared into her eyes, unable to look away. She kept at it, though he could've told her she didn't need to be so gentle. He could take it. But if he said that, then it might be over too quick.

"What happened?" she asked. "How did they get the drop on you?" She'd moved to the cut on his lip and Kade bit back a groan at her soft touch.

"I was . . . distracted," he said, forcing his thoughts away from the path they wanted to drift down. "My own fault."

"Distracted by what?" she asked.

I was consumed with thoughts of you was on the tip of his tongue, but Kade knew he couldn't say that. She was dabbing at the cut above his eye now. She was so close, just a breath away. What would she do if he leaned forward those few scant inches and kissed her? Would she push him away? Would she be disgusted that Blane's brother would cross that line? He couldn't claim that someone had been watching them tonight.

"What was it?" she asked again when he remained silent.

Kade abruptly turned away before he did something colossally stupid. Grabbing the glass of bourbon, he downed it in two swallows, ignoring the slight tremor in his hand. Kathleen just watched in silence.

"Bowers's place was cleaned out," he said roughly, setting the glass back down. "I watched and waited for a while, thinking he might show, but nothing."

"What about the phone records?" she asked, gently turning his face back toward her and swiping at his jaw. His hand tightened on the glass. He wanted to tell her to stop touching him, for God's sake, but was unable to force out the words that would push her away.

"Tracing numbers even as we speak," he said. "I was headed back in when they jumped me. Then this Playboy Bunny showed up with a gun and scared the bad guys away."

Kathleen smiled a little at his teasing, but it quickly faded. "I'm so sorry, Kade," she said. "If it weren't for you helping me the other night, this wouldn't have happened."

As if she should apologize for those douche canoes. They weren't fit to breathe the same air as her. "Don't mention it," he said, cutting off any further apologies. "Want me to get the rest? You're squeamish, aren't you?" He didn't know how much longer he could take her touching him, her being so near and yet so utterly beyond his reach.

"Of course not," she said, wringing out the towel and turning back to him. "Can you lift your arm?"

Shit.

Kade hesitated, knowing how close his control was to snapping, and wondered if she could read the longing in his eyes. Bending his elbow, he stuck his hand behind his head so she could get to the cut.

She moved closer to him, stepping right between his spread thighs as he sat on the stool. Her eyes dropped to his chest and Kade saw the column of her throat move as she swallowed.

Every sense was focused on her, the pain of the cut a distant throb. Her hair was close enough for the scent to drift toward him. The delicate curves of her neck and shoulder drew his eyes and he clenched his hand into a tight fist so he wouldn't touch her.

"You should really get stitches for this," she said quietly, her fingers brushing softly at the damaged skin in something more like a caress.

"Forget it," he said roughly.

"What's the deal, Kade? It only hurts for a second when they numb you and then—"

The mere mention of it brought back the anxiety he always felt when needles were involved and Kade abruptly lowered his arm, forcing Kathleen back. "And we're done here," he said.

"You are kidding me," she said, staring at him as though stunned. He frowned. "What?"

"You're afraid of needles, aren't you?" she asked.

Damn. Perceptive little thing. "Right," Kade snorted, lying through his teeth. As if he wasn't already a total wimp in her eyes now because of the beating, being "afraid of needles" would surely seal the deal. She'd never look at him the same way again.

Kathleen laughed, the sound like music to Kade's ears. "It's okay," she said, holding up three fingers. "I swear I won't tell anyone. Girl Scout's honor."

"I am not afraid of needles," Kade said.

She nodded, still grinning. Kade liked the sight too much to be angry that she'd guessed.

"Fine. But I'm not afraid of needles. I just . . . don't like them. That's all." And if she knew the horror story behind that dislike, she wouldn't laugh at all. But Kade had no desire to tell her that. He'd rather have her disdain and contempt than her pity.

Grabbing his empty glass, she rounded the bar and refilled it before setting it in front of him. "And yet, you have a tattoo." She got a first-aid kit from under the bar, coming back around to him and glancing at the dragon on his bicep.

Dammit, she was up in his space again, close enough to trace the inked edges with a slender fingernail. The touch shot right to his dick, and injured or not, Kade had a brief mental image of picking Kathleen up and setting her on one of those tables behind him, pushing her skirt up to her waist, and—

"What does it mean?" she asked, breaking into his fantasy.

Those blue eyes met his, so innocent and trusting, and guilt immediately chased away the images inside his head. The need to touch her was nearly overpowering.

Finding control he didn't even know he possessed, Kade turned away and grabbed the bourbon again. "Tattoos are different," he said. "Not like the needles they use in hospitals." He swallowed the bourbon in one gulp. And he told no one what the tattoo meant. Not even Blane knew.

She sighed, then said, "Lift your arm again."

Kade did as he was told, assuming she had a bandage, but then her hand was on him, skin against skin, and he stiffened. She was rubbing some kind of ointment into the cut and it burned like fire, but that didn't even begin to compare to the heat in his blood at her touch.

Then it was over and she was using butterfly bandages to hold the skin together.

"There. That should work for now. Though you need a real bandage. We should stop at the drugstore on the way home."

Kade merely grunted and turned away, though inside he reeled. *We* she'd said, meaning her and him. Like they were a couple and would be going *home* together. It struck a need in him so deep and strong, it was overwhelming.

He needed another drink. Glancing behind the bar, Kade was searching for the bottle of bourbon when he heard her.

"Kade—"

She sounded weird, so he glanced around, but she looked fine, just staring at him. "What?"

"Your back . . ." Reaching out, she touched him, and Kade realized what she meant.

She'd seen the scars.

Yeah, yet another story she didn't need to hear. She didn't need to know the shit people did to those more helpless than themselves. To kids. And once upon a time, to him.

"It's nothing," he said. "Just chicken pox scars. No big deal. Not everyone has perfect skin like you, princess." Though *perfect* seemed inadequate for the strawberries and cream of her flesh.

But she didn't smile, and the look on her face was now one of horror. "I know those aren't from chicken pox," she said in a pained whisper. "Who did that to you, Kade?"

The pity in her eyes was the final straw of his crumbling control. He was pissed. Pissed at those assholes who'd jumped him. Pissed that the woman he was supposed to be protecting had been the one to save him. Pissed that he had these . . . feelings that he didn't know what to do with. And pissed that the one woman he wanted, the one he couldn't get out of his head, was the one woman forbidden to him.

Kade snatched her wrist, jerking her toward him to wedge her between his knees. She caught herself, her hand bracing against his chest. The touch only infuriated Kade more. Did she know what she was doing? How insane she was driving him?

"I don't want your pity," he snarled past his clenched jaw.

"I'm not . . . I don't—" she stammered.

"What are you doing, anyway?" he snapped, cutting her off. "This playing nursemaid crap?"

"I'm just trying to help you—"

"Well, I don't need your help."

"Everybody needs somebody," she said softly.

Her body was pliant, so soft and warm, her skin soft like velvet in his grip. Her eyes gazed into his, the pity gone, replaced by a tinge of fear.

"I. Don't."

"Okay, fine, you don't need anybody," she blurted, the blue of her eyes shining with unshed tears.

That's all he needed. Her fucking *crying* over him.

Kade let her go, grabbed his shirt, and jerked it on over his head. Time to get the fuck out of here before he did something she'd regret.

"Maybe you could talk to someone," she said. "There are people who specialize in that sort of thing."

God help him, she was out of her fucking mind. "Why the fuck would I want to do that?" he growled at her. Blane had tried that shit, too, taking him to some psychiatrist. That hadn't lasted long.

Kathleen didn't answer and Kade pulled on his jacket. Grabbing his glass, he approached her until he stood right in front of her. Holding her gaze, he swallowed the last of the bourbon. She didn't speak.

"I'm going to pretend this conversation never happened," he said, his voice cold. "I suggest you do the same." Hell, this whole damn night for that matter.

"But Kade—"

His temper snapped. Kade threw the empty glass on the floor, the sound of it shattering giving him some measure of satisfaction. She gasped, staring at the shards that crunched under his boots as he got closer. His hands came down on her shoulders, gripping too hard, but he couldn't seem to stop. She had to know; he had to make her understand.

"Do you think I want to relive it?"

She shook her head, her eyes wide and frightened.

"Do you think I want Blane to feel guilty for what happened?"

"No, Kade—"

"I don't want Blane to know anything—"

"I won't—"

"—and I don't need you feeling sorry for me—"

"I never said—"

"—and I don't want you inside my head!"

Kathleen was trembling, shaking all over, as tears spilled down her cheeks. Guilt hit Kade hard, crippling in the face of his rage.

He had to leave. He had to get away from her. This woman who he'd already let get too close. Kathleen, she fascinated and terrified him at the same time.

Without a backward glance, he was out the door. Seconds later, the Mercedes was roaring down the street.

CHAPTER SEVEN

Kade didn't get far before he slammed to a stop, his car fishtailing on the side of the road. What the hell was he doing? He was supposed to protect Kathleen, not go running in the opposite direction.

"Fuck!" He slammed his hand against the wheel once, twice. He had no choice. He had to go back.

Stomping on the gas, he swung the Mercedes in a sharp U-turn, the tires leaving rubber on the asphalt as he sped back to where he didn't want to go.

He couldn't see her, though, couldn't handle another conversation with her. The pity in her eyes, the tears shining in the blue depths—it made him hate her and want her at the same time.

Kade parked around the block from the bar, this time making sure no one was around no one was around to get in another fight. Though in the mood he was in, they'd end up regretting it.

What the fuck had he been thinking, letting her get so close? He was supposed to make her hate him, keep that wall of distrust and hostility firmly between them.

The problem was . . . he didn't want Kathleen to hate him. What he wanted was so far from that, it was nearly a physical pain to think of some of the things he'd said to her. But he had to keep her at arm's length. Not only was she off-limits, Kade knew in his bones that somehow, some way, he'd managed to stumble onto the one woman who could destroy him. And the more he knew about her, the more he knew *her*, the more certain of this he became.

Sticking to the deep shadows, he watched the bar until he saw Kathleen step outside. She'd thrown her coat on, but Kade could still see a flash of the red Santa costume underneath. Tracking her movements to her car, he watched as she got in, then he went to his and followed her.

Kathleen was oblivious to his presence about four car lengths behind her as she drove home. Kade rolled his eyes. Some investigator she was. She needed training, skills in observation second only to self-defense.

He parked across the street and watched as she went into her apartment. His hands tightly gripped the steering wheel. He wanted to talk to her, apologize for being such a dick, but he couldn't. She needed to know he was dangerous, to think he didn't want anything to do with her.

A light came on in Kathleen's apartment and Kade watched, imagining her stripping off the Santa outfit before showering, then climbing into bed in that little T-shirt she always wore. What color would her panties be tonight?

It was almost an hour before the lights went off, and Kade let more time pass before he deemed it had been long enough for her to fall asleep. Entering the apartment, he was drawn to her room like the sick fuck he was, standing in the shadows and watching her sleep.

The cat twined around his legs, his purring a low rumble in the quiet bedroom. Kathleen gravitated to one side of the bed, the other side empty and taunting him. Kade's hands clenched into fists so he wouldn't be tempted to touch her. He did ease closer—closer than he had before.

Shafts of light from the streetlamp fell through the slatted blinds, illuminating her face and body every few inches in an amber glow. She was a restless sleeper, and the covers were all tangled. Her hair was splashed across the pillow like a river of molten gold. She lay on her side, the swell of her hip giving way to the deep valley of her waist, and Kade remembered how well she'd fit in his arms and hands.

He didn't know how long he stood there. It calmed him, just being in her presence, even if she wasn't aware. He knew this obsession was getting out of hand, but he was helpless to stop it.

Exhaustion finally drove him to the couch. He pulled off his shirt and dragged the same quilt over himself, falling asleep with the echo of Kathleen's touch drifting across his skin.

～

Kade woke automatically at six in the morning as he'd programmed his body to do. He ached all over from the ass-kicking he'd taken last night, and he spent a long time standing under the hot water of Kathleen's shower.

He could have easily just gone back to his apartment and showered, but there was something about using Kathleen's that made him ignore that. Knowing it was *her* shower, that she stood in the same spot every day, made it . . . intimate somehow.

He was seriously losing it.

After shaving and dressing, he made a pot of coffee, expecting and yet dreading Kathleen's waking. But she didn't. He should be glad; she needed the rest and he needed less face time with her. The disappointment he felt was ridiculous.

Grabbing a pen and a pad of paper, he scrawled a note.

Have business to take care of. Stay put. I'll be back to take you in tonight.

Would she obey? He doubted it. But he had to go. No way in hell could he take another day of constantly being with her. The tracker he'd put on her cell would tell him if she went anywhere.

He grabbed his jacket and was shrugging it on when something caught his eye. He walked to the Christmas tree and removed the locket ornament. He flipped it open and stared at the photo of Kathleen's parents. After a moment, he snapped it closed, then stuffed the whole thing in the pocket of his coat.

Kade locked the door behind him on the way out, did a quick recon of the place and her car before getting behind the wheel of his Mercedes.

His cell rang and he glanced at the display before answering. Blane.

"Yeah."

"Hey, how's Kat doing?"

"You mean after you were such a dick to her yesterday? She's just peachy."

Blane cursed. "I hate that fucking bartending job," he said. "Then she got pissed because of Kandi, thinks I'm just using her . . ." He sighed.

"Can you blame her?" Kade shot back. "I'm not even that into you and *I* hate Kandi."

"Give it a rest," Blane groused. "Are you coming to Kandi's Christmas party tonight or not? I have a feeling whoever's doing this is going to show."

"I thought you were sure they wouldn't."

"That was before I knew she'd invited half the damn town," Blane said. "Better to be safe than sorry. Make sure you're packing heat."

"Have you ever known me to go without?"

Blane snorted a "Bye" and ended the call.

A few minutes later, Kade was pulling into the parking garage of his apartment building. Opening an app on his phone, he checked the GPS on Kathleen. Yep, working perfectly and showing her still in her apartment.

He lived on the top floor, which didn't prevent him from leaving quickly if he had to. Tossing his keys on the counter, Kade set his weapon down, then bent to retrieve the knife strapped to his leg and the other semiautomatic in his ankle holster.

Shoving a hand through his hair, he went into his office, and toggled the space bar on the computer keyboard, causing the four monitors to come to life.

The trace was still going on Bowers's phone numbers, as well as a search Kade had running for all his credit card and ATM transactions. If Bowers used either one anywhere in the world, Kade would know about it within seconds.

Sitting back in the chair, Kade reached for a folder on a stack by his desk. It was something he looked at way too often.

Flipping it open, a photo of Kathleen stared back at him. Kade hadn't taken it. He'd paid someone else to.

She'd been leaving the firm a few weeks ago, the afternoon sunshine making her hair shine like gold. She'd slipped on her mirrored sunglasses, which made her look like the total badass she *wasn't*, but were still smokin' hot on her.

Kade had paid the guy to follow her, tell him her routine, and he'd been thorough. Every day nearly the same. Work at the firm from eight a.m. to six p.m. Some nights she went straight from there to The Drop, depending on her schedule. When she did work at The Drop, she closed, not getting home until after one in the morning.

Other than dating Blane, her social life was nonexistent, not that she had time for much of one. For a month straight, every minute of her day had been documented, right down to the nights Blane stayed over.

Kade had known by then that Kathleen was everything she appeared to be, that she held no threat to Blane. If anything, the reverse was true: Blane was a love 'em and leave 'em type, always going back to Kandi, time and again. Why, Kade didn't know, though he supposed Blane's uncle (Kade refused to claim the relation) often pushed them together, pressuring Blane to marry.

Even knowing she wasn't a threat, however, Kade hadn't stopped the surveillance or his own obsession with finding out everything he could about her. He'd watched as she'd sent nearly every dime of that twenty grand he'd left her to the bill collectors. He'd watched her bank account dip so low he wondered how she could afford to buy food. Even now there were only a couple of hundred bucks in it.

It pissed him off that Blane hadn't done more for her, that he was just using her to fuck until he grew bored. Then he'd dump her—or have Clarice do the dumping for him—and that would be that. Kade had never before spared a thought for the broken hearts Blane left in his wake. Until now.

Granted, she'd lasted longer than most, but Kade would be willing to bet part of that was this case and the threat to her. Nothing quite brought out the protective side of Blane like a damsel in distress. Kathleen had no one. No family, not a lot of friends. That punched about every button Blane had. Add to that her beauty, her innocence, and Kade could see why Blane was totally sucked in. For how long, though, Kade had no clue.

Glancing at his watch, Kade saw it was time to leave. He had a meeting set up with Donovan about a favor. Since Kade had been asking for a lot of favors lately, it was time to pay up.

The nondescript bar chosen for this meeting was nearly empty at this hour, the bartender still taking chairs off tables as Kade walked through the door. Special Agent Donovan was already there and Kade sat opposite him, back to the wall and facing the door. He slid a folder across the table.

"Grey Goose martini, straight up," Kade said to the bartender, who'd approached. He waited until he was out of earshot. "There's the code you wanted broken," he said.

"That was fast," Donovan said in surprise, flipping through the pages.

Kade shrugged as the bartender set down the glass in front of him, filled nearly to the brim with ice-cold liquid. His thoughts weren't on the code, which had been dead simple to crack, but on Kathleen. His skin practically itched to call her, go back to her apartment. He'd checked the GPS about a dozen times already just on the drive over here. Lifting the glass, he downed the vodka in one swallow.

"Little early, isn't it?" Donovan said, a ghost of a smile on his lips.

Kade had always liked Donovan. They'd worked well together as partners for over a year. They'd had each other's backs, keeping the other alive and earning mutual respect, which was something hard-won from Kade. Things were always professional, but occasionally Donovan liked to give him shit. Like now.

Kade answered without thinking. "It takes the edge off."

"What edge is that?"

Glancing up from the empty glass, Kade saw Donovan studying him, his brow drawn in a slight frown. He seemed genuinely interested in what Kade would say.

Kade wasn't the type to spill his guts, not even to his brother, but he suddenly had the urge to talk. Maybe it was the vodka, or maybe it was the beating he'd taken last night. Either way, Donovan felt like someone who'd listen, and maybe he'd have some advice.

"There's this girl," he said, glancing away from Donovan and staring at nothing. Kathleen's face swam in his mind's eye. He spoke without thinking. "She's . . . beautiful. Sweet. Nice. Way too fucking nice. I can't stop thinking about her. It's an obsession I can't seem to kick. I want to *be* with her, not just fuck her, but really talk to her, you know? Listen to her tell me about her shitty day at work or the joke someone told her. Smell her perfume on my clothes before I go to bed at night and know she'll be there when I wake up in the morning. And it's insane, it's crazy, but I can't stop imagining it, picturing it inside my head . . ." Kade's voice trailed away as he realized he'd probably said way too much. He glanced back at Donovan, who now sported a shit-eating grin.

"What's so funny?" Kade asked.

Donovan chuckled. "Never thought I'd live to see the day, man. Kade Dennon. Lovestruck."

Kade snorted, hiding the note of panic that flared inside him at the word *love*. "Fuck that shit." He signaled the bartender for another round. "I just need to get laid, that's all."

Donovan frowned in mock seriousness. "Yeah, really? So tell me, how long has it been? A few weeks? Months? Must've been a while if she's affecting you this much."

The bartender set a new glass in front of Kade. "Three days," he muttered, throwing back the shot as Donovan laughed out loud.

"Nice," he said, still smiling. "And what was her name again?"

"What's your fucking point?" Kade retorted. He had no fucking idea what the girl's name in Buffalo had been.

Donovan raised his hands slightly, palms out. "Nothing. I have no point." He grinned. "Except that you're drinking before noon, waxing poetic about a girl, and have a dreamy look in your eyes."

"You're an asshole," Kade said without heat. Donovan laughed again. "I do not have a 'dreamy look' in my eyes."

Donovan shrugged, still chuckling. "Whatever you say, but I'm starting the pool on wedding dates."

Now it was Kade's turn to laugh, though his held more bitterness than humor. "Yeah, because a girl like that would marry a dick like me. Right?"

Suddenly Donovan wasn't laughing anymore. He hesitated, then said, "Man, I know you don't like to talk about it. But it wasn't your fault. No one blames you."

There weren't many who could stand up to the kind of glare Kade was sending Donovan's way, but he didn't flinch.

"You got part of that right," Kade said. "I don't want to talk about it."

"You don't have to listen to me. Read the files, read the reports. They did an investigation and found nothing wrong—"

"Are you done?" Kade interrupted.

Donovan sighed in defeat. "Yeah, I'm done." His eyes narrowed and he leaned forward. "Just tell me one thing—this case you're on with the woman being threatened, the one you've been having me send the uniforms over to keep an eye on—is it her?"

When Kade didn't answer, Donovan gave a short nod. "I'm going to step up the forensics on that eye, see if we can come up with anything for you. If you need more uniforms, just let me know."

"Thanks. I owe you one."

Donovan left, but Kade barely noticed. He was lost—lost in the drag of his memories.

It was a warm spring evening, and Kade was glad he'd managed a couple of days off from his job with the FBI to stop in Indy to visit his brother. Blane had only just returned from his last deployment three weeks ago and Kade had yet to see him.

He parked his car, hopped out, and went around back to enter through the kitchen of Blane's house. Although Kade himself had called this place home since he was ten years old, inwardly he still referred to it as Blane's. The old man had bought the place and would've turned over in his grave if he'd known Kade had lived there. Not that Kade gave a shit.

"Hey, Mona," Kade said, greeting the woman standing over the stove stirring a pot of something that smelled mouthwatering. He pressed a quick kiss to her cheek.

"It's about time you made it home," she said, though the reprimand in her voice was softened by her smile.

"Well, if you'd told me you were making your world-famous homemade chicken and dumplings, I'd have come sooner," Kade teased. "Where's Blane?"

Mona's face clouded, her smile fading. "He's in the den," she said. "But make sure you holler first, let him know you're coming."

Kade quirked an eyebrow in question as he snagged a chocolate-chip cookie off the rack where more than a dozen of them sat cooling.

"Those will ruin your dinner," Mona scolded, half-heartedly reaching to take it from him. Kade evaded her easily, grinning as he shoved it in his mouth, and grabbed two more.

"They're fabulous," he mumbled, rolling his eyes heavenward, mouth full of gooey cookie.

Mona huffed in exaggerated frustration, her smile indulgent.

"How long are you staying?" she asked.

"I've only got the weekend," Kade replied.

Mona looked disappointed at this, but said nothing more as Kade left the kitchen and headed down the hall. He shoved the two cookies in his mouth as he pushed open the door to the den.

Then immediately dove to the ground as Blane swung a Glock in his direction.

Kade froze, gazing up at Blane, who looked as surprised to see him as Kade was to see a gun pointed at his head. Gingerly, Kade got to his feet, swallowing the cookies in one lump.

"I'd say 'Welcome home, brother,'" Kade said, "but what the fuck?"

"You startled me," Blane said, putting the Glock back in the holster at his side.

"So you pull a gun on me?" Kade asked.

Blane shrugged. "Sorry. Reflex."

And Kade realized why Mona had warned him.

His brows furrowed as he walked over to one of the leather wingback chairs by Blane's desk and sank into its cool confines.

"So how do you like being back?" he asked. Blane had been deployed many times over the past several years, but this last one had been longer than the others, manpower seeming to be in short supply.

"It's taking some getting used to," Blane admitted, sitting in the chair opposite Kade. "But it's good to be home." His skin was a dark bronze, his hair burnished gold from the desert sun.

Kade abruptly realized that Blane looked . . . older. It was sobering. He'd tried not to think very much about all that Blane was enduring while overseas, but looking at him now, it was obvious the years in combat had taken their toll.

He forced a careless smile. "Well, your little brother's come to visit. Let's go paint the town."

Blane grinned, a spark coming back into his eyes. "It'll have to wait until after dinner. Mona will be pissed if we skip out on her chicken and dumplings."

Three hours later, he and Blane were parking the Jaguar outside a club downtown. It wasn't the nicest of places, the clientele rough-and-tumble, but it wasn't a dive either. Kade paid the cover and snagged a high table in the corner. He sat on one barstool while Blane took the other.

Signaling for a cocktail waitress, Kade asked, "So have you been to see Kandi yet?"

Blane shrugged, his gaze flitting around the room. "Once," he said.

A waitress came by and Kade ordered two beers and four shots. When she left, he said, "Thought you and her would be settling down sometime soon. Start poppin' out little blond brats." He grinned at the look Blane shot him.

"She wants to, but I'm not ready for that," Blane said with a snort, taking a long pull of the beer the waitress sat in front of him. She wasn't a bad-looking brunette and Kade noticed Blane eye her ass as she walked away.

"To my big brother," Kade said, picking up one of the shots. "Hail the conquering hero and shit."

Blane huffed a laugh, downing the shot with Kade before they finished off the second one. The beer was a nice, cool chaser to the whiskey, burning a path to Kade's stomach. He signaled the waitress for another round.

Kade knew he and Blane made a striking pair, and more than a few interested female gazes were sent their direction. Blane's golden-boy good looks were polar opposite to Kade's inky-black hair and bad-boy demeanor. The part of Blane that had always made people somewhat wary of him had been honed to a steel edge by the SEALs, which would no doubt attract the women like candy.

While Blane and Kade's outward appearance might have been dissimilar, they both now carried an aura of danger. It was in the way Blane sat in the chair, seemingly at ease, but his eyes were constantly moving and his fingers played with the beer bottle, as though ready at any moment to turn it into a jagged weapon. The FBI training Kade had been given had made his instincts razor sharp. Though he'd convinced Blane to leave his gun in the car, Kade had a gun strapped to his ankle. He had learned to never, ever, be without a weapon.

Forty minutes and six shots later, Kade was studying the bar. Two women in the corner caught his eye. One was a blonde, the other a brunette. Two men were flirting with them, but the girls kept shooting looks at him and Blane, whispering to each other. Giving them a lopsided smirk, Kade crooked his finger, beckoning them.

"What are you doing?" Blane asked as the two girls started heading their way, leaving behind the two guys they'd been talking to.

"Entertainment," Kade said simply, setting aside his beer. He was well on his way to being drunk, and by the look in Blane's eyes, so was he.

"I'm not in the mood," Blane said.

"Bullshit," Kade shot back. "You need to get laid. And from what I've seen, the sooner, the better."

The girls arrived then and Kade randomly picked the blonde.

"Hi," she said. "I'm—"

"Beautiful," Kade interrupted smoothly. Names were unnecessary. She smiled. Kade slid his arms around her waist, his hands gliding under the semitransparent shirt she wore to touch her skin. Pulling her between his spread knees, he leaned forward to whisper in her ear.

"My buddy and I could buy you and your friend a drink and waste time playing the game like those losers you were just with. Or we can get out of here, get a room, and I can spend the next few hours making you come so hard you'll forget every other man who's ever fucked you."

She sucked in her breath, her brown eyes widening, then she smiled and nudged her friend. They exchanged looks.

"I hope you're not all talk," the blonde said.

Kade's answering smirk spoke for itself. He tossed some bills on the table. "Let's go," he said to Blane.

"Just a minute, dickhead."

Kade turned to see that the two guys had approached them. Their stances were belligerent. The one who'd spoken was in front, his friend standing behind him and off to the side, backing him up.

Kade stepped into the guy's personal space. They were the same height. "'Just a minute' is your problem," he said with a twisted sneer. "I'm guessing the ladies want things to last a bit longer. I hear there's medication that can help with that, not that I know from personal experience."

Kade turned away just as the guy grabbed onto his arm.

"Go fuck yourself," the guy said. "We saw them first."

Spinning around, Kade grabbed the guy's wrist, broke his hold, then twisted his arm around behind his back, using the momentum to plaster the guy face first on the table he and Blane had just vacated. Out of the corner of his eye, he saw Blane step up to the remaining dude, who didn't look like he was going to try to bypass Blane to help his buddy anytime soon.

Leaning down, Kade whispered in the guy's ear. "You may have seen them first, but we'll be fucking them first. Have a nice night. Dickhead."

Abruptly releasing him, Kade stepped back. Stopping at the bar, Kade exchanged a hundred for two fresh bottles of Jack before leading the way outside. Blane brought up the rear behind the two girls tottering on their high heels, giggling to each other. With a sharp whistle, Kade summoned a passing cab and they piled in the back. Giving the driver the name of a nearby hotel, Kade pulled the blonde onto his lap.

He was horny as hell and he didn't give Blane and the brunette a second thought as he began kissing the blonde. She was a good kisser, turning so she straddled his lap, her short skirt climbing to her waist.

"Your friend's got the right idea," Kade heard the brunette say to Blane, her voice a husky murmur.

"It would appear so."

Kade's lips twisted in a smile when he glanced over and saw Blane had gotten in on the action, the brunette busy sliding her hands underneath his shirt.

They arrived at the hotel and ten minutes later unlocked the door to a suite. The girls were as drunk as Kade and Blane, laughing uproariously when one of them tripped and nearly went down. They stumbled, helping each other into the bedroom, while Blane and Kade followed.

"One room?" Blane asked Kade with a derisive snort. "We're brothers, but some things I don't need to know."

Kade shot him a wicked grin. "Take a walk on the wild side, brother, and trust me." Unscrewing the bottle of Jack, Kade took a long swig, then handed it to Blane.

Blane sighed, then shrugged and tipped the bottle to his lips.

When they entered the bedroom, the girls were already down to their underwear, both clad in tiny thongs. The blonde wasn't a real blonde, not that Kade cared. And he was pretty sure her breasts were fake, but he wasn't going to complain.

"Care for a drink, girls?" Kade asked, handing the blonde the bottle he'd opened.

The blonde laughed, took a drink, and passed it to the brunette. While the brunette drank, the blonde unhooked her bra, helping the brunette slide the straps down her arms while she kept drinking. The blonde began touching the brunette's breasts, her palms cupping them while her thumbs brushed the pink nipples. The brunette tossed aside the now empty bottle, and they started kissing.

"Holy fuck," Blane breathed quietly.

Kade's dick was hard as a rock. He didn't turn away from the scene when he answered Blane. "You can thank me later." Digging in his pocket, he handed a couple of condoms to Blane.

The alcohol in his bloodstream made disrobing slightly more difficult, but it wasn't too long before Kade was naked and kneeling on the bed behind the blonde. Out of his peripheral vision, he saw Blane mirroring his movements.

Then the brunette was on her back, and Blane was fucking her. Kade pushed himself inside the blonde, his hands cupping her fake boobs. The room began to spin, the booze hitting him hard, and he closed his eyes.

The next few hours were a haze of sweat and skin, the blonde sucking him off as Blane fucked her from behind, the brunette straddling Kade's face, his hands gripping her ass while he ate her pussy. Blane passed out at some point and the last thing Kade remembered was screwing the brunette while she used her fingers on the blonde. Feminine moans and sighs filled his ears, his orgasm making him groan, then he collapsed on the bed, spent.

When Kade next opened his eyes, it was almost four in the morning and the room was still spinning. He sat up, blinking as he got his bearings. The girls were sprawled together, their naked limbs entwined. They were sleeping . . . or passed out. Blane was asleep at the end of the bed, his leg hanging off the side.

Getting up, Kade shook Blane awake.

"Wha—" Blane groaned, but Kade shushed him.

"Let's get out of here, bro," he said quietly. The last thing he wanted was to wake the girls.

Kade dressed, finding the buttons on his shirt more difficult to do up than usual. He had to help Blane, who he thought had drunk most of that second bottle of Jack.

They exited the hotel from a side entrance.

"That was one for the books," Kade said, flashing a grin to Blane. "Am I right?"

Blane laughed, scrubbing a hand across his face. "My little brother's a bad influence on me," he joked.

"Damn straight."

They scanned the deserted street for a moment. "No way are we getting a taxi at this hour," Kade said. "We'll have to hoof it back to your car."

The streets were silent and nearly empty. Kade knew the layout and alleys of downtown Indy like the back of his hand. He turned into a side alley shortcut, Blane close behind.

The alley was dark with shadows, meager light filtering through the blackness. Kade was as alert as he was able to be with as much alcohol in his system as he had. Which wasn't good enough.

A sound behind him made him turn in time to see a figure fly at Blane from the shadows. Kade had no time to help Blane as another attacker came at him, catching him in the gut and making him double over.

"You may have fucked them first, but we're gonna fuck you over," the guy hissed.

Kade realized it was the two guys from the bar. They'd waited for him and Blane to show? What losers.

"Fuck you," Kade rasped. He brought his fist up, knocking the guy in the jaw. Blane was punching his attacker while Kade wrestled with his.

The darkness of the alley didn't help and Kade didn't see the glint of a knife until it was already coming at him. He leapt backward, but not in time. The knife swiped across his chest, leaving a slice in his shirt and skin in its wake. The cut burned, but Kade could tell it wasn't that deep. Blood oozed a trail down his stomach.

A roar of rage made both Kade and the guy with the knife look back. Blane had caught sight of them, his attacker on the ground.

Blane's gaze was locked on the blood on Kade's chest, his eyes glinting with fury. He launched himself at the guy with the knife, his hands locking around the man's neck. The guy dropped the knife to tug uselessly at Blane's hands. Blane let go, crouching down to grab the knife from where it had fallen. The man came at Blane, who, with one hard, upward thrust, buried the blade in the man's chest.

He stared at Blane, his mouth open in surprise, then looked down at the hilt protruding from his body. The light faded from his eyes and his body dropped to the ground and was still.

Kade stared in shock, his mouth agape. It had happened so fast.

"Holy shit," the remaining guy breathed. "You killed him! You sick motherfucker!" Scrambling to his feet, he began running down the alley.

Kade made a split-second decision. Reaching down, he pulled the gun from the holster around his ankle. Taking quick aim, he squeezed off a single shot. The man dropped to the ground and didn't move.

Breathing hard, Kade looked over at Blane, who stood, looking down at the man he'd killed, his chest heaving from exertion. His hands were clenched into fists and he was shaking.

Survival instinct kicked in and Kade hurried to Blane. "Careful not to touch him," he said. "C'mon. We've got to get out of here." Reaching down, Kade grabbed the switchblade and yanked it from the body before flipping it closed and shoving it into his pocket.

Blane didn't respond and Kade had to call his name twice more before it seemed to get through.

Moving quickly, they were back in the Jag in five minutes.

"Gimme the keys," Kade said. Blane handed them over without a word.

They didn't speak on the way home. Blane stared out the window.

The enormity of what had just happened hit Kade as he drove. The two men had been looking for a fight, not looking to die. Blane's reaction to Kade getting hurt, the blood seeming to set him off, scared Kade. He'd never seen Blane so . . . out of control.

And Kade himself had done worse. He didn't have the excuse of blind rage or what he now suspected was PTSD in his brother. Kade had assessed the situation, had known the man would be a witness to the murder of his friend, and had done what he had to do. Kade would protect his brother, no matter what.

An officer of the law, an FBI agent, he had just killed a man in cold blood.

Kade pushed the thought away, his attention returning to Blane, who still hadn't spoken.

After parking in the driveway, Kade got out. He went around the car and opened Blane's door, too, when his older brother didn't step out. Taking his arm, Kade led Blane upstairs to his bedroom and sat him on his bed.

Finally, when Blane was still silent, Kade said, "Hey man, are you all right?"

Blane blinked confusedly, looking up at Kade. His face blanched when he saw the cut across Kade's chest. The bleeding had stopped, but it'd left a helluva mess behind.

"What the hell happened to you?" Blane asked.

Kade was so surprised, it took him a moment to reply. "The . . . fight," he said finally.

"Shit," Blane said, jumping to his feet and heading to the bathroom. "What have I told you about getting in those damn bar fights?" He returned, holding a small med kit. "What if he'd stabbed instead of sliced? You could be dead right now."

Kade stared as Blane opened the kit, taking out some antiseptic wipes. Could Blane really not remember what had happened?

Blane carefully cleaned the cut, the antiseptic burning like a sonofabitch, but Kade ignored it. "You were in the fight, too," he said carefully.

Glancing up at him, Blane said, "Obviously I didn't hold up my side if you got hurt like this."

"You don't remember?" Kade persisted.

Blane sighed, pausing in his ministrations to rub his forehead. "My head hurts like there's a jackhammer in there and all I remember is a brunette— no, wait—a blonde? I do know there was booze." He cracked a grin at Kade. "Guess if you can't remember the details, that must mean it was good, right?" He laughed lightly.

Kade forced a smile. "That's right, brother," he said. "Hey, I'm gonna hit the shower, then the sack. I'll catch you in the morning."

"Afternoon, more likely," Blane said with a snort.

Kade didn't reply as he left the room and headed downstairs. He went into the den, closing the door behind him, and pulled his cell from his pocket. He dialed a number and when a man answered, Kade said only four words.

"Blane needs your help."

⁓

"What happened?" Senator Keaston asked once he'd slid into the passenger seat of Kade's car. He hadn't wanted to discuss anything over the phone, agreeing to meet Kade instead.

Kade quickly explained, ending with how Blane had no memory of the incident with the men in the alley.

"Did anyone see you?"

"No, I don't think so," Kade answered.

"Did you take the knife?"

"Yes."

"Are the bodies still there?" Keaston asked.

"Probably."

"Okay, here's what's going to happen," Keaston said. "I'm going to have the bodies taken care of and we're not going to speak of this again. You will never, ever tell Blane what happened, do you understand?"

Kade swallowed. "Yeah."

"In return, I want something from you," Keaston said, his eyes narrowing as he studied Kade.

Kade's brows lifted in surprise. Blane's uncle had barely given him the time of day over the years, tolerating him solely for Blane's sake. It hadn't escaped Kade's notice that Keaston thought Kade was a blight on Blane's life, and he'd helped convince Blane to go along with Kade's request to not tell people they were brothers. Blane hadn't wanted to do that, but Keaston had taken up Kade's argument for the secrecy and eventually Blane had reluctantly agreed.

"What do you want?" Kade asked.

"I want you to quit the FBI and come work for me."

Kade had spent too many years knowing that people wanted to use him to think that this was going to work in his favor in any possible way. With a sinking feeling, he asked, "Doing what?"

"You're a smart man, Kade," Keaston said. "A clever and dangerous man. The skills you have, the additional skills you could acquire, would be extremely . . . useful . . . to me."

"Why me?"

"Because you have nothing to lose," Keaston answered flatly. "And a lot to gain. Agree, and I'll take care of this problem for you with Blane none the wiser."

"And if I refuse?" Kade asked.

"Refuse, and I can't help what'll happen," Keaston said with a sad shrug. "Two dead bodies are hard to run from, especially when there are witnesses to an altercation you had earlier with them. Blane will be caught, as will you."

"I can say I did it," Kade replied. "I killed them both."

"And do you really think Blane will believe you?" Keaston asked. "You and I both know he'll figure out the truth, maybe even remember it. Then not even I will be able to stop the wheels of justice from turning."

"He's your nephew," Kade protested. "Why do I have to do anything? You'd really let Blane go down for this if I don't do what you want?"

"Perhaps," Keaston said, his calculating gaze glittering in the near darkness inside the car. "Are you willing to take that chance?"

Kade stared at the man. The same blood ran in their veins and for the first time, Kade recognized some of himself in Keaston. A ruthlessness and coldness that Kade had tried to pretend didn't exist in his own soul. The only person who'd ever looked beyond that, had seen something else inside Kade, was Blane.

"All right," Kade said. "I'll do it."

"Excellent." Keaston smiled, his lips thin. "Do you have the knife?"

"I ditched it," Kade said. "And the gun."

"Good thinking," Keaston replied. "I trust somewhere they'll never be found?"

Kade nodded.

Keaston smiled again. "Get Blane back to normal, then I'll be in touch," he said, before getting out of the car.

Watching Keaston walk away, Kade felt as though he'd just agreed to a deal with the devil. Everything he'd wanted, dreamed of—it was all dust now, collateral damage from the choices he'd made tonight.

But better Keaston destroy Kade's life than Blane's. Blane deserved nothing but happiness and success, and if Kade had to be the darkness lurking in the shadows to make sure that happened, then he would be.

Kade had e-mailed his resignation to the FBI that very night, breaking the news to Blane the next day. Blane had been stunned, then furious.

"Why the hell would you do something so stupid?" he'd raged at Kade. "You just threw away your entire career!"

"It's my life," Kade replied stonily. "And there's no money in law enforcement. You know that."

"If you need money, then just say so," Blane said.

"I don't want your money."

"What's mine is yours. I've been telling you that for years—"

"I don't want to live by the rules, Blane," Kade interrupted, grasping at straws. "It's boring. You may be able to handle it, but I can't."

Blane was quiet for a moment. "What do you mean?" he asked finally.

Kade glanced away, unable to see the look on Blane's face. "People pay a lot of money for the stuff I can do," he said.

"Please tell me you're just talking about hacking," Blane said in a low voice.

Kade didn't reply and Blane cursed.

"Hunting people for a living is not a career," Blane argued. "It's a death wish."

"I've made my choice," Kade said flatly. "I'm not ten anymore. So you can either accept it, or throw me out. Which is it going to be?"

Blane had studied him, his lips pressed tightly together. The disappointment in his eyes had pierced Kade, but there was nothing Kade could do about it, nothing he could say. He couldn't tell Blane the truth, so he just met his gaze and waited.

Blane sighed. "You're my brother, no matter what," he said. "Even if you're making a shitty decision."

And that had been the end of it. Blane had refrained from any lectures over the years, though Kade had certainly deserved them. What had remained was Kade's task—getting Blane to a state of normalcy.

CHAPTER EIGHT

Kade spent the rest of the day digging up everything he could on every single person involved in the case Blane was defending. Kyle Waters was a decorated SEAL, as had been the men with whom he'd served on the ill-fated mission where a US citizen fighting for the other side had been killed. The ex-wife was a piece of work, though Kade supposed she was entitled to a little bitterness after her miscarriage. The divorce had come swiftly after that, Kyle deployed for the entire proceeding.

He kept tabs on Kathleen and saw when she left her apartment—as he'd told her not to do—ending up at some hotel downtown where she stayed most of the day. Kade briefly entertained the thought of calling her to see what the hell she was doing, but then she'd know he had a tracker on her.

What was she doing at a hotel? Was she seeing someone else behind Blane's back? The thought should have irritated him. Instead, a little voice inside his head said that if she wasn't into Blane any longer, then maybe Kade had a shot . . .

Kade shoved the thought away as he surveyed himself in the mirror. Tuxes weren't really his thing, but women seemed to like them. Would Kathleen think he looked good in a tux? He snorted at the thought. Like he should care what she thought. Grabbing the jacket and bow tie, he headed downstairs. He found Mona in the kitchen and handed her the tie.

"I've taught you how to do this a dozen times," she said mildly, wrapping the length of silk around his neck.

"And I've told you, I don't want to learn," he replied.

Mona chuckled and shook her head. Kade's lips lifted in a half smile as she patiently tied the bow tie.

"There. Perfect," she said. "Are you and Blane going to Kandi's party?"

"Unfortunately," Kade said.

"Is he taking Kathleen, too?" she asked.

Kade shook his head, snagging a meatball from the plate where Mona had set them and popping it into his mouth. "She's gotta work," he mumbled.

"Don't talk with your mouth full," Mona automatically chastised. "That's too bad. I'm sure she would have enjoyed it. The Millers' Christmas parties are always nice."

"They should be for how much she spends on them," Kade said with a snort.

Just then, Blane entered the kitchen. Of course *his* bow tie was already perfectly done. Spying the meatballs, he grabbed one.

"Will you boys stop?" Mona said, slapping at Blane's hand. "I just made those."

"And we're just eating them," Kade said, sneaking another one while she was occupied with Blane.

Mona huffed, but wasn't successful at hiding a smile.

"When will you be there?" Blane asked.

"Not until I absolutely have to," Kade said. Blane gave him a look. "I've got to take Kathleen to work first, then I'll show," he said. The GPS had shown her returning to her apartment an hour ago. He waited to see if Blane would ask about Kathleen, but it seemed he didn't want to open that particular can of worms again.

"Gotta go," Kade said to Mona, pressing a kiss to her cheek. "See you later." He snagged another meatball as he passed by.

"You boys have fun," she called after him. "Kade, tell Kathleen I said hello."

Kade didn't bother knocking when he reached Kathleen's, he just let himself in. He was nervous after last night. Would she look at him differently? Would he see the pity again in her eyes? He didn't know if he could handle that.

He heard her in the bathroom. The door was open, so she must be doing her hair or putting on her makeup. Kade hoped she was doing her hair. He'd like to watch that. Maybe she wouldn't think it was too weird.

Kade silently leaned against the doorjamb to the bathroom. Damn. She was already done with her hair. But she was wearing that cock-tease Santa outfit again, so that was a definite plus.

"Nice night, princess," he said. He couldn't help a smile. It was strange, how he felt when he saw her. No one else made him feel that way. Anticipation and pleasure—and all he was doing was talking to her. Donovan's words echoed in his head before he shoved them away.

She spun around in surprise and Kade caught a flash of relief cross her face. Why? Was she glad he was there? And if so, was it because she was afraid? Or maybe, just maybe, she'd wanted to see him, too?

"Hey," she said. Her gaze dropped to the tux he wore and Kade was gratified to see a flicker of appreciation in her eyes. "Going somewhere?"

This should be interesting. "Kandi's Christmas party is tonight," he said. He noticed her mouth was swollen and hope flared briefly inside him. She'd been kissing someone else today—she *was* having an affair.

"Is Blane going?" she asked with forced nonchalance that didn't fool Kade for a second. She brushed past him on her way to the living room. He caught a whiff of her perfume.

"It would seem so," Kade said, taking her coat from her and holding it so she could slide her arms into the sleeves. It was an excuse to touch her. Now that he was close, he could see that yes, her mouth was swollen, but it was cut, too, which meant someone had hit her. Someone who'd just put themselves on Kade's shit list. People on that list had a nasty habit of dying, usually in a painful, drawn-out kind of way.

"What happened today?" he asked, sliding his hands under her hair to lift it from underneath the collar. The strands were so soft, his fingers lingered longer than they should have.

"What do you mean?"

Kade lightly grasped her chin, forcing her to look at him. His thumb touched her abused lip, and she winced. "This is what I mean," he said. How the hell had this happened? "I told you to stay put today. I see you did your usual bang-up job of not listening."

"It's nothing," she said, pulling away from him. "And you gave me a promotion, remember? I had a job to do."

Yeah, he was already regretting that promotion.

"Aren't you going to be late for the party?" she asked.

"Wanted to take you to work first," Kade said. "Make sure you arrive alive." His eyes narrowed as he tried to think of how he could figure out who'd hit her.

"Great, let's go," she said.

Although Kade had already checked outside and knew there were no lurking threats, he didn't tell Kathleen that. Instead, he used it as an excuse to wrap an arm around her and pull her close, shielding her with his body as they walked to her car. It seemed she'd come to accept it, and she didn't protest.

Kade followed in his car, then walked her into The Drop and settled at the bar while she clocked in and stashed her purse. She set a cup of coffee in front of him while his gaze roamed down to her thighs, covered in thin nylon that would feel like silk against his hand.

"You don't have to stay, you know," she said. "I can take care of myself."

There was nothing Kade could say to that ridiculous assertion that wouldn't piss her off, so he just looked at her over the rim of the coffee mug. She had no trouble reading his unspoken thought.

"I ran into some trouble today," she said defensively, "but I'm fine. So go. Have a good time tonight." Her smile was fake, but hey, at least she made the effort.

It was better to leave now. She was safe here and he could go put in his appearance at the party and leave in plenty of time to take her home. "I'll be back by closing," he said, taking one last sip of the coffee. Sliding off the stool, he headed for the door.

Kandi's father's house was overflowing with people, as Kade had known it would be. Kade's perfectly done bow tie lasted exactly thirty minutes. By that time, he'd undone it and the top button on his shirt. He hated the constriction of a tie around his throat.

Drink in hand, he clung to the outer edges of the ballroom, avoiding people if at all possible. He didn't have to try very hard. Most had enough sense to stay away from the man with the cold and deadly look in his eyes.

Kade watched Blane dancing with Kandi. They made a striking couple. She was clinging to him like a vine, and it didn't seem like Blane minded. When the strains of music faded, Kade saw Kandi take Blane's hand and lead him out of the ballroom through one of the side doors.

Kade finished the rest of his drink in one swallow. He'd never before cared what Blane did in his love life, who he screwed or how many hearts he broke. Until now. Now there was an angry ball of bitterness in the pit of his stomach.

Kade wanted to follow Blane to wherever Kandi had led him for what he was sure would be a private room for fucking. Then he wanted to kick Blane's ass for cheating on Kathleen, as well as thank him, because if he was cheating on her, then Kade could move in.

But he didn't follow them, because as much as he wanted Kathleen to be available, it scared him, too. Was it just because he hadn't slept with her? Was that why he couldn't get her out of his head? What if Donovan was right? What if it was something . . . more?

"You seem awfully lonely, over here by yourself."

Kade turned from where he'd been staring at the door through which Kandi and Blane had disappeared and saw a woman had approached him. She was pretty, with dark hair and dark eyes, and perhaps older than him, but very well preserved. A divorcée, maybe, or a rich, bored housewife.

"Being alone doesn't make me lonely," Kade said, handing his empty glass to a passing waiter.

"And not being alone doesn't ensure you're not," she shot back.

Kade's lips lifted in a smirk. She had sass. He liked that.

"So you came over to talk to me?" he asked, his sarcasm thick. "Keep me company?" His gaze traveled deliberately down her body and back up, lingering on the lush amount of cleavage on display. He'd seen better—Kathleen's immediately sprang to mind—but this one would do. Maybe she'd help rid him of this fixation he had.

"Talking wasn't the first thing on my mind, no," she replied.

Her bluntness was appreciated, and not something Kade usually saw in the women who approached him.

"Good, because I'm shitty at small talk." Taking her hand, he led her swiftly from the room, finding an empty place as close as possible, which happened to be a bathroom.

Her dress was unzipped and on the floor before she'd managed to undo his fly. She stretched up to try to kiss him, but Kade evaded her, turning her around and fastening his mouth to her shoulder. She wore no bra and his hands cupped her breasts, making her moan.

If he closed his eyes, he could pretend it wasn't some nameless woman who didn't give a shit about him. He could pretend it was a girl with blonde hair kissed by the sun and blue eyes so pure they could see right through him.

Slipping a condom from his pocket—never leave home without one—Kade rolled it over his erection as the woman shimmied out of her panties. Using his knee to spread her thighs, he pushed her down, bending her over the counter, then thrust inside her.

He pumped hard and fast, his eyes tightly shut and the image of Kathleen behind his lids. He felt the woman come before him, which was good because he didn't care enough to make sure she came once he was finished.

Discarding the condom in the trash, Kade rearranged his clothes. The woman was panting, still bent over the counter. Placing his hands on her waist, he slid them up her sides, pulling her back until she stood upright, her back to his chest. Kade focused on their reflection in the mirror. She was naked, he fully dressed. Her eyes were sated as she gazed back at him.

Lifting his hands, he cupped her breasts, his thumbs flicking lightly over her erect nipples. Bending, he placed a kiss to her shoulder, trailing his lips up her neck to her ear. She smelled nice.

"Thanks for keeping me company," he whispered. She shivered at the touch of his breath, her eyes slipping closed, then Kade was out the door and gone.

He felt better, but it hadn't helped that he'd pictured Kathleen during that. If he wanted to get her out of his head, thinking of her while having sex with someone else probably wasn't the best way to go about it.

As if his thoughts had conjured her out of thin air, a door across the ballroom burst open and in walked Kathleen.

Well, not walked. She was speed-walking, almost running. What was she doing here? He'd left her at work a few hours ago and she'd obviously just come from there, because she still wore the Santa outfit.

People scurried to get out of her way and now Kade saw Blane enter the ballroom in hot pursuit of Kathleen. Kade frowned, wondering what the hell was going on, then he spotted Kandi. She stood next to Senator Keaston and seemed unsurprised at the scene playing out in her ballroom.

Several people followed Blane and Kathleen, including Kade, who pushed his way to the front of the crowd in time to see Blane grab Kathleen's arm when she reached the front door. She swung around, her fist nailing him right in the jaw.

That had to hurt—her, of course, not Blane—but it was her face that held Kade's attention. She was paler than he'd ever seen her, and tears coursed down her cheeks.

Everyone seemed to stop breathing for a moment, including Kathleen, who looked horrified that she'd hit Blane. There was no doubt in Kade's mind that whatever Blane had done, he probably deserved it. Then she was out the door and everyone began talking at once. Kade went up to Blane, who still stood by the door.

"What the fuck did you do?" Kade hissed, his temper raging. He felt a consuming need to protect Kathleen and to hurt whoever had hurt her.

"Not now," Blane said in a low, tight voice. The look he shot Kade told him something was going on, but damned if Kade gave a shit right now. This hadn't looked like the scene at the bar the other night, where Kathleen had known Blane was setting her up. This had looked pretty fucking real.

"She ran out of here, crying like you just shot her fucking cat, and you tell me 'not now'?" Kade retorted. He got in Blane's face. "You told me to protect her. Am I protecting her from a psycho who wants to kill her? Or a sociopath who wants to rip her fucking heart out?"

Blane said nothing, the two of them caught in a stare-down. Kade's hands curled into fists and he turned away first, mostly so he wouldn't coldcock his own brother. Without another word, he walked out the door, following the path Kathleen had taken.

The night was bitter cold and still. Kade thought of what Kathleen had been wearing, realizing she had to be freezing in that getup. Had she gone? He searched for her car, finally spotting it. She hadn't left yet, hadn't even started the engine.

Worry dogged him as he hurried toward the piece-of-shit Honda, a little voice in the back of his head asking him what the hell he thought he was going to do when he got to her. It wasn't like comforting crying women was something he did. Ever. But he shoved the thought away. He'd think of something. Right now he just had a burning need to make sure she was all right.

He could see her behind the wheel, staring straight ahead as though in shock. Kade's gut twisted.

"Kathleen," he said, talking through the window to her. She jerked in surprise, her red-rimmed eyes wide as she turned to look up at him.

"Kade—"

"Open the door," Kade ordered. "You're in no condition to drive." The last thing he needed was her wrecking the car on her way home, and he tried not to think about that driving urge to protect her that still burned white-hot in his gut.

"No! Wait!" Her shout was laced with panic and made Kade freeze in place. "Look," she said, pointing to the windshield.

Kade's brow creased in a frown as he tried to see what she was pointing at. It took a moment, but he finally made out the word some-one had written on the glass.

BOOM.

"Fuck." Someone had planted a bomb on her car, or wanted her to think they had. Only one way to tell for sure. "Don't move," he ordered, then crouched down on the cold, wet asphalt.

He saw the device immediately. Strapped to the underside of her car was enough C4 to make sure she didn't walk away. Wires led from the explosive up into the car, but without more light and time, Kade couldn't see where. What he did see were the red, glowing numbers counting down.

Getting back to his feet, he spoke through the windshield.

"Okay, now don't panic," he said. "There is a bomb underneath your car."

Those words had an immediate effect as Kathleen slumped in her seat. Shit!

"Don't you pass out on me, Kathleen!" He'd never get her out if she was unconscious, and watching her die was out of the question.

Kathleen jerked upright at his yell and Kade spoke again.

"Listen to me. The bomb is rigged to something inside, but I can't tell what it is. It could be the door, ignition, radio, anything."

"That's not helpful," she said.

A visceral part of Kade appreciated the fact that she had a sense of humor even under these dire circumstances. God, he loved this woman.

"It's also on a timer, Kathleen."

Her eyes slid shut and Kade could practically see the despair slide into her soul.

"How much time?" she asked. He barely heard her.

No sense lying. "Three minutes."

She took a breath and resignation replaced the despair. "You should go," she said, her voice choked. "Back off. I can try to open the door."

Yeah, not gonna happen. "I'm not leaving you, Kathleen."

She glanced back at him, and the strangest thing happened. She looked at him—really looked at him—the way other women had looked at him a thousand times, but never before by her. A slide of her gaze from his head down his torso and back up, like she was drinking him in. Then the moment was gone.

"Don't be ridiculous, Kade," she snapped, looking away again. "You don't even like me. Now go."

As if she could order him around. "I don't have to like you to save your life," he retorted. "Now roll down the window." Blane had said to keep her safe, so that's what Kade would do. For Blane.

Right.

"Can't," she said. "Not without turning on the car."

It figured. The one time an ancient piece-of-shit car could be helpful with manual windows and hers didn't have them.

"Turn away then," he said.

She obeyed and Kade bent his elbow before sending it hurtling against the glass. The collision sent a jolt of pain through his arm, but he ignored it and tried again. The glass splintered, but stubbornly held together. Fuck. There had to be something around that he could use to help break that window.

Kade began searching the ground. A big chunk of asphalt would probably do the trick—

"Wait!" Kathleen's shout made him whip around. "I forgot something," she said. He saw her dig underneath her seat and a moment later, she brandished something in her hand, a slim device about six inches long. "This!"

She pressed one end of the emergency hammer to the window and it shattered immediately. Kade wasted no time in reaching through the window for her. Luckily, she was tiny enough to fit through the opening. Once she was on her feet, Kade grabbed her hand and pulled her backward. The clock inside his head said they had only seconds remaining.

"Run!"

They both ran and the explosion followed moments after, the shock wave knocking them off their feet. Kade grabbed Kathleen, pulling her into him and twisting so her body landed on top of his. She was small, but big enough to knock the wind out of him. They both lay there for a moment, the night sky lit from the fiery blaze engulfing her car.

Kade sat up, pulling her still form onto his lap. Was she okay? Had she been hurt? She wasn't talking.

"Are you all right?" he asked anxiously.

Her entire body was wracked with tremors and she didn't speak, just gave a nod.

The ground was cold and hard, so Kade got to his feet, helping her up as well. She didn't look so good. Her face was deathly pale and the shaking was even worse now. She was going into shock.

Shrugging out of his tuxedo jacket, Kade swung it over her shoulders and pulled it closed. She was too cold.

"Kathleen!"

Kade turned to see the explosion had brought the party outside and Blane was running toward them, the expression on his face one of stark fear that changed to relief once he saw Kathleen standing next to Kade. He skidded to a halt a few feet away, his breath coming in harsh pants.

"Keep him away from me. Please." Kathleen's whispered plea only just reached Kade's ear, but it had the same effect as if a switch had been thrown. The burning in his gut that wanted to protect her flared, solidifying into one all-consuming purpose.

Kade pulled Kathleen into him, shielding her with his body. Blane took a step toward them, his eyes on Kathleen. Kade wanted to growl at him, like a dog staking its territory.

"She's fine," Kade said, his eyes narrowing as he watched his brother. It was a warning veiled inside a statement, but Blane heard it loud and clear. He stopped in his tracks.

Kade and Blane stared at each other, something shifting between them, but Kade was too far gone to care. He was furious and inches from losing control.

Another ten seconds and Kathleen would've been dead. But he had her now. She was in his arms, her weight almost fully resting on him—trusting that he would keep her standing. Trusting Kade to protect her from harm . . . from Blane. And if Blane took one more step toward her, he would regret it. And he knew it. Kade could see in Blane's eyes that he'd read Kade's body language.

She was gasping now, pulling Kade's attention away from Blane and back to her. "Breathe, princess. Just breathe," he said, but the wheezing gasps continued.

"She's going into shock, Kade. We need to get her to the hospital." Blane spoke but remained where he was, keeping his distance from Kade as one would give a wide berth to a rabid animal.

"Haven't you done enough?" Kade's hissed accusation was laced with fury.

Kathleen's knees gave out and Kade whipped his head around to see her eyes roll back in her head as she lost consciousness.

"Kat!"

Blane's cry seemed far away as panic burned away the fog of blind rage inside Kade. He scooped her up in his arms. She weighed next to nothing, her head lolling back against his arm, exposing the column of her throat.

"Let me take her," Blane said from behind Kade.

"Fuck that shit," Kade shot back. "She doesn't want a damn thing to do with you right now." He bypassed Blane and headed for his car. Blane followed and pulled open the door to the backseat. Kade carefully arranged Kathleen's limp body on the leather. Blane opened the passenger door, preparing to climb in.

"I don't think so," Kade said, slamming the door shut and going toe-to-toe with him. "You're in this shit up to your neck, brother, and whoever's behind this nearly turned your girlfriend and me into a matching set of charcoal briquettes."

Blane's jaw tightened as he stared at Kade. "You think I don't know that?" he ground out.

"So get your head out of your ass and find this guy," Kade snapped, stepping away and rounding the car to the driver's side.

"And what are you going to do?" Blane shot back.

Kade pulled open the door. "What I was told," he said. "If they want to kill her, they'll have to get through me." He slid behind the wheel and a moment later was speeding toward his apartment, Kathleen unconscious in his backseat and his brother in the rearview mirror.

CHAPTER NINE

It was no easy feat, juggling an unconscious woman in his arms while unlocking his apartment door and getting inside, but Kade managed. She wasn't heavy—it was just awkward. Finally, he laid her on his bed, still unconscious.

He tugged the boots off her feet, then the shredded nylons covering her legs that he'd fantasized about touching just hours before. The tuxedo jacket had fallen off in the car and now Kade could see the Santa outfit Kathleen wore was torn and dirty. It bothered him. It was too much of a reminder of just how close she'd come to dying tonight.

Reaching into his pocket, Kade took out a switchblade. A practiced flick of his wrist and the knife appeared, its edge wickedly sharp. Sure she would wake, Kade grasped the velvet fabric at the top and sliced between her breasts straight down her torso all the way to the hem. He was exceedingly careful, lest he accidentally nick her skin. But even with the sound of the fabric rending, she didn't open her eyes.

The crescent of skin revealed by his cut teased him and the velvet slid away. Kade swallowed.

She was as perfect as he remembered. She wore no bra, not with that outfit, and Kade could only be grateful for small favors. Her breasts were full and plump, the nipples rosy against her pale skin. Her waist was narrow, the indentation of her navel drawing his gaze. Tiny, black bikini panties was all that was left, coyly hiding the paradise between her thighs.

Forcing himself to turn away, Kade quickly undid his shirt, yanking the tails from his pants. It took only a moment to whisk away the ruined Santa costume before easing her arms into the sleeves of his shirt. He probably should get her a clean shirt, but the instinct deep inside him wanted to brand her as his and mark her with his scent.

Fantasies took hold in his mind at the sight of her in his bed, her hair spread in a river of gold on his pillow. All of it seemed surreal. Things like this didn't happen to him, not good things.

Starting at the top, he began doing up the buttons, concealing her body from his gaze. Not that anything would ever erase the image from his mind. His fingers brushed her skin more than was necessary, the satin texture so soft, it made him wonder how much softer the center of her would be.

Imagining made his hands shake and his cock stiffen. He lingered over the buttons, trying not to think about all the reasons he had for not touching her even as his hand drifted over her abdomen. His fingers trailed lightly across her ribs and down her side.

His skin was darker than hers, and in the low light of the lamp, his hand looked dirty against the pure ivory of her flesh.

Kade yanked his arm back, a cold sweat breaking out on his forehead. What was he thinking? She was out cold and he was going to touch her without her knowledge or consent. The thought made his stomach roll and he swallowed down the bile that rose in his throat.

Quickly, he finished buttoning the shirt, then went to his closet, discarding his tuxedo slacks, shoes, and socks for jeans and a long-sleeved

Henley. He cast one last glance at Kathleen, still sound asleep, and left the room. He'd make her some tea or something. They did that, right? Like in the movies and shit? Hot tea was supposed to help.

But he didn't have tea, only coffee. Ten minutes later when he returned with two steaming mugs, Kade saw Kathleen had woken and was sitting up. She was looking around the room as though poised to bolt.

"Take it easy now," he said, sitting next to her on the bed. He handed her a mug, which she took automatically.

"Where am I?"

"My place."

She frowned. "Your place? I thought you lived with Blane."

Kade snorted. "Not likely. As if I could stand living with him for more than a few days."

He watched as she took a few careful sips of the coffee. Kade knew how she took it—too sweet and too much cream. After a moment, she spoke again.

"Um, how did I get into this?" She tugged at the hem of the shirt he'd dressed her in.

Best to avoid that question. "Yeah, that little red outfit's a goner. Sorry."

She blushed, her cheeks turning rosy. Kade wasn't surprised. Modesty wasn't a trait he often ran across, which made it even more charming when he did. She looked down, letting her hair swing forward to conceal her face. Kade couldn't have that. He brushed her hair back so he could see her, tucking the silky strands behind her ear.

"Would it help if I said I didn't look?" he lied through his teeth. The image of her body spread out on his sheets would haunt him forever.

Kathleen smiled a bit at that, though it quickly faded.

"Are you going to tell me what happened?" he asked.

She looked at him in surprise. "You don't know?"

Did he have an idea of what Blane had done? Yes. Did he want her to spell it out so she would be forced to deal with it? Yes.

She set aside the coffee. "I'm going to need something stronger."

Kade watched the shape of her body through the thin cotton of his shirt as she rose from the bed and walked into the kitchen. Her legs weren't long, but had curves in all the right places. He followed her, leaning against the counter as she began searching through his cabinets.

He knew what she was looking for, but decided to wait it out. She seemed completely oblivious to the way the shirt rose up her thighs when she reached, or how exposed she was when she bent to open the lower cabinets. Kade caught flashes of the black panties and he abruptly set his mug down before the death grip he had on it broke the ceramic.

Finally, she gave up and turned toward him. "Where's your liquor?"

Kade dragged his gaze up from her legs to her hips and breasts, finally reaching her face. Holding on to his control felt as though he were trying to keep from falling over a cliff. He took two steps, right up into her space, and heard her breath catch as she looked up at him.

"It's where it should be," he replied, reaching behind her to open the freezer door. He took out a bottle of vodka, pulled the stopper, and set it on the counter. "Straight?"

"Please."

Grabbing a couple of shot glasses, Kade filled them, then handed one to Kathleen. "Cheers," he said, clinking his glass against hers.

They both tossed back the liquor and she didn't even flinch, just sucked in another breath, set the glass back on the counter, and tapped it.

Kade filled their glasses again as Kathleen rounded the bar and climbed onto one of the barstools. It was only after they'd both downed the second shot that she spoke.

"I walked in on Blane and . . . Kandi."

Anger flooded through him, and his voice was tight when he asked, "Doing what?" He wanted her to say it out loud, so it was good and real.

Blane didn't deserve her, would only lie to her and hurt her, and she'd do well to remember it.

But she wouldn't answer, just tapped her glass for another refill. Kade obliged and they drank in silence.

He watched her, but she didn't cry, thank God. Kade could handle a lot of shit, but crying women wasn't one of them. She seemed lost in thought, her eyes gazing off into the distance, but seeing nothing.

"You all right?" he asked.

"I'm fine," she said.

Yeah, Kade had been *fine* once, too. It sucked.

Kade emptied the bottle into their glasses, then got another from the freezer. The vodka was hitting his veins now, which was why he didn't see anything wrong with giving in to the urge to be closer to her. He slid onto the adjacent stool, his eyes drawn to the length of her bare thigh alongside his denim-clad one.

"People leave, you know?" she said. "They desert you, forget about you. People hurt you, betray you, don't love you anymore. They get hurt. They die. I don't know why I thought it might be different with . . ."

But she didn't finish, just reached for the fresh bottle and gave them both refills. A little spilled on the counter.

"Well, aren't you the cynic," Kade said, reeling. Every word she'd said was true, and more than enough reason to not allow anyone inside. To hear it spelled out so plainly, especially by someone like her, was a shock. He'd thought darkness hadn't touched her soul. He'd thought wrong.

"When has anyone you've been close to not left?" she asked.

Kade took a moment before he answered. "I don't stick around long enough to give them the chance." The one time he had stuck around, he'd had to watch his brother leave for a war from which he might not have returned.

"Why is that?" she asked, jerking his thoughts back to the present.

Shrugging, Kade tossed back the vodka. "I'd rather be the one leaving than the one who's left behind."

"Why am I here?" she asked, changing the subject. "Why not just take me home?"

The thought hadn't even occurred to Kade, not that he could tell her that. The burning need to have her near, keep her safe, had overridden any other logical thought. He scrambled to come up with a believable answer.

"You've nearly gotten yourself killed several times in the last few days," he said. "It's easier to keep you safe here." And keep himself sane.

She snorted. "What do you care? Blane and I are through, so no one's making you play bodyguard anymore. You can't stand me as it is—you should be glad to be rid of me. I'm just the white-trash gold digger, remember?"

Ouch. Her words twisted like knives. "I never said that."

"Which part?"

Their eyes caught and Kade couldn't look away. The hurt and despair written on her face made him want to beg for forgiveness. He'd been wrong. He'd hurt her, just as Blane had, and he was so fucking sorry. But the words wouldn't come, and deep down he knew he could never say them. He'd finish this case, keep her safe even if Blane was through with her, and then he'd get the hell out of town and as far away from her as possible. She made him feel things, want things, and it was too much.

"You need some food in you," he said, desperately searching for safe ground. "When was the last time you ate?"

But she just shrugged and reached for the bottle of vodka.

"Nope," Kade said, snatching it from her. "Not until you eat."

"But I'm not hungry!"

Was that a whine?

Kade went to his cabinets and pulled out a box of moon pies. That sounded awesome right now. He dumped a pile of them on the counter in front of her.

"Moon pie?" she asked, gingerly picking up a package as though it was going to bite her. "Where did you get these?"

"I have my sources." Kade ripped open a package and took a bite. Best junk food ever. He caught Kathleen staring at his mouth with enough interest to make his jeans suddenly uncomfortable.

"Try it," Kade said. "You can't have that much booze on an empty stomach or you're going to be puking, and I'm not holding your hair for you." Another lie. He totally would.

She still hesitated, eyeing the pie he held.

"Here, just try," Kade said, then an impulse struck him. Before he'd even thought it through, he'd dipped his index finger into the marshmallow fluff, scooped out some, and held it out to her.

Kathleen glanced up at him in surprise. Kade held his breath, wondering what in the hell he was doing. He hoped she'd take the bait, and dreaded what it would do to him if she did.

She leaned forward and wrapped her perfect pink lips around his finger.

Kade sucked in a breath, the hot slide of her tongue brought fantasies to mind immediately. She was very thorough, and when she lightly sucked, he had to swallow down a groan. He gripped the counter, grounding himself so he wouldn't move, wouldn't cross over to her and do something he couldn't take back.

Kathleen leaned back and his finger slid from her mouth. She raised an eyebrow, then took a bite of the moon pie. Kade scrambled to think of what to say, and ended up saying the first thing that came to mind.

"If I'd known you'd do that to anything covered in marshmallow, I would have put it in a different location."

She laughed, not realizing of course that he was dead serious. Finishing the pie, she licked the chocolate from her fingers. Kade couldn't look away, the sight mesmerizing him.

"Are you going to take me home now?" she asked.

Kade tore his gaze from her mouth to look her in the eye. "Wasn't planning on it."

"I need to go home."

That was so not happening. He needed her here, where he could be sure she was safe. Not that he could tell her that. But logistics worked in his favor. "And then what? In case you haven't noticed, you have no car. No car means no transportation."

As soon as the words left his mouth, he regretted them. A not-uncommon occurrence. Kathleen looked as though he'd hit her. Her face was white and her mouth open in a little O. Then her blue eyes filled with tears that spilled over and down her cheeks.

"Dammit," Kade cursed himself, hurrying around the bar. He took her in his arms, an instinctive gesture, and at first he thought she might push him away. But she didn't. She just leaned into him and cried like her cat had just died.

Kade tucked her head under his chin and held her, mindlessly running his hand over her hair and murmuring, "Shh. I'm sorry, princess. Don't cry. Please," over and over.

Her sobs tore through him like a knife, and if slicing his gut open would have made her stop crying, Kade would have wielded the blade himself.

"Please, Kathleen," he begged. "Please don't cry." He'd do anything, just so she'd stop crying as though her heart were breaking, which maybe it was. The thought made him want to slam his fist into Blane's face.

Finally, she was all cried out. The tears stopped and she lifted her head. Her eyes were swollen and her nose was red, but Kade saw none of this. All he saw was the most beautiful creature he'd ever seen, staring up at him with heartbreak in her eyes.

"There, that's better," he said, brushing away the tracks of her tears from her cheeks. "I'm sorry Blane's such a bastard. And I'm not any better. But you're not alone, okay?"

"But I am," she whispered. The sadness in her voice had Kade tightening his grip on her as he gazed into her eyes, purity and innocence shining through her tears.

"You have me," he vowed.

Kade wasn't worth much, but he was loyal. He never offered anything to anyone, so the fact that he'd just impulsively offered this woman a piece of his soul would have been earth-shattering to him, if he'd paused to dwell on it. So he didn't.

She was so close, her eyes full of trust and gratitude, as though he were her hero. The idea was absurd, but it sure did feel good for her to look at him like that.

Kade pressed his lips to her forehead in a gentle kiss, then smiled at her. He'd gotten her to stop crying, made her feel a bit better. He, Kade Dennon, had done that. No one else.

She gave him a tremulous smile back, sniffling. The touch of her skin against his lips was like silk and Kade didn't think before pressing another kiss to her cheeks, first one side, then the other, her skin like warm velvet. His hands cupped her jaw, his fingers buried in the long strands of hair at the nape of her neck. His eyes settled on her lips again, and without thinking, he kissed her.

It was an impulse, one born of the need to comfort her, to see that smile last just a bit longer. He should have known better. Everything he touched ended up dark and twisted. Corrupt. This was no different. He could tell the moment their lips touched that he'd been lying to himself.

Kade lifted his head and their eyes locked. She looked surprised, shocked even, her eyes wide as she stared at him.

Would she be angry? Appalled that he'd kissed her? He didn't want to see her face fill with disgust and contempt, hear her tell him how sick and twisted he was to kiss his brother's girlfriend.

But she said nothing.

Her gaze dropped to his mouth. He didn't move away. He couldn't. Kade barely breathed as she tentatively reached up, her fingers sliding through his hair, pushing it back off his forehead.

Kathleen's touch felt like sweet acceptance and it broke what little restraint he had.

He kissed her again, only this time, it wasn't to comfort her and it wasn't the perfunctory prelude it had always been with other women. It was different. *She* was different. He wanted to explore her, know everything about her taste and touch. Hear her little sighs and feel the warmth of her breath.

"Kiss me back, princess," he murmured, needing to feel her respond to him. To his awed amazement, she did.

Kade could have stood there and kissed Kathleen for hours. She'd settled her arms on his shoulders, her hands sliding to the back of his neck and threading through his hair. Her nails lightly scraped his scalp, a uniquely feminine touch that sent a shiver down his spine.

She tasted sweet, like marshmallow and chocolate, and Kade took his time, memorizing the contours of her lips and the timid slide of her tongue against his. She relaxed against him, her body pressed into his from chest to knee. The soft fullness of her breasts made his hands itch to touch.

The darkness inside him was already planning, calculating. All she wore was his shirt and a tiny pair of panties. It wouldn't take but a moment to slide his hands underneath the fabric and between her legs. As much as he wanted her, he wouldn't even bother taking her into the bedroom. The stool at her back was about the right height, or hell, he'd just press her against the fucking wall. She'd be gasping his name while he buried himself inside her wet heat.

And then what?

Kade wanted to ignore the question whispering through his mind. He wanted to do what his body was urging him to do and screw the rest. He'd never worried or cared about what happened *after* he fucked someone, other than making sure he didn't take their number because there was no sense in them entertaining the possibility that he might call. He never did.

But Kathleen didn't fit into that equation. There were a lot of consequences if they had sex, not the least of which was that Blane would kick his ass. And as for Kathleen . . .

Even now he could taste the vodka on her tongue. Her tears were barely dry from what Blane had put her through tonight. And if they did this, tomorrow morning she'd see it as nothing more than a drunken one-night-stand rebound that she would no doubt deeply regret. She might even hate him for taking advantage of the situation, and of her.

The thought was a cold dose of reality.

Before, Kade had wanted her antipathy and her hatred. Now, the thought of her seeing him that way, feeling like that, cut him like a knife. He didn't want that any longer. A moment ago, she'd looked at him like he was her hero. Kade wanted to see that look in her eyes more than he wanted to have sex with her.

He raised his head, breaking their kiss. Her breath was coming in little pants that made him want to see what other noises he could get her to make, but he resisted the urge.

"Why'd you stop?" she whispered. Her eyes were heavy-lidded and dark with desire.

"You're drunk," he said, combing a hand through her hair. Her eyes drifted closed at the touch. "And I have no interest in being your rebound guy." What he did have an interest in . . . he couldn't put into words, not even for himself.

She didn't reply, but she did sway, which told him the alcohol was definitely a factor in what had just happened. He swallowed down bitter disappointment. Maybe she would have kissed anyone tonight, given these circumstances. Maybe there was nothing particularly special about Kade to her.

"Come on," he said. "You need to get some rest."

But she resisted his tugging her toward the bedroom. "No," she protested, trying to pull away. "I don't want to sleep."

There was fear in her eyes, fear that Kade knew well. Sometimes sleep and dreams held more terror than staying awake.

"All right," he said, instead leading her into the living room.

She looked around, taking in the decor and furniture. Kade had the absurd thought that he hoped she liked it. It should be universally appealing, at least that's what the interior decorator had said when he'd written her an exorbitant check for her services. He hadn't really cared at the time about the aesthetic properties of "warm earth tones," but now he found himself craving Kathleen's approval. She didn't say anything though, just sank onto the couch and crossed her legs, tucking her feet underneath her. Kade got a quick glimpse of satin between her thighs before she tugged his shirt down to cover herself.

"Where's your Christmas tree?" she asked as he sat down beside her.

Kade looked at her. Didn't reply.

"What?" she asked. "Everyone should have a Christmas tree, even if it's only a little one."

"I'll keep that in mind," Kade said. He didn't own a single holiday decoration and it hadn't occurred to him to buy something. He wouldn't even be in this city, this state, if not for Blane asking him to come back.

He reached for her, giving in to the temptation to touch her again. She came willingly into his arms and settled beside him on the couch. She trusted him, the silly, foolish girl. He could give her a list of names as long as his arm who could tell her that trusting Kade Dennon was a bad idea.

The feel of her ass pressed against his crotch as they lay spoon-style made his still-hard cock twitch inside his jeans. Nothing he could do about that, and if she noticed, she didn't let on.

She was flipping through the television channels, finally settling on some cartoon, of all things. She seemed engrossed in the tale of Charlie Brown and his sad-looking Christmas tree. Kade glanced at the screen a few times, but mainly he just watched her. His elbow was braced on the cushion, his head resting in his palm, so he had a good view of her face.

Kathleen was so pretty. Pretty in the true sense of the word, the way you'd describe something that needed no adornment, but just . . . was.

Her face was perfection, from the high cheekbones to the wide blue eyes and her lips, pink and full. She fit against him as though they were made for each other, and she didn't seem to mind the fact that he had his hand on the curve of her hip. He could feel the warmth of her skin through the fabric of the shirt she wore.

Kade hadn't even noticed the cartoon was over, so consumed was he with memorizing every feature, so he was surprised when she spoke.

"Thank you," she said.

He frowned. "For what?" For not screwing her against the wall the way he'd wanted to?

"Saving me. Again."

Kade's lips twisted. "I have told you you're a shitload of trouble, right?"

He drank in her answering smile. "I believe you may have mentioned that."

Their eyes were locked together, the moment growing heavy between them. At last, she glanced away, and Kade knew she was sobering. He was suddenly glad they hadn't had sex. She would've regretted it, and that would have nearly killed him.

"Did you used to watch this as a kid?" she asked, changing the subject.

Watch Christmas cartoons? Hardly. "I don't really remember," he lied, hoping she'd drop it.

She frowned. "You don't remember?"

"I spent the days and nights just trying to survive when I was a kid. Holiday specials weren't a big part of that." He was blunt, hoping she'd take the hint. But instead of glancing away in discomfort and changing the subject again as he'd expected she would, she turned, wriggling until they faced each other on the couch.

"Tell me?" she asked, punctuating the plea by reaching up to push her fingers through his hair.

Kade's brow furrowed as he tried to puzzle this out. Why did she want to know? Why did she care? Blane had never asked him about the time after his mother's death and before he'd come to live with his newfound brother. He'd seemed to understand without Kade saying that he didn't want to talk about it.

For the first time, Kade *did* want to talk about it. He wanted to tell Kathleen, though why, he couldn't say. Maybe it was just because she'd asked.

"Not every one was bad," he said finally, "but a few were the stuff of nightmares. Those, I ran away from. But there was one . . . I couldn't run away."

"Why not?"

"There was a little girl there, too, younger than me." The image of Branna when he'd first met her drifted through his mind. "She didn't know, didn't understand, and he'd go after her." Kathleen's blue gaze was steady as she listened, and Kade couldn't look away. Confessing this to her felt like he was stripping his soul bare.

"I figured out I could distract him, make him stop, if I pissed him off," he continued. "Kind of like a diversion. He was a mean sonofabitch. Liked to do the cigarettes and the belt. His fists when he was too drunk to find something else. A few times, a broken bottle, a knife." And each time Kade had bit the inside of his lip until he bled, vowing he would not cry. And he hadn't. That had really pissed the guy off, but it had been worth it. Because fuck him.

Branna had been safe, and at the time, that was all Kade had cared about. The guy had gotten his in the end, and no one and nothing would make him regret shoving that bastard down the stairs.

But tears were leaking from Kathleen's eyes, so Kade cut his story short.

"Eventually, the girl left. The state took her away. Blane found me shortly after that."

"What happened to the girl?" she asked.

"You've met her," he said. "It was Branna."

That surprised her, he could tell, and Kade wondered briefly at how pissed off Branna would be if she knew he was telling someone about that time in their lives, but he gave a mental shrug. It's not like she'd ever know.

More tears spilled down Kathleen's cheeks and Kade frowned. God, he was such a dick. After what she'd been through tonight already, he was telling her shitty sob stories from his past? He'd really lost his touch if he thought tales of woe would make her want to sleep with him.

Reaching out, he brushed the back of his fingers against her cheek. "I didn't tell you that so you'd feel sorry for me," he said.

She shook her head. "I don't feel sorry for you, or pity you. I feel . . ." She seemed to struggle for the right words. "Rage and helplessness. Sorrow and despair. I hate that you had to endure such things and I *hate* the people who did them to you."

If she'd said she wanted to strip naked and paint his toenails, Kade couldn't have been more shocked.

No one had cared for him enough to feel those emotions on his behalf. Only Blane. To hear Kathleen tell him so passionately how she hated those who'd hurt him . . . it rocked him, made him want to lay his head against her and let her put her arms around him, soothe him. Her fingers still trailed through his hair as they stared at each other.

That elusive feeling of peace settled over him. It was something particular to Kathleen and not a state of being he'd felt with anyone else. There was something about having someone so pure look at him as though she could see into his soul, and what she saw didn't frighten or disgust her. It was the look of a woman who could stare into the face of overwhelming odds . . . and smile. She amazed him, humbled him, which was a dangerous place to be. Because she wasn't his, and would never be his. The realization was more painful than all the trauma he'd endured that had left scars on his body.

"I lied, you know," he said, desperate to change the subject.

She went still, her eyes wide.

"I did look."

It took her a second to get it, and when she did, she laughed. The sound was one Kade prayed he'd never forget.

Something on the television caught her attention and she turned. "Oh, I love this movie!"

She squirmed again, turning until her back was once again pressed to his chest. The movie was *It's a Wonderful Life*, a sentiment Kade would take issue with, if he cared enough, which he didn't.

She seemed content though, absorbed in the black-and-white scenes playing out on the screen. After dropping way too much of his emotional baggage on her, she'd made no move to leave his arms or the couch, just turning back to the television and snuggling.

He couldn't remember the last time he'd honest-to-God snuggled with a woman where sex wasn't involved. He couldn't recall the last time he'd *wanted* to.

Kade paid half his attention to the movie, listening to the dialogue, but his gaze was on Kathleen. His arm still rested in the curve of her waist, his hand flat against her abdomen, but she didn't seem to mind. Her cheeks were flushed rosy from the vodka she'd consumed, making her skin appear flawless. Her hair lay in long waves against his chest, the strands tickling slightly at his neck.

Kade loved her hair. The color was so rare, like the horizon at dusk just as the last ray of sunshine was set to disappear. He wanted to touch the wavy lengths, but he was afraid that if he moved, she'd move, too. Maybe she'd sit up and go to the other end of the couch away from him. He didn't want that. So he just watched her.

"This part gets me every time," she said quietly, and Kade looked up at the screen.

It was some scene with a kid talking to an old man, pleading with him. Mr. Gower? As Kade watched, the old man hit the kid on the side of the head.

"You like this?" Kade asked in disbelief.

"Well, no, I don't like him hitting the kid," Kathleen said. "I hate that. But the kid is George Bailey, and he's trying to save the old man. The guy just lost his son in the war, so he's upset and hurting. George is taking the abuse because he refuses to let the old man push him away, not when he knows he can help him."

The words hit a little too close to home. Kade had treated Kathleen like shit, and she'd let him, coming back for more until he'd finally let her in. He wondered if that's how she saw him, as a charity case who needed her help. He'd warned her already that he was beyond saving. He hoped for her sake that she'd heed that warning.

Kade tuned out the TV as he studied Kathleen, memorizing every minute expression that crossed her face as she watched the movie. Sadness. Concern. Amusement. Joy. They didn't talk, and that was fine. Just being here, with her, was more than he'd ever expected . . . or thought that he'd want.

Blane was a fool, he decided.

She sighed, nestling more closely against him, and Kade realized she'd fallen asleep. The vodka had probably helped with that, not to mention the emotional and physical shocks of tonight. His lips twisted slightly as the image of her tossing back a shot ran through his mind. He liked a woman who could hold her liquor.

Carefully easing the remote out of her hand, he turned the volume down on the television.

Kade wasn't usually the type of man to take the high road, if given a choice, and tonight was no exception. Kathleen's squirming had twisted the shirt she wore so that now it gaped at the neck, offering him an unobstructed view of her incredible breasts.

He lifted his hand, his gaze returning to her face, and softly brushed the back of his knuckles down her cheek. She didn't wake, so he did it again, savoring that he'd been handed an opportunity to hold her, touch her.

He'd nearly lost her tonight, had escaped with seconds to spare.

It was the first time he'd really allowed himself to dwell on what had happened. He'd risked his life for her and would have died right there beside her. And he'd done it without hesitation.

It gave him pause.

Kade didn't just lay his life down for anyone, yet tonight he hadn't thought twice. And if things had turned out differently and they *had* died, he couldn't make himself regret that the last thing he saw would have been Kathleen's face. That sounded pretty fucking perfect, actually, and that thought brought back another that he'd had in the heat of the moment when they'd been trying to escape.

He loved her.

He remembered now. He'd thought it, just a split-second thing when they'd both realized a bomb was going to go off. *God, he loved this woman.*

Kade's hand paused in its fourth trip down her cheek.

Donovan was right. Somehow, someway, he'd fallen for this little slip of a girl with blue eyes and sun-kissed hair.

And there wasn't a damn thing he could do about it.

Chapter Ten

A knock on the door roused Kade from where he was sleeping on the couch. He rubbed his eyes and glanced at his watch. Almost ten in the morning. Shit. He hadn't slept that long in a while.

The knock came again and Kade got up, grabbing his shirt and pulling it over his head as he went to the door. Only a handful of people knew of his apartment, so he wasn't surprised to see Blane on the other side.

He didn't greet him, just left the door open as he turned away, pushing a hand through his hair to arrange it from a sleep-tousled mess. Blane followed him inside.

"Is Kathleen all right?" he asked. "I've been by her apartment. She's not there."

"Why would you think she'd want to see you?" Kade countered, filling the coffeepot and grabbing some coffee grounds from the freezer.

"I'm her boyfriend. I have a good reason for what happened last night. I just need to see her and explain."

"Why don't you give her some space," Kade said, hitting the button on the coffeemaker. He'd made twice as much as usual, to accommodate Kathleen, but Blane hadn't noticed.

"It's driving me crazy," Blane said, heaving a sigh. "This case, my witnesses disappearing, some crazy fuck stalking Kathleen."

"Bowers has cleared out," Kade said. "I went by his place the other night. He won't be back anytime soon."

Blane nodded absently, as though he'd expected that. "I don't know if she's going to take me back," he mused, and it was obvious he meant Kathleen. "Not after last night."

Dread and bitter disappointment filled Kade's gut. This was new. Blane had never given a shit before whether some woman would *take him back*.

Naturally, that was the moment the woman they were both thinking about chose to open his bedroom door and step out.

Kade winced. She hadn't put on the clothes he'd left for her. All she was wearing was his shirt. Her cheeks were flushed, her eyes still heavy-lidded with sleep, and he would swear he'd buttoned that shirt up further last night than it was buttoned this morning.

So riveted was his attention on Kathleen, that Kade didn't see Blane swinging his fist until it connected with his jaw.

Kathleen shrieked and for a moment, Kade was too stunned to react. Then all the anger and frustration and regret boiled up. He flew at Blane.

They collided, grappling, fighting like they hadn't fought in years. It felt good to get it out, and his knuckles slammed into Blane's face. Blane got him in the side, right in the cracked rib. Sonofabitch, that hurt.

"Stop! Stop it! Both of you!"

Kade ignored her, as did Blane. Kade landed another blow in Blane's gut, which was like hitting a brick wall, and Blane shoved him away.

Kathleen darted between them, putting her back to Kade as though to shield him, just as Blane threw another punch. Kade had no time to react, no time to shove her out of the way. He just knew that if Blane so much as laid a finger on her, Kade would rip him apart.

Somehow Blane stopped at the last possible second, his fist a hair's breadth from Kathleen's face. They all stood there, frozen in shock at what had nearly happened.

"What the fuck are you doing?" Blane yelled at her. "Do you know how close I came to hitting you?"

"Well, if you hadn't been fighting, you wouldn't have almost hit me!" she yelled back. Kade had to hand it to her, standing her ground with Blane in a towering rage took balls. "Why would you do that anyway?" she continued berating him. "Why would you hit your brother?"

Kade knew why.

"I didn't sleep with her," he said, slipping out from behind Kathleen and heading for the freezer. His jaw ached and he took out an ice pack.

"Is that what you think?" Kathleen asked Blane, her question deceptively quiet and calm. "That I'd screw your brother to get back at you? That's the sort of person you think I am?"

Kade didn't bother explaining that Blane didn't think *she* was that type of person, he just knew Kade *was*.

"Like you have any room to talk, brother," Kade said. "Or are you the only one allowed to fuck around?"

"Kathleen, I—"

"Save it," she snapped, cutting him off. She stomped back into the bedroom, slamming the door behind her.

Kade waited a beat. "I'm not great at reading women, but she didn't really seem in the mood to talk things out. What do you think?"

Blane glanced at him and it took a second, but his lips twitched in an almost smile, which faded quickly. "I'm sorry, Kade," he said. "I just—I saw her and thought the worst. But I should know you'd never do that to me. Not my own brother."

Guilt nearly choked Kade, but he forced his lips to curve in a tight smile.

"No worries. Just finish this case so we can shut the psycho down and I can get back to my real job. All this drama is killing my street cred."

Blane grimaced and shoved a hand through his hair. "Yeah. I'm working on it. You come up with anything? Bowers, maybe? Finding him is about the only shot I have left."

"Not yet," Kade said. "But I'll have the FBI check what's left of her car for anything they might be able to find."

"If Freeman was being threatened, then chances are, Bowers was, too. I'd buy that he took off rather than betray Kyle. Those guys may not be brothers by blood, but they're brothers just the same." He gave Kade a look that spoke volumes.

"I'll do what I can."

Blane nodded and headed for the door. Just before he left, he turned and said, "Thanks. I don't know what I'd do without you."

"Ditto." Then Blane was gone.

Kade didn't want to think about what had just happened, or how he was feeling, so he pushed it all to the back of his mind and went into the guest bathroom to shower and shave. He had to go into his bedroom to get more clothes and was both relieved and disappointed that Kathleen was still in the shower.

After he dressed, he poured himself another cup of coffee and sat at the bar in the kitchen, waiting. He prayed she'd put on the clothes he'd left for her, clothes that would cover every square inch of her skin. What he hadn't counted on was how much smaller and more feminine she'd look wearing them.

She must've had to roll down the waist to get the sweatpants to stay on her hips, and the thought of how easily he could slip them off had Kade averting his eyes. She wore no bra, which was obvious, and he wondered if she'd discarded her panties as well.

She seemed oblivious to his discomfort, pouring herself a cup of coffee and sliding onto the stool next to him.

"How's your jaw?" she asked.

"I'll live." Frankly, for the thoughts he'd been having lately, he deserved far worse from Blane—his brother just didn't know it. And hopefully, he never would.

Kade glanced at her. A bruise darkened her cheek. His eyes narrowed, anger burning away everything else going on inside his head. Someone had hurt her, marked her. They'd regret that. He'd make damn sure of it.

"You have a bruise," he said, his fingers brushing her cheek. "Are you going to tell me who hit you?"

"And what will you do if I tell you?" she asked.

"Kill him." Obviously.

She smiled like he'd made a joke. "Well, I'm not going to say, so just forget about it. It doesn't matter anyway."

It bothered Kade, the way she said that as if she believed it—that someone hitting her didn't matter. It mattered to him a whole helluva lot.

"You need to take a self-defense course or something," he said. "You're too little to take chances." And it wasn't like he or Blane could be around her one hundred percent of the time.

She snorted. "Little? Please."

"You're five-foot nothing, have bones I could break with my bare hands, and no doubt weigh about a buck ten. You couldn't stop an overgrown fifth grader from pushing you around." All of which worried him.

"I'll have you know I'm five foot one and three-quarters," she said, proving his point.

"Exactly."

"Like a self-defense course would have stopped Blane this morning?"

"I didn't say it would make you smarter," Kade retorted. "Interfering was a bad idea."

"I had to do something," she said, flushing. "I couldn't just watch you two kill each other."

"Next time, leave it alone." And somehow Kade knew, deep in his gut, that there would indeed be a next time. "I'll set up the class. The firm will pick up the cost. It's cheaper than a hospital bill."

She got the joke, raising an eyebrow. "How pragmatic of you," she said dryly. "I went to visit Adriana Waters yesterday."

Kade's mind switched gears. Blane's client's ex-wife. It was on the tip of his tongue to ask her how she knew where Adriana had been staying, then he remembered. The intercom. Clever girl must have written down the address Blane had given him, which hadn't even occurred to Kade when he'd seen Kathleen's GPS at the hotel all day yesterday.

"And?" he asked, hoping there was more to the story.

"And she's working with whoever is doing this. I broke into her hotel room and—"

"You what?" Kade interrupted. "You broke into her room? How?" This should be interesting.

"Well, I got a maid to let me in, so I guess that's not really breaking in," she said.

Nice. Kade couldn't help admiring her ability to think on her feet. It was a trait he rarely came across, especially in a woman.

"Anyway," she continued, "she came back with a man. I didn't get to see who he was, but they talked about getting Blane to lose this case. I think they're behind the threats that made Ron Freeman change his testimony."

Kade didn't want to think about how she'd overheard all that. He wouldn't sleep for a week. "Did they say anything else?"

She shook her head.

"Blane wants me to find Bowers," Kade said. "He thinks Bowers might have been threatened as well, into changing his story, but decided to go into hiding rather than betray Kyle."

"Do you know anything about him? What his hobbies are? His friends? Maybe he's hiding out with a girlfriend."

"I'm going to do some digging today," he said.

"What about me?"

"You are going to chill here, relax, and stay safe." The last part being the one that concerned him the most.

"I can't just sit around all day and do nothing," she argued.

Ah, the sound of a perpetual workaholic. "Of course you can," he said, getting up and tucking his gun into the holster attached to his jeans. "You've had a rough couple of days. Take it easy today." Grabbing his leather jacket, he slipped it on.

"Kade."

The urgency in her voice had him turning back around. She'd slid off the stool and stood close to him.

"Want a kiss goodbye?" He wished.

But she only smiled a tight little smile. "I just wanted . . . just . . . be careful today, okay?"

Kade frowned, wondering at the change in her voice. She sounded worried, tense, almost afraid. For him? Surely not. That beating he'd taken must have warped her view of him worse than he'd thought.

"No worries," he said. He brushed his lips against her forehead because he wasn't allowed to kiss her the way he wanted to, then left quickly before he did anything else that would betray how he really felt.

And because she'd already proven herself as someone who refused to do what she was told, Kade stopped by the doorman on his way out.

"Hey, Paul," he said, pulling a twenty from his wallet. "There's a girl in my apartment, about yea tall," he held his hand at slightly less than his shoulder, "reddish-blonde hair, blue eyes. If she leaves, text me and let me know."

"Absolutely, Mr. Dennon," Paul said with a smile, pocketing the money.

Today was going to suck, there was no getting around that. If Bowers wasn't on the grid, then he was under it, and looking for him meant he'd be going to some sketchy places. Places he hadn't been to for years.

But first, he needed to call Blane. Today was Saturday and judging by what had happened last night, he sincerely doubted Kathleen had told Blane about the five grand Simone wanted to collect.

"Kirk," Blane answered.

"Hey, something I forgot to mention," Kade said. "I don't suppose Kathleen told you how Simone says she owes her five grand and if she doesn't pay up by tonight, she has to work it off?"

"Excuse me? Work it off? Tell me that doesn't mean what I think it means."

"Wish I could. She's supposed to meet a john at the Crowne Plaza tonight if the money isn't paid in full."

Blane's response to that was a streak of colorful cursing that Kade envied. Only the military could give someone the proper skills to weave a pattern of vulgarity that stood above the commonplace.

"I'll take that as a no," Kade said when Blane paused to take a breath. "I'm assuming you want me to take care of it."

"No, I will," Blane replied. "I want to make sure we don't hear anything more from Simone after this."

Kade frowned. "May not be the smartest idea," he said. "Don't say or do something you'll regret. She's a clever broad."

"I know. Don't worry. You just find Bowers."

"I'm on it." Kade ended the call.

His phone buzzed and he glanced at it. A text from Paul.

Your friend left in a taxi.

Fucking shit!

Kade slammed his hand against the dash in a fury. Kathleen hadn't waited fifteen goddamn minutes before leaving. Her listening skills were for shit.

Punching up the GPS app on his phone, he waited impatiently for it to zero in on her tracker. Finally, it showed him her location. She was home. Kade breathed out a sigh of relief.

He was going to have a come-to-Jesus with her about following directions.

Since she was home safe and sound for the moment, Kade headed for the outskirts of downtown off Washington. He parked a good distance away and spotted a teenage boy hanging nearby. Sliding on his sunglasses, he got out of the car and locked it, pocketing the keys.

"Hey, kid," he called out, beckoning the boy over.

The kid approached, wary. His eyes narrowed as he studied Kade, then glanced around. His hands were shoved into the pockets of his jeans. He looked about fifteen.

"Yeah?"

"You see this car?" Kade asked. "It's nice, right?"

The kid nodded.

"I bet you keep track of all the nice cars that come by. And I'm sure there's someone you're supposed to call if somebody's dumb enough to leave a car like this parked here."

The kid shrugged, not meeting Kade's eyes, but he didn't have to. Kade knew how the streets worked. He wouldn't get two blocks before his Mercedes would be stripped or gone entirely.

Taking a hundred-dollar bill, he held it up. "See this?" The kid nodded, his eyes glued to the money. Kade carefully tore the bill in half and handed one side to the kid. "When I come back, if my car is still intact, you get the other half."

The kid grinned, his teeth very white in his face. "Man, you flash that kinda cash 'round here, you won't make it an hour."

Kade took a step closer to the kid. "I grew up on these streets, so I know all about the homeboys coming up behind me. They're about fifteen feet back now, right? So if you don't warn them off, I'm going to do it the hard way." Moving aside his jacket, he let the kid get an eyeful of the metal at his side. He watched the kid's throat move as he swallowed, then the kid flicked a hand in a wave-off gesture.

Glancing in the side mirror of the Mercedes, Kade saw the two teens who'd been creeping up behind him hesitate, stopping in their tracks. The lookout waved again, this time more urgently, and they backed off. Kade smiled.

"Good choice," he said. "Make a bad choice, I'll find you and make you wish I hadn't. Do what I ask and you get a hundred bucks. Easy money. Understand?"

The kid nodded. "Yeah, man, I got it."

Kade had printed out the service photo of Bowers, sizing it to something he could slip in his pocket. Now he pulled it out and showed the kid. "Ever seen him before?" he asked. "Take a good look."

The boy frowned, squinting as he studied the photo, then shook his head. "Nah, man. I ain't seen him."

One down, God knew how many left to go. Kade heaved an internal sigh. Too much to hope that he'd get a hit on Bowers right away.

"Alright," he said. "See you soon."

At this hour, the streets hadn't yet come fully awake, the residents still recovering from the deeds done the night before. Kade slipped inside a dingy bar that advertised three-dollar beers and "fully naked girls." The "girl" in question looked more mid-forties and wore a G-string, perhaps in concession to the fact that it wasn't yet noon.

She danced on a stage, clinging to a pole, and swayed to the strains of George Strait. It was an odd pairing that made Kade pause, raise an eyebrow, then give a mental shrug before heading for the bar.

The man serving up drinks looked as tired and droopy as the dancing woman's breasts and he cast a jaundiced eye Kade's way before sidling over.

"What'll it be?" he asked.

"A bottle of Bud and some information," Kade replied, sliding a twenty across the bar.

The bartender grabbed a frosty brown bottle and popped the cap. He set it in front of Kade, eyeing the money. "You a cop?"

"Do I *look* like a cop?" The man didn't reply. "I'm looking for someone." Kade flashed the photo. "Seen him around?"

The guy didn't even look at the picture. "Nope."

Kade stared at him. The man didn't bat an eye.

Picking up the bottle of beer, Kade drank it down. It was ice-cold. When the last drop had been drained, he flipped the bottle, catching it by the neck, then smashed it against the bar. It took some skill, breaking a beer bottle. They're tougher than they look and mostly just bounce right off whatever they're hit against. But Kade had a lot of practice from a time in his life when weapons were whatever was handy and his life depended on his own creativity.

Reaching over, he fisted a handful of the bartender's shirt and hauled him off his feet, pressing the jagged edges of the bottle to his throat.

"I ain't a cop, so I won't have any problem slicing you from ear to ear," he snarled. "So maybe you wanna look again."

The man's rheumy eyes were wide, their bloodshot depths filled with fear. He gave a jerky nod. Kade let him go and he slid back down until his feet touched the floor. This time, he gave the photo a good, hard stare.

"I seen somebody kinda like him," the bartender said. "But it's been a few days."

"How many is 'a few'?"

"I seen him Tuesday night," he said. "Yeah, Bev was workin' that night. He came in, looked like he was waitin' for somebody, but they never showed. He left after an hour maybe?"

Well, that was more than Kade'd had before. He gave the bartender a chilly smile. "Thank you for your cooperation."

And so it went. From bars to strip joints to dealers on the street, Kade flashed Bowers's photo all around the underside of Indy, but he got no more hits after that first one until early that evening.

He was sitting on a barstool in a place that looked like the health department hadn't visited in at least a decade, sipping another beer from the bottle. At least with a bottle, he could be moderately certain the contents were what they were purported to be.

Kade had forgotten, or maybe just hadn't wanted to remember, the feeling of despair and hopelessness that hung in the air of these kinds of places like a cloud of cigarette smoke. It covered him like an invisible film, filling his lungs as he breathed it in, sat like a thousand-pound weight on his back.

This was where he belonged, where his future lay. It didn't matter if Kathleen and Blane were over. How could he possibly hope for someone to overlook his past, especially someone as pure and innocent as Kathleen? If she knew some of the things he'd done, she'd be horrified. Revolted. She'd never look at him the same way again.

That's what he couldn't get out of his head. The kiss last night, the way she'd gazed up at him with those blue eyes so full of trust. How she'd cuddled in his arms—the arms of a killer—and asked him about his past.

She'd cried for him.

There were many things a woman like that would cry about, and Kade was the least deserving of her tears. He'd made his choices and he didn't flinch from the consequences. If it hadn't been for him quitting the FBI and sticking next to Blane like his shadow for the next six months, who knows what would have happened?

"So you're just going to hang out here?" Blane asked. "Two weeks ago you quit the FBI, tell me you're going 'freelance,' then you move back into your old bedroom?"

Kade shrugged. "What can I say? I miss Mona's cooking. How'd you sleep last night?" He'd heard Blane cry out in his sleep, then get up and pace the floor. It had been nearly four in the morning before the sounds had quieted.

Blane looked away. "Fine." His abrupt reply fooled neither of them.

"You know, maybe you should talk to someone," Kade said.

"I'm fine."

The way he said that had Kade dropping the subject. "Hey, let's go to the shooting range today," he suggested instead.

Blane seemed to think about that for a moment. "All right," he said at last, which was how the two of them found themselves alone at the shooting range at ten o'clock in the morning on a Wednesday.

Cautious and edgy at first, Blane took a while to relax. Kade gave him a hard time like he always did, comparing his target to Blane's and dishing shit.

"I think you've lost your touch, brother," Kade teased. "I'm definitely the better shot."

"Bullshit," Blane retorted. "Fifty bucks, best of three."

"You're on."

They loaded new targets and Kade saw a few other men come into the range and set up not far from them. Blane did, too, but he didn't say anything.

Things were going fine, he and Blane competing to see who could land the best round, until the other guys got to shooting. The range echoed with their shots. Kade barely noticed, until he saw the sweat beaded on Blane's forehead and upper lip.

Concerned, he stopped shooting and set aside his weapon. Blane was reloading but he seemed to be having trouble. When Kade stepped closer, he saw why. Blane's hands were shaking.

"Hey, man, you okay?" Kade shouted over the noise of the gunshots. The earmuffs made hearing difficult, so he touched Blane's arm. Big mistake.

Blane reacted instantly, spinning around and shoving his elbow into Kade's chest, then smashing the back of his fist into Kade's nose. The blows took him by surprise and knocked the wind out of him, but Kade stayed on his feet. He grabbed Blane's arm just as Blane raised his gun. Pushing Blane's wrist back but stopping short of breaking it, Kade got close, shoving Blane into the confines of the shooting gallery cubicle until they were eye to eye. The gun was between them, the deadly muzzle pointed toward the ceiling and Blane's finger on the trigger.

"It's me, man," Kade said urgently. "Take a breath. It's me." He kept as tight of a hold as he could on Blane's wrist, the heavy bones and muscle straining against him. If he had to, he could stop Blane, but Kade would have to hurt him and he didn't want to do that.

Blane's eyes darted around before finally landing on Kade's. Now that he was up close, Kade could feel the heat radiating off Blane. He was sweating, and it wasn't even hot in there.

Kade waited, tense, but Blane's gaze finally cleared and he relaxed. Gradually, Kade loosened his grip on him, then took the gun from Blane's hand.

"Get me out of here."

Kade barely heard Blane's hoarse request, but he could read body language well enough. He didn't even pause to collect their weapons, just tossed a "Grab our gear for us, Johnny, I'll be back" to the guy behind the counter on his way out the door with Blane. The other men had paused in their shooting and watched silently as the brothers left.

Once in the car, Kade started the engine and turned on the air, then let it sit idling with the air-conditioning running full blast. Blane had his elbows braced on his knees, his hands covering his face. He didn't speak.

Flipping the mirror down on his visor, Kade looked at his reflection. Blood dripped from his nose and he felt carefully at the cartilage. Sore, but not broken. He'd like to keep it that way. It was a point of pride for him that, as many fights as he'd been in, he'd never had his nose broken. And it would totally suck if it happened to be his brother who finally did the honor.

"You okay?"

Kade glanced over at Blane, flipping the shade back up as he did so. He frowned. "Dude, I'm fine. I think you're the one we should be worried about. It's time we talk about it, like it or not."

"If I talk about it, I have to relive it."

Kade could relate to that. There were parts of his past he never wanted to talk about either, but then again, his past wasn't encroaching on his present. Blane couldn't say the same. So Kade was brutally honest.

"Next time, I may not be able to stop you," he said. "Another second— any hesitation on my part in there—you would've dropped me. And while I realize that there've been times you've wanted to kill me, I'd always hoped you didn't mean that literally."

Blane was pale underneath his tan, his green gaze steady on Kade's.

Kade reached in the seat pocket behind him, pulling out a pack of cigarettes. He offered one to Blane, who took it, before he shook one out for himself. Thumbing the lighter, he lit the cigarette, then tossed the lighter to Blane, who did the same.

"I keep having this dream," Blane said after a few minutes of silent puffing. "It's you and me. We're in some alley fighting off a couple of guys."

Kade went still.

"One of them has a knife, goes after you. Next thing I know, he's dead at my feet."

Forcing himself to act normal, Kade took a drag of the cigarette. Blowing out the smoke, he said, "Well, that sucks. Maybe you should watch some porn before you go to bed or something. You'd have better dreams."

But Blane didn't laugh and the silence between them grew thick. Kade took another drag, glancing out the tinted window.

"It's not a dream, is it?" Blane said. "It happened. That night, two weeks ago, when we went out. I didn't notice until the next day. My knuckles were bruised and there was blood on my clothes. Not my blood."

Shit. Kade slipped on his sunglasses, still staring out the window as his mind raced, trying to figure out the best way to handle this.

"I told you we got in a fight," Kade said, keeping his gaze averted.

"But you're not telling me everything."

Kade didn't reply. Heat radiated off the asphalt of the parking lot, the midday sun cooking the blacktop. It was a stark contrast to the chill of the air inside the car.

"Tell me what I did," Blane insisted. "Did I hurt someone and just can't remember it? Kade—" He grabbed Kade's arm, forcing Kade to look at him. "Did I kill that guy?"

Kade stared at his brother, at the man who'd given up so much, who'd saved him, taken him in with only the bond of blood between them. That bond had grown from blood into trust, loyalty, and brotherhood. He opened his mouth.

"You didn't kill him. I did." The words fell out of their own accord, though once he'd said them, Kade was glad of it.

"What are you talking about?"

Kade shrugged. "Those jerks were waiting for us, ambushed us. The guy had a knife and slashed at me. I retaliated. You tried to stop me, but were too late. I hadn't intended to kill him. It was just a heat-of-the-moment kind of thing."

Blane stared. "Are you telling me the truth?"

"Why would I lie about this?" Kade asked, avoiding the question. Lying to Blane wasn't something he enjoyed doing, but he'd much rather take the fall than his brother. If Blane knew he'd killed someone, he'd want to turn himself in to the cops. No way in hell that was going to happen, no matter what Kade had to do. Blane wasn't going to spend the next twenty years of his life in a prison cell.

"So is that the real reason you quit the FBI?"

Kade shrugged again. "Kinda hard to enforce truth, justice, and the American way when you've slit someone's throat in a back alley brawl. I may be a murderer, but I'm not a hypocrite."

Blane winced at the word "murderer," but Kade knew he wouldn't turn him in, not his little brother. It was a ruthless move, to use Blane's love and loyalty for Kade against him, but it was also necessary.

"Can we get back to what we're going to do about your little problem?" Kade asked, anxious to move away from the topic of that night in the alley. "What happened in there?"

Blane shook his head. "I don't know. The sound, the smell, it was making me tense. Then you grabbed me and it's like I just . . . reacted."

Kade considered this. Nodded. "We need to expose you to civilian life again, bro, or you're never going to get used to it. Until you know there's not a threat lurking behind every corner, you're dangerous to me and everyone around you."

Blane shook his head. "There's no 'we.' You need to take off, go somewhere. I don't want to do something stupid."

Yeah, that ship has sailed, Kade thought. "Bullshit," he said. "I'm not leaving you alone. I'm the only one who can stop you when you get like that, so that means I'm not leaving your side, whether you like it or not."

Their eyes caught and Kade saw something akin to relief flash across Blane's face, then it was gone.

The drive back to the house was quiet, Blane retreating to his study while Kade flipped open the cell he'd palmed from Blane's pocket. Scrolling through the contacts, he came across one that sounded promising. No last name, just a first: Todd. Kade hit the button to dial the number, walking into the empty kitchen as it rang.

"Yo, Cap'n! What's up? Long time, no see."

Kade frowned, pulling the phone away from his ear to glance at the number. Yeah, he'd dialed the right one. He put the phone back to his ear.

"Cap'n?" the voice asked.

"Yeah, it's not 'Cap'n,'" Kade said. "Is this Todd?"

"That depends on who's asking," the guy said, his voice guarded now.

"I'm . . . a friend . . . of Blane's," Kade replied. "I'm looking for some more friends of Blane's. Are you one of them?"

"Why? Is he all right? Is he in trouble?" The anxiety in his voice told Kade he'd hit upon the right guy.

"You could say that," Kade said. "He just got back, you know, a few weeks ago. I think he's been having some . . . issues adjusting to civilian life. Thought I'd look up some buddies of his, see if they might have some good advice for him."

"Yo, man, you did the right thing," Todd said. "I've been back a year, and it sure as hell ain't easy, especially at first."

"Maybe I could bring him to you, just something informal, you know? I thought it might help."

"Absolutely. I'll call a couple other guys from our unit, we'll all meet up, have a few beers and talk." He gave Kade the name and address of a bar in Indy. "Bring him tomorrow night," Todd said. "That'll give me time to round up the crew."

"Sounds good," Kade said. "Thanks." He felt relieved. God knows he'd do anything for Blane, so long as he knew what to do. This PTSD was like walking blindfolded through a minefield, though. If Blane wouldn't talk

to a professional, maybe talking with other men he'd served with would be just as good.

"We'll see you tomorrow night," Kade said. "Seven o'clock."

"Wait, you didn't tell me your name," Todd said.

"That's right. I didn't." Kade ended the call.

The next night, Blane didn't protest when Kade wanted to go out for dinner. He was tense, Kade could see that, but seemed to trust that Kade wouldn't let him get out of hand.

Blane looked questioningly at the bar Kade pulled up to. It did look like a dive. Kade checked the address. Yeah, this was the place.

"This isn't really my style," Blane said, raising an eyebrow.

"You should branch out," Kade said, pocketing the keys and getting out of the car. Blane followed suit.

"You figure, if I go apeshit and bust a few things in this place, no one could tell the difference, right?"

Kade laughed at Blane's self-deprecating joke. At least he wasn't denying that he couldn't control his reactions. That was a good sign. "Something like that."

The inside was as dingy as the outside, just with a soundtrack, since the jukebox in the corner was blaring out AC/DC. Kade spotted a table full of guys and headed in that direction. Blane fell into step behind him. Once they were close enough for the men to turn and spot them, Blane's hand landed heavily on Kade's shoulder, pulling him to a halt.

"What did you do?"

Kade glanced back at him. "You'll have to be more specific."

"Hey! It's the Captain! Yo, Cap! Over here!"

Kade recognized the voice as the one on the phone, Todd. He was a big guy, but not the largest in the group. He was waving them over.

"Why do they call you 'Captain'?" Kade asked. "You know what? Never mind. I don't wanna know." He headed toward the table, leaving Blane no choice but to follow.

Todd jumped to his feet, bypassing Kade to reach Blane. "Man, it's good to see you!"

"Same here." Blane was smiling, but it seemed forced.

"Hey, look who's here," Todd said, turning to the table where three other men sat. "You remember Rico and Sammy? Erik made it, too."

"You all just happened to be in this particular bar, on this night, at this specific time?"

Blane's dry question made Todd squirm a bit, and he cast a nervous glance Kade's way. Stepping up to Blane, Kade turned his back to the table and spoke so only Blane could hear.

"I called Todd," he said. "You won't talk to a shrink and you won't talk to me. I thought you might talk to them. Chances are they've been through the same thing."

Blane didn't reply and Kade couldn't read his expression. He shifted his weight and waited before finally saying in exasperation, "Just give it a chance, will you? I don't want to get shot by my own brother, for Chrissakes."

That got through to him, Kade could tell. Blane didn't say anything, just gave a curt nod. Kade turned back to Todd and slapped Blane on the back.

"Yeah, I got a date with some hot chick, so you have fun." He pointed at Todd. "Don't keep him out past curfew, boys, he has to work tomorrow."

Blane just shook his head, his lips tipping up slightly at the corners. They all watched Kade leave, but he didn't go far. He didn't know those guys, even if Blane did, so he stuck around, parked his car in a shadowed lot across the street, and kept an eye on the place. It was several hours later before he saw the group come out, Blane getting into a pickup with Todd.

Kade was relieved, and hopeful, because there was nothing Blane could do that would drive Kade away. He was in it for however long it took to get his big brother back to being himself. Knowing that he'd hit upon a way to help him made Kade feel like a hundred-pound weight had just been lifted from his shoulders.

Blane didn't say much about the meeting, but he started hanging out with his SEAL buddies more often, at least twice a week. Kade kept up his *normal routine, making Blane go out and experience civilian life in all its unpredictable forms. Sometimes those nights ended better than others, but each time got a little easier.*

Six months later, Kade entered Blane's study one Friday evening. No longer did Blane react by pointing a gun at him. He still tensed slightly, but his reactions were much more measured and controlled. Kade could only admire the strength of will and determination Blane had to retrain himself like that.

Kade plopped down on the leather sofa, propping an ankle on his knee. "So I'm leaving tomorrow," he said without preamble.

Blane's brows flew up in surprise. "That's awfully sudden. Why?"

Kade shrugged. "Been on vacation long enough. Time to get back to work." The senator, who'd also been monitoring Blane's progress, had sent him a plane ticket that morning. The destination was Venezuela and the flight left at 7:00 a.m. tomorrow.

Blane hesitated. "You don't have to go it alone," he said. "The law firm could use an investigator. That'd be right up your alley."

Yes, it would, but his future was already spoken for, Kade thought. Regret whispered to him, but he ignored it. He refused to regret the choice he'd made, and he'd make the same one again to spare Blane.

"Thanks, but I already have plans," he said. "I leave pretty early in the a.m., so tell Mona goodbye for me, would you? I didn't have a chance to tonight."

"Bullshit," Blane snorted. "You just hate seeing her cry."

Kade didn't reply, just shifted uncomfortably. It was quiet in the room, the weight of Blane's gaze resting on him felt like the beam of a spotlight.

"When will you be home again?" Blane asked.

Kade shook his head. "I don't know." Which was the truth. The airline ticket was one-way. For all he knew, he could end up rotting in a god-awful Venezuelan prison for the next fifty years. All he had to go on was the agreement he'd made with Keaston. Kade had taken the fall when Blane remembered some of that night, and he'd keep taking the fall so long as it kept Blane out of Keaston's claws.

"Kade."

Forced to look at Blane, blue eyes met green.

"Thank you," Blane said. "For being here. For staying. For not giving up on me. I couldn't have made it without you."

Kade's lips twisted in a half smile. "What else are brothers for?"

The moment grew heavy, so he got to his feet before he did something stupid, like spill his guts to Blane. He'd made a deal and it was time to pay the piper, no matter how much it terrified him.

"I'll be in touch," he said as Blane also got to his feet. They shook hands, as Kade preferred.

"You'd better be." Blane's voice was rougher than usual and he clasped Kade's hand longer than was necessary.

Kade cleared his throat. "Don't do anything stupid while I'm gone," he said. "Like marry Kandi, or some dumbass shit like that."

Blane let out a low chuckle. "Couldn't do that without you anyway," he said. "Who else would be my best man?"

Kade rolled his eyes and headed for the door. "That'll be the only time you see me walking down the aisle, that's for damn sure," he tossed over his shoulder.

He cast one last look at Blane, standing by the fire in his slacks and shirt. His tie had been discarded but he still looked every inch the lawyer. Kade found new resolve in that last look at his brother. Blane deserved a good life, the very best it had to offer him, and if Kade could ensure some of that, then he would.

That image of Blane was burned into Kade's memory, and that's what kept him anchored in the years to come. The senator had taken Kade and honed him into a deadly killing machine, having him train with men who hadn't said what they did for a living, and Kade hadn't dared to ask.

Kade had first killed at the age of ten. He found that it just got easier as time went by. He should've known that whatever was inside him, whatever it was that allowed him to feel nothing but ice when holding someone's life in his hands, wasn't ever going to change, never going to get better.

The jobs were delivered to Kade in different ways. Sometimes by messenger, other times through dead drops. Payment was sent upon completion of the job, that is, when the target was dead.

Keaston hadn't sent Kade many hits over the years, just enough to remind him of the deal they'd made. Eventually, Kade had begun taking on independent jobs, some of them hacking, even as his reputation as an assassin grew.

He'd stayed in touch with his buddy Donovan, who'd been promoted through the ranks in the FBI. Donovan had asked for Kade's help once or twice, then began bringing more and more jobs to him that the bureau either didn't have the will or resources to pursue.

It had been years before Kade had been able to tell Keaston to go to hell—hacking into the Social Security Administration and deleting every record that ever existed on the two men who'd died that night—but by then, it was too late. There was no turning back from what he'd become, no redemption from the demons that plagued his soul.

CHAPTER ELEVEN

Someone slid onto the stool next to Kade, pulling him from his memories. He glanced around. It was a guy who looked to be in his mid-twenties. A tough guy, with a brutish face and clothes that could've used a trip through a washing machine. He was looking at Kade.

"Ain't seen you in here before," he said, and it sounded like an accusation.

Kade didn't reply. He took another drink of his beer, which was warm now. Ugh. He hated warm beer.

"Hey man," the guy persisted. "I said, I ain't seen you in here before."

Kade still ignored him, until the guy laid his meaty hand on Kade's shoulder. In a flash, Kade had a grip on his hand, the pinky bent back at an unnatural angle. The guy grunted in pain.

"Don't touch me," Kade said. "And 'I ain't seen you in here' isn't a question, so it doesn't require a response. Touching me gets a response, but not a pleasant one. Understand?"

The guy's face was a white grimace and he nodded. Kade released his hand.

"I hear you're looking for somebody," the guy said, his tone much more cautious, though his eyes were resentful. "Is that true?"

"Possibly," Kade replied.

"Mike said he mighta seen your guy. Said you was to meet him behind the Rusty Nail."

It was what Kade had been waiting for. Anyone shows up on this turf, eventually the man running it is going to find out. Add to it Kade's persistent questioning today, and it was damn near impossible to miss. If anyone, "Mike" would be the one to know if Bowers had been here and what had happened to him. But trolling the streets asking to meet with the boss usually ended up with somebody in a body bag.

"Then I wouldn't want to disappoint him." Kade stood, leaving the guy behind as he headed for the door. He saw two other guys get up and follow him out.

He knew what was happening. They were setting him up to "meet" with their boss, who of course wouldn't actually be there. People asking questions were viewed with hostility in this environment, and they knew he wasn't a cop. An unknown quantity on their turf was asking to get his ass handed to him, or to be killed outright, neither of which sounded appealing.

Kade walked down the block to the Rusty Nail, knowing the guys were still behind him. Chances were there were a few more waiting to ambush him when he emerged into the alley.

Stepping around the corner, Kade paused and waited. As he'd expected, the guys were close behind him, turning the corner only moments later.

Coming out of nowhere in the dark, Kade slammed his fist into the first guy's solar plexus, punching the air out of him. The trick was to punch first and punch hard. He bent over, as Kade had known he would, just as Kade's knee came up to slam into the guy's nose. Down he went, out cold.

The second guy had time to prepare, the element of surprise gone now, and punched Kade in the side. Slamming back his elbow, Kade got him in the shoulder, then went for the knee, nailing it with his heavy boot. It bent the wrong way and the guy went down, clutching his leg and groaning in pain. His position left his crotch exposed and Kade nailed him there, too.

Breathing hard, Kade stared at the two men on the ground. The whole thing had taken eight seconds, maybe less. Now to deal with the ones waiting for him.

There were three waiting when Kade stepped into the deserted lot behind the Rusty Nail. The place had been shut down a few years ago, but the sign out front remained.

"Hey, fellas," Kade called. "Nice night."

One of the men, the leader, stepped forward. His eyes shifted behind Kade.

"They're not coming," Kade said. "Had a bit of trouble along the way. They'll be all right. Wait, I take that back, one of them probably will have a limp the rest of his life." He smiled in a thin, cold way.

The leader stiffened, his eyes narrowing. "Who are you?" he asked.

Kade's smile faded. "I'm someone you don't want to fuck with," he said. "And I've had a shitty day. So be good and go tell Mike that Kade Dennon is here to see him."

The leader beckoned one of the others over and spoke to him in a low voice. They both looked at Kade and the lackey nodded, then hustled away.

"We'll see if Mike wants to talk to you," the leader said. He watched Kade, his gaze wary and suspicious.

Kade blew out a breath, as though his time was too valuable to be dicking around with this shit, and glanced at his watch. He wanted to have his hands free so he resisted the urge to pull out his cell and check on Kathleen again. She'd been home all day. He'd have preferred her at his place, but it was probably for the best that she wasn't.

A few minutes later, the lackey returned. He was hurrying and he spoke in hushed, urgent tones to the leader, who turned to Kade with newfound respect in his eyes.

"Mike said he was available," he told Kade. "Follow me."

They went inside the Rusty Nail. Though it was closed for business, it was apparently open for Mike and his base of operations. Kade passed two dealers, collecting their stock for the night ahead. At the end of a dark corridor, the guy who'd led him inside turned to Kade.

"Mike says you have to be unarmed if you want to meet with him."

A huge guy, obviously meant to be a bodyguard, waited for Kade to hand him his weapons. He glowered at Kade, who just shrugged and handed over his gun.

"Do I have to wash my hands first, too?" Kade's smartass question didn't get a response from either man, not that he'd expected it.

The bodyguard opened the door and Kade went inside.

The room wasn't much, and neither was Mike, but that's usually the way these things worked, Kade knew. The guys you had to watch out for the most weren't always six foot four and weighing two-fifty. It was the guys who'd been bullied and roughed up for being the smallest in the class. Those guys had learned early how to fight tooth and nail, how to survive through any means necessary. And Kade should know. He'd been one of them. They grew up to be more dangerous than any of the bullies.

There were two other guards in the room who looked like they had a bit more brains than the one outside. They were twins and Kade immediately thought of Thing One and Thing Two from the Dr. Seuss book. They eyed him, which was smart. Because while Kade had given up his weapon, that didn't make him any less dangerous.

"Word is you been asking around my streets today," Mike said. "We don't like people who ask questions."

"And I don't like people who waste my time," Kade said. He moved slowly—didn't want Things One or Two to get jumpy—and pulled out the photograph of Bowers. He slid it across the table to where Mike was sitting. "You know this guy?"

"I don't give a shit if I know him or not," Mike sneered. "I run my streets, and I don't care who you are, but you ain't gonna rile up my people askin' 'em a bunch of questions all fucking day about a guy I don't give a fuck about."

Kade's eyes narrowed. "Now you're just pissing me off, Mike." He said his name hard and slow, enunciating each consonant. "I've been real polite, except for those guys you sent to ambush me, and besides wasting my time, you're being a dick."

"Fuck you, asshole." Mike made a motion with his hand to Thing One and Kade reacted instantly, diving down as the sound of the gunshot echoed in the small room. It missed him by an inch, but he didn't stop moving, going straight for Thing Two. He'd been too slow, assuming his brother would take Kade out, and was only now pulling a gun from his jeans. Kade grabbed his wrist while the muzzle was still stuck in his waistband and pulled the trigger. The guard shot himself. He yelled in pain and grabbed his thigh, dropping the gun as his leg collapsed underneath him.

The sheetrock above Kade's head shattered as Thing One fired again, but the wounded twin's body fell over Kade, effectively acting as a shield. Kade bet he wouldn't fire on his own brother, and he was right. The guy quit shooting and ran toward him. Kade waited until he was close, then heaved his brother off him. Instinctively reacting to catch his twin, Thing One wasn't watching Kade, who lashed out with his boot, catching the guard in the side of the knee. The crack was loud and he went down in a tangle of limbs with his brother.

Kade grabbed the gun the first twin had dropped and shot the still-armed brother, one round right between the eyes. He didn't pause before another round finished the other brother. No sense leaving one of them alive to come after Kade for revenge.

The door slammed open and the thug who'd taken his gun barreled in. He didn't make it two steps.

Suddenly, it was quiet. The sounds of the bullets echoing had faded. Kade was on his feet, the weapon aimed at Mike, who was also standing. He had the blank look of someone in shock.

"Things get messy when I get pissed off, Mike," Kade said. "Now you wanna answer my question? Take a look at that photo. Take a real good look."

Mike swallowed, his gaze dropping to the gun in Kade's hand, then down to the photo on the desk.

"Yeah, man," he said at last. "He was here a few days ago. Looking to buy papers. My boy didn't trust him, so he got nowhere. Last anyone saw of him, he was gettin' in the back of a cab."

Kade squeezed the trigger. The bullet landed an inch from Mike's hand, resting on the table. He jerked it backward.

"You're sure that's all you remember?" Kade asked.

"Fuck, man, yeah! That's it!" He stared at Kade, anger and fear warring in his eyes.

Kade's lips twisted in a smirk. "See ya around, Mike." He retrieved his own weapon from the dead bodyguard and walked away. No one accosted him as he left and twenty minutes later, he was back where he'd parked his Mercedes.

The car was untouched and Kade glanced around for the kid, who appeared within seconds of Kade's arrival.

"Good job," Kade said, holding up the other half of the hundred between two fingers. The kid snatched it.

"Anytime, bro," he said, his eyes on the money.

Kade slipped inside the car, started the engine, and peeled away from the curb.

A reaction time even a half second slower, and he would've been dead. Normally, that wouldn't be something he'd dwell on, but tonight was different. If something happened to him, who'd be around to keep Kathleen alive and safe?

The anxiety that thought produced was new to Kade, and he tried to shake it off as he headed toward his apartment. If he began worrying for his own life, it would cease making him effective. Part of what made him good at what he did was that he didn't care if he lived or died, other than the slight concern that he'd prefer a quick death over a long and drawn-out one.

Pulling out his phone, Kade opened the GPS app, expecting to see Kathleen still at home. But she wasn't. She was at the Crowne Plaza Hotel.

What the—

And he remembered.

Cursing, he dialed Blane's number and didn't even greet him when he answered.

"I told you to pay off Simone," Kade bit out.

"I did," Blane said. "It looks like she didn't bother passing that information on to Kathleen. I just went by there and her neighbor said she went to the hotel."

Kade bit back the part of him that wanted to ask why Blane had been stopping by to see Kathleen. It wasn't any of his business anyway. "Tell me you're on your way there now," he said instead.

"Two blocks away."

Closer than Kade was. A tinge of disappointment whispered through him and he told himself it was because he wouldn't have the chance to beat up the asshole trying to use Kathleen as a prostitute tonight rather than the fact that Kade wouldn't be the man riding to her rescue.

"Call me once you have her," Kade said.

Blane confirmed and ended the call.

Kade headed toward his apartment. He felt dirty from being on the streets and in dives all day, not to mention he had blood on him. He'd shower at home, then head over to Kathleen's.

Abruptly, he realized he missed her. An odd feeling, and one he wasn't sure what to do with. It had been hours since he'd spoken to her, and now he identified the itch under his skin as being a subtle anxiety for her safety.

But Blane was going to get her, bring her home.

There was a sinking feeling in his gut as Kade thought about Blane and Kathleen. Blane wanted her back and Kade didn't know why. He didn't know if it was just because Kathleen had basically told him to fuck off and Blane wasn't used to getting dumped. Maybe it was because of her intense vulnerability, or perhaps she was an attraction he hadn't yet grown tired of.

As for Kathleen, she didn't seem to be one of those women who took betrayal so lightly as to forgive and forget. She'd seen Blane with another woman. Surely she had enough self-respect to not go back to him after that.

It shamed him, how much he hoped she told Blane to take a long walk off a short cliff. He should be pulling for his brother, not the woman he'd wronged. And it wasn't like Kade was going all righteous. He knew exactly why he hoped they didn't get back together.

Kade wanted her.

He wanted her so much, it was an obsession. He liked her. He liked the way she joked with him, the way she laughed at the things he said, how she wasn't afraid of him when she damn well ought to be, and he liked how she made him feel. Around her, he wasn't Kade Dennon, cold-blooded assassin. He was just Kade. A man who wasn't any better or worse than any other man. The anger and dark emptiness inside weren't so all-consuming when she was there.

The anticipation of seeing her made him hurry and he felt uncomfortably like a teenager looking forward to seeing his favorite girl at the football game. Which lasted right up until he stepped into his office and saw the file he'd had on Kathleen scattered all over his floor.

Shit.

The little sneak, snooping through his things, and then obviously having a fucking temper tantrum when she found something she didn't like.

Typical woman.

He picked it all up, carefully rearranging the pages, and set the folder back on his desk. He took a quick shower and changed into clean clothes. His cell rang as he was pulling a shirt over his head. It was Blane.

"You have her?" Kade asked.

"Sort of. Not really."

Kade frowned. "What the hell does that mean?"

"It means I got there and she'd already been to the guy's room."

Kade let loose a string of profanity, furious anger riding him hard. "Is there any other way you can possibly fuck up her life?" he snapped at Blane, ending the call before he said something he couldn't take back.

So she'd slept with some guy, a stranger, to pay off her debt. The debt Blane had already paid, but obviously hadn't bothered to tell her about. As always, too wrapped up in himself to make sure she didn't go through with it. Blane had no doubt just assumed Kathleen would never do something like that.

Kade could've told him differently.

Kathleen was honorable and brave. If she had a debt, it didn't surprise Kade at all that she'd do what she had to in order to pay it off, even if it terrified her. And Blane had been too late to stop her.

After what she'd gone through in Chicago at Stephen Avery's hands, Kade could only marvel at her courage. Sex was just another weapon in the arsenal, for men and women. Sometimes sex could comfort, other times it was like scratching an itch, but mostly it was about a power struggle and using people. The lovey-dovey shit you saw in the movies was a fairy tale. Kathleen was learning that the hard way.

Glancing at his unmade bed, Kade had a twinge of regret that Kathleen wasn't still there.

But she could be.

There might not be a better time to make a play for her. Blane had fucked up royally. Kathleen was probably feeling vulnerable and lonely, perhaps traumatized after her ordeal tonight. Kade would be as good as anyone else at picking up the pieces, perhaps slightly better, since he knew her.

And he did know her, he thought as he drove toward her place. He knew all about her past, which explained why she did some of the things she did. And he knew that she would come home tonight, wanting the safety and security her apartment represented.

Kade waited for her, sitting in her living room with the glow of the Christmas tree the only lighting. His eyes adjusted as he stared at the door, anticipating her arrival.

She'd fucked somebody else tonight, and it bothered him, in a way he was trying to ignore. It didn't matter. Sex didn't matter, whether it was between two friends or two strangers, so he shouldn't care who else Kathleen had slept with, which is what he kept telling himself.

Finally, he heard a key in the lock and the knob turned. Kathleen stepped inside. She was tired, her whole body seeming to droop, and she limped slightly, as though her ankle hurt. She hadn't seen him and once she'd locked the door, she stopped to take off her coat. The garment slid down her arms and she tossed it aside.

Holy shit.

Kathleen was wearing . . . next to nothing. An outfit that made the Slutty Santa costume seem downright modest.

A tiny black skirt that stretched tight across her ass, the hem barely concealing her crotch. A silvery scrap of fabric that covered her breasts, clinging to the curves and clearly outlining her nipples. There wasn't even a back to it, just a little tie around her neck and another around her waist to hold it on. That alone was enough to make his dick stand at attention, but it was her shoes that made Kade want to pick her up and fuck her against the wall. Or bend her over the couch. Or, even better, toss her onto the bed and hook those legs right over his shoulders.

"What do you want, Kade?"

Her question caught him off guard, so caught up had he been in his fantasy. She sounded . . . pissed and tired. Oh yeah. The file.

"I saw you took a tour of my office. Then left. Something I remember quite clearly telling you not to do." And if she hadn't left, she wouldn't have had to fuck that guy tonight. No one would have found her at Kade's.

The thought made his words come out more harshly than he'd intended and he realized . . . he felt guilty. He'd left her alone all day. If he hadn't, she wouldn't have gone tonight, wouldn't have done what she did.

"Seeing as how you have a rather detailed file on me, I'm surprised you'd expect any different."

Yeah, she was pissed all right.

"Yes, the file currently decorating my floor." Not one hundred percent true. "The file you're all pissed off about. The one I refuse to apologize for making." He couldn't stand not being close to her any longer and got to his feet, heading for her. He stopped when they were just inches apart. She didn't back away.

"And where the fuck have you been?" he asked. His gaze dropped to her breasts all the way down her bare thighs to her toes, peeping out of the best pair of fuck-me shoes he'd ever seen. She looked even better up close and he had to curl his hands into fists so he wouldn't touch her. "Dressed like that, I can only guess you thought you'd keep your appointment for Simone." Would she tell him the truth? Would she tell him she'd fucked a stranger?

"I took care of myself," she hedged.

"I'll bet you did." The lucky bastard. Though Kade had just added him to a list inside his head. A list of people whose lives now had termination dates. Wasn't the guy's fault. He was probably just looking for an easy lay and Simone had provided it. But he'd slept with Kathleen against her will, so he had to die now.

"I didn't screw him, Kade," she said, her eyes flashing. "I black-mailed him."

Whoa, what? Kade was pulled from the fantasy of how exactly he was going to kill the unknown john. "Blackmail? Who?"

"James."

There was only one James and the mere mention of his name sent Kade's temper boiling.

"James Gage?" he asked, just to be sure. Kathleen nodded. "Junior? James Gage—the DA? You blackmailed the district attorney?"

She nodded again.

Well. Kathleen was full of surprises. It embarrassed him that he hadn't thought enough of her to think she'd find a way out of it. But . . . maybe she hadn't, not completely. James was a dick. Even with the threat of blackmail, Kade wouldn't put it past him to molest her, especially if he'd been outmaneuvered by a chick. James's pride was in inverse proportion to his intellect. Kade could imagine how enraged James would have been at Kathleen's blackmailing him. She was lucky to still be standing here.

It scared Kade, even more than if she'd just gone to have sex with a stranger, and he detested that feeling. James was weird with a capital *W* and he didn't think before he acted. He could've killed Kathleen and then poured himself a glass of wine, and she didn't seem to realize that as she stood there looking at Kade with defiance in her eyes.

Take care of herself, my ass.

"And how far did it get before you pulled off your Big Plan?" he asked, angry at how clueless he'd been to the danger Kathleen had put herself in tonight.

"That's none of your business." The little snot was practically spit-ting nails at him.

God, she was hot.

"Dressed like that, I'd be surprised if he let you go before screwing you, no matter what you threatened." Kade certainly wouldn't have.

"Oh, you like my outfit?" she asked, her tone deceptively nice. A tight smile curved her mouth as she ran her hands over her sides down to her hips. Kade's hungry eyes followed the path. "You should—after all, you bought the shoes."

It took Kade a second longer than it should have to catch on. Of course. The money he'd left. She *hadn't* sent every dime to the bill collectors. She'd done exactly what he'd told her to do and bought herself a pair of shoes. And not just *any* pair of shoes, but sky-high stilettos that matched her eyes.

She was absolutely fucking perfect, in every way.

"Then I should take a closer look," he said, latching on to the excuse she'd just handed him to touch her.

Kade crouched down and slid his hand behind her knee, pulling her foot up to rest on his thigh, forcing her to clutch his shoulder to keep from falling.

"What the hell are you doing?"

"Taking a closer look at the merchandise," Kade said. It was pure pleasure and torture to touch her. So much skin was bare, he could slide his hand all the way up the back of her thigh. He made a big show of examining the stiletto. "These are definitely come-fuck-me shoes. They must have set you back some."

A woman who'd spend five hundred dollars to buy a pair of shoes that would live in his fantasies for weeks was his kind of woman.

"Well, you were quite generous the last time you were here." *Sweet* and *nice* Blane had said? Kathleen could give lessons on bitchy.

And it was a complete fucking turn-on.

With her foot raised, her skirt had hiked up further, giving him a delicious view of the scrap of satin panties she wore. She was the perfect height. All he had to do was lean forward and he could fasten his mouth between her legs. He could smell her perfume and just . . . her. He'd never wanted to eat a woman's pussy as bad as he did right then. His dick felt like it was going to explode, he was so hard.

Kade tried to rein in his thoughts. He swallowed. What had she just said? Oh yeah. The money. Speaking of which . . . "It was stupid of you to send all that money to the bill collectors."

She ignored that. "Why the file, Kade? Why would you put me under the microscope like that? Invade my privacy?"

Ah, shit. She'd lost the bitchy and now just sounded . . . hurt. Fuck.

"You were dating my brother," he answered, his voice flat. "I told you once before that I won't take chances with Blane. I needed to find out who you were." He looked up and their eyes met. A beat passed.

"It seemed very . . . thorough," she said at last, and Kade could tell she'd already forgiven him.

She was watching him, her cool blue eyes steady and serene, and Kade couldn't lie to her.

"Yeah, well, that's what it became."

A slight frown marred her brow, but Kade didn't say anything else.

He couldn't take his eyes off her, and it suddenly struck him that he was on his knee. It seemed appropriate somehow that he should kneel for her. Kathleen was so much *more* than him. She looked like a goddess, staring down at him, the silver top making her shine in the lights from the tree. Her hair was long and golden, her skin satin ivory perfection. Her breasts were full, the nipples hard points beneath the fabric, begging for his touch.

Kade slowly stood, his hands wrapped around the back of her legs, sliding up her thighs to her skirt, then dragging the hem up further. To his surprise, he touched nothing but sweet skin.

Fuck. Me.

She was wearing a G-string. Sweet, innocent little Kathleen owned a G-string. And was wearing it. Right fucking *now.*

He cupped the globes of her ass in his palms, ignoring the way she stiffened.

"How about I spend tonight in your bed instead of on the couch?" he whispered in her ear.

"Kade, stop," she said.

God, he loved hearing her say his name. He closed his eyes, inhaling the scent of her hair and perfume.

"You shouldn't . . . touch me like that." She tried to move away, but Kade tightened his grip, pulling her body into his. With those shoes on her feet, his dick was nestled against her abdomen in the sweet spot between her hips.

Kathleen was as turned on as he was. He could tell. Her pulse was racing and her breath was coming in those sweet little pants that he knew he'd never tire of hearing. Both her hands were on his shoulders, and it wasn't to push him away.

"Why not?" he asked. "We're two consenting adults." His lips brushed her ear. "I know you want me, princess." A telling shiver went through her at the slight touch and her eyes slid shut.

"Just because you have a file on me doesn't mean you know me or what I want." Her hands locked around his wrists, moving them from underneath her skirt.

Kade wrapped them around her waist. She was so tiny, he could nearly span the width of her with his hands. More warm skin met his fingertips. She was like a Christmas present, all sparkly and full of promise. He just had to convince her to give him a shot. God, they'd be so good together. It would be a night she'd never forget, he could promise her that.

"I know you better than you think," he said. "I know that you wanted to be a lawyer, which is why you got a job at the firm. I know that piece-of-crap car you had was one of your sole possessions. I know that you avoid sad movies because you hate to cry."

Her wide eyes stared into his. "What are you doing, Kade? Why are you telling me this?"

It was now or never. Time to go for broke and lay it on the line. "I also know that the last thing you want to do is trust someone," he said, "because everyone you've ever loved has left you. And I know this because we're the same, you and me. Trust, love—those things are more dangerous than knives or bullets."

She was trembling. He could feel it. He wanted to pull her close, wrap his arms around her and ease her fears. But he had to get through to her first, make her understand this wasn't just about a quick lay. It was more, *she* was so much more than that.

"Trust is hard-earned, princess, and I didn't mean to break the little trust you had in me." Kathleen said nothing, her eyes still wide. "The file on you started as a background check. Then I met you."

Memories of Kathleen assailed him. Cradled in his arms, gazing up at him like he was her hero after saving her from Avery. Standing in front of a server rack, blinded by darkness, terrified he was going to leave her. Her tongue sliding against his, tasting of chocolate and vodka.

"Then I kissed you, touched you, worked side by side with you. And suddenly, I care about more than just Blane and my own hide. And I didn't want to. I've fought it and I tried to hate you, tried to despise you—but I can't."

So much was in those words and so much more he couldn't say, things he'd never felt for anyone before. Kade gazed into her eyes, his palms cradling her jaw as he willed her to understand, to feel the same way he did. That this wasn't just a one-way thing, but a connection between them that was beyond anything he'd ever known.

He waited, praying to a God he didn't believe in that she'd say yes, she felt it, too. He was vulnerable, too much so, in a way that he hadn't felt since he was a kid. His heart on the line, wishing and hoping for a miracle.

"Kade, I can't. Blane—"

Kade never would have thought that just hearing his brother's name would be as excruciatingly painful as it was, but it just goes to show. Wishing and hoping only got you a fucking dropkick in the gut. He was a fool to think she'd want him—that she'd choose to be with him instead of Blane—even if Kade would treat her better than his brother would. Hell, he'd treat her like fucking gold. All she had to do was say the word.

But Kathleen wasn't a fool. What did Kade have to offer besides a really good lay? Blane may cheat on her, ignore her, lie to her, and treat her like a child, but he was respectable. He had a good job, a home, a career.

"Of course," he said, his voice much too rough. "I should've known you'd still want Blane, even if he is screwing someone else." The words came out and when he saw the hurt in her eyes, he desperately wanted to take them back. But that was the thing. You can't take shit like that back.

"I don't want Blane," she said, "but I can't have you. Don't you see that?"

Her eyes were pleading with him to understand. What was it? Was it because they were brothers? Did she view him as off-limits because she'd slept with Blane? Ethics and morals. Two things Kade didn't give a shit about. He *would* have to pick a woman who did.

"You're the only one who sees that," he said.

He had to stop touching her, needed to put some space between them. His chest hurt, an ache he couldn't place, and his gut felt like he'd swallowed a chunk of lead. He had to get out of there before he did something stupid, like drop to his knees and beg her. Kade headed for the door as quickly as he could without making it look like he was bolting. His dignity and pride were shattered already, but still.

"Wait!"

Fuck. He'd almost been there. His hand was on the doorknob, but he stilled. She had that power over him now. He was helpless to resist her. And she had no fucking clue.

"You said I wasn't alone, that I had you," she said. "Were you lying to me?"

Kade closed his eyes. Maybe he was wrong. Maybe she knew exactly what she was doing. Did it matter?

No.

He was in love with her, an affliction he thought would never happen to him. But he wasn't surprised that it wasn't hearts and roses, not for Kade Dennon. He should've known that it would kick the shit out of him. After all, he deserved nothing more.

On that ironic thought, he turned back to face her. "No. I wasn't lying. I won't leave you alone." More like *can't* than *won't*, but that was just semantics. "It's just better for me to not be in here tonight. I'll be close."

Her eyes slid shut, relief washing across her features, and it was a slight balm to him. She didn't love him, didn't want him, wouldn't choose him . . . but she trusted him.

It was better than nothing.

She opened her eyes again. "Will I see you tomorrow?"

"We have a case to solve and it's not going away," he said. And the sooner it did, the sooner he could get the fuck out of town. Being around her without being able to have her was a torture he didn't need, especially when she wore next to nothing. "Just put some fucking clothes on before I see you again."

"You know I don't normally dress like this!" she called out to him as he stepped outside and closed the door.

Something inside him, a part of him that didn't want to give up and couldn't bear to think this was the last of it, had him opening the door again. She'd turned away but jerked back around. Their eyes met.

"And the next time I see you wearing those shoes, they'll be the only thing you're wearing."

CHAPTER TWELVE

Kade sat in his car for a couple of hours, until he was sure Kathleen was asleep, then went back inside. He couldn't stay away from her, not when he could be close.

He stood in her bedroom, watching her sleep. She'd tossed and turned again, the covers twisting around her legs.

It was pointless to fight it anymore. He'd tried and all it had done was turn him into a confused wreck who couldn't think straight. It seemed somehow fitting, that he'd be destined to fall in love with a woman who didn't want him. How could he have expected her to love him back? It was like asking the sun to stop shining so it could be one with the night.

He was gone before daybreak, replacing the locket ornament on her tree before he walked out the door, and calling Donovan to put a couple uniforms on the place while he was gone.

Mike had said Bowers had taken a cab. Time to find the cabbie who'd picked him up that night, and it was going to be like finding a fucking needle inside a haystack.

It was midmorning when his cell rang. Kade glanced at the caller ID and his heart skipped a beat.

Kathleen.

"Morning, princess," he answered. The endearment was so much how he thought of her, it wasn't even a conscious decision anymore when he said it. Luckily, she'd never said a word, not that he'd know what to say if she did or how he'd explain.

"Good morning," she said, oh-so polite. "I need to run an errand. Stacey Willows called. I think she's being threatened as well. She wants to see me."

And Kathleen had no car, which explains why she'd called him. "I'll come get you," he said.

"I can get a ride. I think I need to get there ASAP. She sounded really freaked out."

So she'd called to get his permission, which was gratifying. "Not cool with that," he said. She'd had one too many close calls for Kade to be comfortable with her going off on her own. It made him nervous and edgy. He didn't even like having to leave her alone inside her apartment.

"I'll be fine," she said. "Isn't this what you're paying me to do?"

She had a point, but still. "I'm paying you to investigate, not throw yourself into obviously dangerous situations."

"What do you think she's going to do to me? Her fiancé is Kyle's commanding officer. Nothing's going to happen. I'll call you as soon as I'm done."

That phrase, *I'll call you as soon as I'm done*, burrowed inside his gut like a warm, sweet promise. It was an acknowledgment of a connection between them. She was admitting that she knew he cared, and that it was okay. She accepted it without any questions and wasn't trying to use it against him.

Blane would say no. Blane would tell her there was no fucking way she was going anywhere today, then he'd lock her in her room to make sure of it.

But Kade wasn't Blane, and Kathleen was a grown woman who could make her own decisions. He trusted her not to do something stupid.

"Fine," he said. "But don't take chances. Get out if it looks bad."

"Got it." Her tone was pleased and he was glad he'd said yes, not that she probably would have obeyed him if he'd said no, but it was nice to be in agreement for a change.

There were several cab companies in Indy, plus a few owner-operated ones with only a handful of cars in their fleet. It took the better part of the day to visit them all and flash the photo of Bowers. Kade left copies of the picture and his number in case any of the drivers out on their shift came back and recognized him.

He thought he'd gotten a hit at one place, the owner calling out for one of the drivers. "Hey, Frankie!"

A kid—Kade guessed him to be no more than twenty—shuffled into the office.

"Frankie, weren't you on Washington Tuesday night?" his boss asked.

Frankie shrugged. "Th-that w-w-was a few d-days ago," he replied with a pronounced stutter. He glanced at Kade, then looked quickly away.

Kade held up the photo of Bowers. "Did you see this man? Did he get in your cab?"

Frankie looked at the picture, then shook his head. "Nah. I ain't n-never seen him b-before." He pushed his hands in his pockets and shifted his weight from one foot to the other.

"All right. Thanks, Frankie," his boss dismissed him.

Frankie left the office and Kade stared after him. Something about the kid bothered him, but he couldn't pinpoint what it was. Just a feeling, a twitch inside his gut.

Frankie looked back and his eyes met Kade's. For an instant, something calculating flashed across his face, then it was gone. He disappeared around the corner.

"Kinda young to be driving a cab, don't you think?" Kade mused, still staring at the spot he'd last seen Frankie.

"He's properly licensed, if that's what you're implying," the man said, defensive. "Nice enough, good manners. The stutter's a bit unusual, but there's nothing wrong with him."

Kade turned around, pushing thoughts of the strange kid aside. "Okay, thanks for your help. Let me know if anyone recognizes him."

"Will do."

He checked the GPS on Kathleen as he left. She was still at Stacey Willows's house. She'd been there all day. He wondered if she needed a ride. Maybe he should swing by and pick her up . . .

No. Not him. Blane.

She'd made it pretty clear last night that she was still hung up on Blane, despite his cheating on her with Kandi. Kade wouldn't have pegged her for that kind of woman, but apparently you never knew. But she was attracted to Kade, so maybe he'd just wait it out. Blane was bound to fuck it up again, or grow tired of her, whichever came first.

He called Blane on his cell.

"No hit on Bowers," Kade said, forgoing the preliminaries. "He's in the wind. We're never going to find him."

Blane sighed. "Yeah, all right. Thanks for trying. How's Kat?"

"She's been visiting Stacey Willows all day," Kade said. "She called Kathleen this morning, said she wanted to talk to her. She's been at her house ever since. I'm thinking you should swing by and pick her up, maybe see what Stacey had to say that's taken all day."

"Good idea. I was just leaving work so I'll get her and take her home."

Jealousy struck and Kade struggled to push it aside. A part of him didn't want Blane anywhere near Kathleen, even as the logical side of him said it had to be this way.

"Yeah, sure," he said easily. "Let me know when my shift starts." The joke was lame, but the best he could come up with at the moment.

"Will do." Blane ended the call.

It wasn't until Kade was driving past a car dealership that it occurred to him, *if Kathleen had a car, she wouldn't have needed Blane to come pick her up tonight.*

He swung into the dealership without thinking twice.

It was fifteen minutes until closing and the salesman wasn't that into working late, but when Kade said the magic word, "Cash," suddenly he was all kinds of helpful. An hour later, Kade had wired the money to the dealership and walked off with the keys to a shiny, new, fully loaded black Lexus SUV. He was just giving them Kathleen's address for delivery when his cell rang.

Blane.

"Gimme a minute," he told the sales guy, then stepped outside. "That was quick," he answered, though he was secretly pleased. If Blane had only spent an hour with Kathleen, she must not be feeling overly forgiving at the moment.

"Why the *fuck* did you let her go see Stacey by herself?"

Blane's furious yelling caught Kade off guard, and pissed him off.

"Because she wanted to," he retorted.

"Well, she was nearly killed," Blane shot back. "Stacey's dead. Kathleen spent the better part of the day knocked out cold and locked in a closet."

Kade's eyes slipped shut as a wave of cold washed over him, stopping him in his tracks. Fuck. Someone had gotten to her. And where had Kade been, her bodyguard, the man who was supposed to protect her? Trolling cab companies looking for a ghost.

"Did you take her to the hospital?" Kade asked.

"She hates hospitals," Blane said, still angry. "She went in to work at that *fucking* bar."

"Then I'll go there," Kade said.

"Ya think?" Blane shot back, his sarcasm grating. "You know, she's saying all this shit now about how she's an *investigator*, for Chrissakes, and that's why she went to talk to Stacey. So if she'd been killed, it would've been *your* fault."

Kade gritted his teeth. "She's not some kid," he argued. "Yeah, she was trying to do her job. Give her some fucking credit, will you? After everything that's happened the past week, she's holding her shit together pretty fucking well. She's been shot at, her car was blown up, somebody sent her a fucking *eye*, and on top of all that, her boyfriend's been a total fucking *dick*."

He was breathing hard, his blood pressure and temper hitting new highs.

They were both quiet for a moment, and Kade could sense Blane regaining his control. He took a deep breath as well. Nothing would be solved by them fighting.

"Shit," Blane finally said. "This fucking blows. It's killing me, the danger she's in, and I can't do a damn thing about it."

Kade could relate to that. Blane was a protector, a man who took action. Inherent in his nature, being a SEAL had only sharpened and honed that side of him. To be forced not to do anything—not to protect Kathleen himself—had to be driving him nuts.

"No worries," Kade said. "I got it. I'm on my way now."

"Thanks."

A lot was unsaid there, but it didn't have to be stated outright. Sometimes you just needed an outlet for your frustration. If Blane's current outlet was Kade, so be it.

Kade pocketed his cell and went back inside, telling the guy to follow him with the SUV. He drove to The Drop and watched the salesman get in a cab for a ride back to the dealership before going into the bar.

It was a relief to see her, whole and unharmed, even if she was wearing that scrap of a Santa costume. Leave it to that shitty bar to have extras. The knot that had formed in the pit of his stomach when Blane called finally eased and he could breathe again. It was new . . . and disconcerting . . . to worry about someone, and a woman at that.

"I see you didn't listen to me," he said to her, cocking an eyebrow. "You're going to catch pneumonia wearing hardly any clothes in the middle of winter." If she dressed like this in subzero weather, Kade wondered what the hell she wore in July. And if he'd ever be lucky enough to see it.

"If only I could be so lucky," she retorted.

That was funny and Kade hid a smile. Damn, he liked her. He really wished he didn't.

"Brought you an early Christmas present," he said, and tossed the keys to the SUV at her. She caught them neatly, then looked up at him in confusion.

Kade slid onto a bar stool. "Well, I'm certainly not going to chauffeur you all over town," he said by way of explanation. Reaching across the bar, he grabbed a bottle of beer from where he'd seen Kathleen pull them. Twisting off the cap, he took a long swallow.

It should be interesting to see her reaction to this. Kade hadn't really considered the *how* of giving the car to her, he'd just wanted to get it for her. Now, though, she was looking at him like he was nuts.

"You . . . got me a car?"

Kade scrambled for what to say, how to do this. He took another drink to buy time before replying. "Thought you could use a little Christmas cheer."

She looked skeptical.

"Consider it an advance on your salary and a tax deduction for the firm." Maybe she'd buy that and just let it go.

Her jaw hung open as she stared at him. "Kade, I don't know what to say—"

He relaxed slightly. Okay, easier than he thought. "Thank you is customary," he said, unable to stop a small smile. It had been a long time since he'd been able to give someone a gift like this. Blane and he rarely exchanged gifts anymore. If they wanted something, they just went and bought it. It felt good, really good, to do this for someone else. For Kathleen.

"Thank you," she said. "But I can't accept this. It's too much." She tried to hand the keys back to him and Kade's smile faded. She was really sucking the fun out of this.

Of course. The answer came to him in a flash. She wouldn't accept a car from him, but she'd take it if she didn't know it was a gift. And what did it matter, really? Hadn't he bought it for her to use? Buying a car was expensive, and she didn't have the money to buy even another piece of shit like the Honda had been.

"Please," he scoffed. "It's not like I bought it for you." He took another swig of beer, forcing himself to be casual.

She looked at him, a question in her eyes as well as a little bit of hope, which sealed it.

"The firm bought it," he lied. "An investigator has to have wheels. It's a company car." That only she was licensed to drive.

He could see the indecision on her face. "Are you sure?" she asked.

"You really think I'd just go buy you a car?" he asked. It was both expected and yet depressing when that sentence seemed to be what convinced her.

Then . . . she did something amazing.

Stepping out from behind the bar, Kathleen put her arms around him and squeezed.

For a moment, Kade did nothing. He was too surprised. Kade didn't get hugged. He just . . . didn't. He wasn't *huggable*. Mona persisted now and again, but a hug from a woman in a gesture of friendship and warmth . . . it never happened to him. Ever.

Shaking himself free of his frozen shock, Kade raised his arms and gave Kathleen a tentative squeeze back. It felt awkward and good at the same time, though she didn't seem to notice, or if she did, she didn't mention it.

"Thank you, Kade," she said. "This is a huge load off my mind."

Pulling back slightly, Kade looked down at her. With him on the stool, they were closer to the same height. Her blue eyes stared trustingly into his. The relief in her gaze made him ache to do more for her. Buy her a half a dozen cars, a house, a fucking yacht—pretty much anything she could possibly want, just to have her keep looking at him like he was her knight in shiny fucking armor.

"No problem," he said, swallowing down words he shouldn't say. He wanted to pull her close again, and not just for a hug, but knew he shouldn't. Yet he was incapable of pushing her away. "And if you'd like to thank me further, I could give you a few ideas, several of which prominently feature those shoes you wore last night."

That did the trick. She stepped away, slapping him lightly on the arm as her face flushed rose. "Drink your beer," she said.

Moving back behind the bar, she took something out of her purse and handed it to him. "I took this cell phone from Adriana's hotel room," she said, "but it has a code on it. I thought you might be able to break it."

"No problem," Kade said, slipping the phone into his pocket. "I was able to trace the phone calls made to Freeman."

"Who called him?"

"Someone with a lot of resources. Government resources." That even he had been unable to trace to their origin as of yet.

"Blane said he thought that might be the case, that the Defense Department budget is supposed to be cut by billions next year."

"Yep," he said, pleased she'd made the connection. "Always follow the money, princess. Nine times out of ten, it's all about the cash."

"And the tenth time?" A smile played about her lips, entrancing him. She was playing with him. It made him smile a little, too.

"The tenth time is personal," he said. "Everyone knows that."

Kathleen grinned outright, and was quiet for a moment. Kade sipped his beer. It was nice, just being with her. He didn't feel a pressing need to be something he wasn't. He could just . . . be. He recognized the feeling as something unique to her, and was grateful for it.

She was wiping down glasses and Kade watched her work, admiring the smooth efficiency of her movements. That outfit showed a helluva lot of skin, and he committed all of it to memory, right next to the image of her wearing those peacock stilettos.

"Ryan Sheffield came by tonight," she said, pulling him out of his thoughts. "I'm going on a date with him tomorrow night."

Kade tensed. The words *I'm going on a date* were some of the last ones he wanted to hear come out of her mouth, much less if they involved someone on this case.

"You realize he works for the government," he said. "He could be our mysterious caller. Or our shooter. Why the date?"

She shook her head. "No, I don't believe that. He doesn't strike me as the type. And why not a date? Maybe he knows more than he's telling, though. If he does, I'll get it out of him."

There were so many things wrong with that statement, Kade didn't know where to begin. First, Kathleen was a woefully bad judge of character, as evidenced foremost by her trust in him.

Second, she couldn't date him because Kade would have to beat the shit out of him. That was a given.

Last, *she'd get it out of him?* Please. Kathleen was about as threatening as a Chihuahua.

"And how do you plan on doing that?" he asked, electing not to piss her off by saying any of that to her. This should be good for a laugh.

"Men the world over have the same weakness," she said with a shrug of one perfect, naked shoulder.

"Really? Do enlighten me, princess."

Leaning over the bar as though to tell him a secret, she crossed her arms under her breasts, pushing them up and together. The Santa outfit already barely contained her feminine assets and now it seemed they were nearly overflowing the fabric's ability to cover them. It made for an impressive display and Kade couldn't stop his eyes from dropping to enjoy the view.

Glancing serenely up at him, she laughed, then said, "Breasts, of course."

Kade swallowed, forcing his gaze back up to meet hers. Yeah, he'd tell her just about anything she wanted to know if she dangled the chance to get his hands and mouth on her.

"Point taken."

She laughed again as she stood and Kade mourned the loss of the amazing view.

"What about Stacey Willows?" she asked. "You know she was murdered today."

It didn't escape Kade's notice that she didn't mention her close call. "So Blane said. What happened?"

"I walked in, said about five words, and she hit me from behind. Next thing I knew, I was waking up inside a closet. I managed to get out, and that's when I found her. Dead. She said she was being threatened, too, that she was supposed to testify against Kyle."

"And you were so sure she wouldn't hurt you," Kade couldn't help reminding her. Her lips thinned but she didn't respond. "I'll check her phone records, too. But why would she knock you out? Were there signs of a struggle?" He was thinking out loud.

"You mean other than her slit throat?" Kathleen's dry retort had Kade smirking again.

"Smartass," he said. His brain was working, playing out the scene from what she'd told him. "If she knew her killer, she would have trusted him, let him into the house. Otherwise, there would have been signs of forced entry, a struggle, something to signify she'd fought."

Kathleen frowned and Kade could practically see her thinking, remembering what had happened. "I don't think there was any kind of a struggle," she said at last. "Her body was right outside the door of the closet she'd stowed me in. Maybe she was going to show him she had me when she turned her back and he took advantage of the moment, killing her before she could tell him about me."

Kade had come to the same conclusion, and he wondered if she realized just how close she'd come to dying. He'd felt the breath of death on his neck too many times to not feel its cold whisper now. "So it seems you're lucky to be alive this evening," he said.

She just shrugged, though her face paled, and guilt rose in him again. If he'd been there, she wouldn't have gotten in that situation. And yet, she wasn't dumb. She knew this case was dangerous and had elected to go anyway. It was a no-win situation for him.

"Any luck finding Bowers?" she asked.

Kade shook his head. "These guys are good. If he doesn't want to be found, I don't know if I'll be able to find him." Finishing his beer, he dug a ten from his wallet and tossed it onto the bar. Kathleen immediately snatched it back up and handed it to him.

"The drink's on me," she said. "It's the least I can do."

"The sooner I can track down who's making these calls, the sooner we can catch whoever's doing this," he said. He'd slip the money in her purse later.

"Then go do it," she said, waving him away. "I don't need you dogging my every move anyway."

"Since when?"

"Go home, Kade," she said, taking him by the elbow and steering him toward the door.

He wasn't letting her out of his sight, not after today, but if it made her feel better to think he had, then Kade didn't see the harm.

The thought again of how she could be dead on a slab in the morgue right now had him pausing on his way out the door. She looked up at him, her hair curling softly around her bare shoulders, her eyes so blue they appeared silvery in the low light.

Kade pressed his lips to her cheek. Her skin was like downy velvet and he lingered longer than he should have.

"Car's parked out front," he murmured in her ear. His hand brushed her shoulder and he felt a shiver run through her at the touch. "I'll see you tomorrow."

He felt her eyes on him all the way to his car.

Not too long after that, he saw her leave. He wanted to watch her reaction when she saw the car and he wasn't disappointed. At first, she looked around as though expecting something else. Then she pressed the key fob and the SUV's lights flashed. Her mouth dropped open in a little O and then she hurried as fast as her little legs would take her over to the vehicle.

She looked ridiculously tiny inside it, which was a good thing. If she got in an accident, chances were good she'd walk away. Kade imagined her checking out the interior—fully loaded, of course—and adjusting the seat and mirrors to suit her stature.

He followed at a respectable distance as she drove home and he waited in the lot the usual amount of time after her light went out before getting out of his car. He was nearly at her door when he saw a car swing into the parking lot.

Easing into the shadows, he watched as a man got out of the car and jogged up the steps.

Blane.

"What the hell are you doing here?" he blurted as Blane stepped onto the landing.

Blane looked just as surprised to see him. "What are you doing out here?" he asked, ignoring Kade's question.

"I always wait until she's asleep before I go in," Kade answered. "It's not like she's rolled out the welcome wagon for me." The words popped out without him really thinking about it first, and he wondered at his instinct to lie about the state of his and Kathleen's relationship to his brother. Blane thought Kathleen hated him, and suddenly Kade didn't want to alert him otherwise.

"I thought you two had declared a truce," Blane said.

Kade shrugged. "You didn't answer me. What are you doing here? It's the middle of the night."

"She called me."

Kade's gut twisted and it felt as though someone had sucker punched him.

Kathleen had called Blane. Her ex. She wanted *him*, not Kade.

It seemed Kade had been quite thoroughly friend-zoned.

Fuck.

"Yeah . . . yeah, sure, man," he said finally. "You, uh, want me to stay?" *Please say yes please say yes please say—*

"I've got it from here," Blane said, passing Kade to stand in front of Kathleen's door. "I'll call you tomorrow."

It was hard to breathe, a sharp pain digging into the center of his chest, but Kade forced himself to nod, act normal. "Got it. Okay then. Later."

Jogging down the stairs, he didn't turn to look back as he heard Kathleen's door open and close. Gazing up at the apartment windows, Kade started the Mercedes. No way was he going to stick around, knowing Kathleen and Blane were having make-up sex just yards away from him. With one last glance to her darkened windows, he peeled out of the lot.

Chapter Thirteen

It was the first night he'd spent in his own bed in weeks. The last person to have lain between the sheets had been Kathleen.

Kade stared at the rumpled covers for a long moment before sliding in. He pressed his nose to the pillow and inhaled deeply. Perhaps he only imagined it, but it seemed he could smell the faint trace of her perfume.

Turning on his back, he folded his arms behind his head and stared at the darkened ceiling.

It seemed impossible that this had happened, that he'd allowed himself to fall for some chick. Worse than that, she wasn't even aware that Kade was in love with her. She still thought she was in love with Blane and hell, maybe she was. Enough women had fallen for Blane before, there was no reason why she'd be any different.

But she was attracted to Kade. She couldn't hide that. And if she'd been a woman with fewer scruples, he would've had her in bed last night.

An image of her naked, Blane pumping between her thighs, flashed in his mind. It made him wince. Jealousy was a hot torrent in his veins, an emotion he'd rarely experienced. To feel jealous implied that he actually cared, and Kade didn't care about much. Somehow, Kathleen had added her name to his very short list, then squirmed her way right to the top.

Tragic, innocent, vulnerable, good. All wrapped up in a package so beautiful, it made his chest ache, and all of it equaled Kathleen—a woman he could never have.

He'd laugh at the irony, if it wasn't so fucking pathetic.

~

Kade was up early. He showered and threw on a pair of jeans before going to work on cracking the password of the phone Kathleen had lifted. He'd also finally gotten a trace on one of the numbers used to call Freeman that had been stonewalled behind a labyrinth of government agencies. He hadn't yet found a name, but it was worth following up on.

He heard from Blane around midmorning.

"Kathleen's staying home today," he told Kade, "so you're off the hook for bodyguard duty."

"Awesome," Kade said flatly, ignoring the twinge of disappointment that he wouldn't see Kathleen today.

"She's got some date tonight," Blane said, "but I don't think she'll be out long."

So they had made up, or were at least well enough on their way to inspire that confident tone in Blane's voice.

"Yeah, I know," Kade said, leaving it at that.

"One more thing," Blane said, then seemed to hesitate.

"What?" Kade prompted.

"Kathleen. I think . . . well, it seems likely anyway . . . that she's pregnant."

Kade's stomach dropped to his feet.

He'd lost her.

"Please tell me you're joking," he said at last, belatedly hearing the rough aggression in his voice.

"Pregnancy is not something I joke about," Blane said. "I just thought . . . with how much you detest playing bodyguard . . . that you should know."

"You think I'd do a better job if I knew she was having your baby, you mean," Kade said bitterly.

"That's not it," Blane said. "I just thought you'd want to know that she may be carrying your niece or nephew."

"I hate kids."

Blane laughed lightly. "You won't hate your own flesh and blood, I guarantee it."

Kade didn't smile. He was still reeling from the fact that Kathleen was now permanently and forever beyond his reach. He'd thought he'd accepted that last night.

Guess not.

"Gotta go. I'm due back in court." Blane ended the call.

Kade stared blindly at the four computer screens in front of him, the dead phone still in his hand.

Kathleen was pregnant. With Blane's kid.

She wasn't his, was never going to *be* his. He'd been deluding himself last night. Deep down, he'd been nurturing a persistent hope that once Blane was through, Kade could make a play for her.

Not anymore. Even Kade drew the line at going after another man's pregnant girlfriend.

It suddenly occurred to him—he assumed Blane would marry her if she was pregnant, but this was *Blane* they were talking about. He'd been on the ropes with Kandi for years. No way was he just going to throw her over for Kathleen, no matter how beautiful she was, pregnant or not.

Which would leave Kathleen a single mom, just like Kade's own mother had been.

Kade tossed down his cell and scrubbed his hands over his face. His loyalty should come first and foremost to his brother. He knew that. So why did he feel like he wanted to kill him?

Pushing aside thoughts that made him feel like the shittiest kind of brother, Kade went back to work, his fingers flying over the keys as he routed his IP address through China and Eastern Europe before attacking the firewalls protecting the network at CIA headquarters in Langley, Virginia.

~

Kade wondered if he'd hear from Kathleen, but not once did she call him. Maybe she wasn't even thinking about him and hadn't thought of him at all today. Pregnant with Blane's child, she probably had other things on her mind, which didn't stop him from reaching for his cell a little before seven o'clock. He hit the number for her speed dial.

"Nice of you to tell me the big news," he said when she answered.

She paused and Kade wondered if she was surprised that he knew.

"I don't know what you mean," she said, and Kade could tell she was lying through her teeth. She knew exactly what he meant.

"I talked to Blane," he said. "He told me."

"I-I'm sorry, Kade," she stammered. "I didn't mean for this to happen. I'm not trying to get Blane to marry me, if that's what you're upset about."

Kade mentally cursed. He wished his anger was so righteous and noble as to be protecting his brother. Instead, he was just mad. Mad that she was pregnant with Blane's kid. Mad that he'd missed his shot. Mad that she was about to become another casualty of the Kirk family.

"Damn it, Kathleen, that's not why I'm pissed. Blane knows better than to be so careless."

She didn't reply for a moment, and when she did, it was almost as though she'd seen through his excuses.

"It's not for sure," she said quietly. "Probably just a false alarm. I've been under a lot of stress, you know."

No shit. "Yeah, I know."

"Ryan's here," she said. "Gotta go."

Ryan Sheffield.

Supposedly a JAG officer, but his interest in Kathleen seemed a bit too . . . convenient.

Kade turned back to his computer. A few minutes later, he'd gotten into the personnel records for the Navy, based out of Tennessee. Ryan Sheffield pulled up okay and he seemed to check out.

Following his gut, which had turned out to be right on more than one occasion, he traced his service record back a few years . . . and hit a brick wall. He grabbed his cell and dialed.

"Hey. Remember me?" he asked when the person picked up.

There was a pause. "Um, yeah," the guy said.

"Remember when I said I'd call one day and you could do that favor you owe me."

"Yeah." The man's voice was hesitant, slightly afraid.

"Today's that day." Kade went on to explain what he wanted to know.

"But I'm not supposed to access those files," the guy protested.

"So be sneaky about it. I'll call back. You have ten minutes." Kade hung up.

The phone's code had cracked while he'd been busy, and Kade picked it up to scroll through its contents.

They'd been careful, whoever they were. There were no e-mails or texts and the dialing history had been erased. Even star-sixty-nine to redial the last number led to a disconnected line with the number blocked.

Pulling up software he'd written himself, Kade accessed the phone's memory. Not something just anyone can do with just any tool, and most people wouldn't know to look there anyway, but it proved fruitful for him.

"Well, look at what we have here," he murmured to himself.

A photograph had been left in memory. A naked woman who didn't seem to mind at all that she was having her photo taken.

Adriana Waters.

The photographer could be seen in a mirror on the wall. It looked like a generic hotel room. Enlarging the photo, Kade scrutinized the somewhat blurry reflection. He'd bet a thousand bucks it was Ryan, but he needed more proof.

Grabbing the phone, he dialed his source again.

"What do you have for me?" he asked when the guy picked up.

"Yeah, that guy is like a ghost," his source said, speaking furtively in an undertone. "His record is bullshit. Says he's served for six years, but none of the places he said he was stationed have any record of him."

Kade digested this, the bad feeling that he'd felt when Kathleen had said Ryan was picking her up now growing.

"So I kept digging," the man continued in a hissed whisper. "And, well, I think the guy is CIA."

Fuck.

"I haven't had a chance to get any further, not enough time, but does that give you enough?"

Kade's reply was curt. "Yeah."

"So we're square?"

"For now. Catch you later."

Kade was already typing on his computer, disconnecting the call with a flick of his finger. Ryan Sheffield may think he was smart, but he wasn't smart enough. He may have deleted the phone numbers he'd called from his phone, but he hadn't been thorough enough to get a burner phone, and the phone company would know who he'd called.

Soon, Kade was staring at the phone number for the Bank of Grand Cayman. This was going from bad to worse to downright shitty. Grand

Cayman was a pain in the ass to hack into and took some time, which he didn't have. So instead, he called a woman.

"Nicole. Guess who."

There was a fluttering of rapid French and Kade had to cut her off.

"You know I love that shit, but I'm short on time, sweetheart. Been shopping lately?"

Nicole was an expatriate from Paris with a taste for the finer things. Her job didn't come with a salary to finance her habits, so she supplemented in some creative ways.

"You know I have not, Kade," she said in a throaty purr. "Perhaps you come take me, no?" Which she meant literally and sexually. As he recalled, she was particularly flexible.

"I'll send you on a spree to Tiffany's if you'll look up a phone number for me and tell me the name on the account," he replied.

She laughed and he could picture her swinging back her long, chestnut-brown hair. Nicole was tall and lean, with bedroom eyes and a smile you could feel.

"Okay, but you promise not to tell," she said.

"Would I do that to you?" Kade drawled before reading her off the number. He glanced impatiently at his watch while he waited. Kathleen had been with Ryan for almost thirty minutes. Pulling up the GPS on his computer, he saw they'd ended up at some restaurant north of downtown, at least thirty minutes from him.

He was up and grabbing his keys before Nicole even came back on the line.

"That account belongs to a Ryan Sheffield," she said. "Perhaps a rich friend of yours? He has over five million dollars in the account, new deposits within the past two weeks."

Shit! "Thanks, Nicole. Hit Tiffany's up this weekend and give them my name. I'll make sure you're on my list."

"Merci, Kade. Though I would prefer if you were to take me." He could hear the French pout in her voice.

"Some other time, sweetheart. Gotta run." He ended the call and hit the door at a dead run.

The elevator seemed to crawl and blocked his signal. He was dialing Kathleen as he ran to his car and jumped inside. To his relief, she picked up on the third ring.

"Get out of there, Kathleen," he said. His tires squealed as they spun on the concrete floor of the parking garage.

"What? Why?"

"I cracked that phone you lifted," he said, burning straight through a red light. Cars honked as he flew past. "It belongs to Ryan Sheffield. From the photo I found, he's been sleeping with Adriana Waters."

"They're having an affair?" she asked.

Duh. Dumb question. Hadn't he just said they were sleeping together? Wasn't that the definition of "affair"? But he bit his tongue when he replied, mindful of the fact that she was in the company of a cold-blooded murderer who, for some unknown reason, hadn't hurt her. Yet.

"It would seem so."

"That must have been him that I heard in the hotel room," she said.

Now she was putting the pieces together. He could only hope she kept her wits and didn't panic. "Right, which is why you have to leave. Now. I found an account in Grand Cayman that belongs to Ryan. It's recently received over five million dollars in deposits. In case you're not aware, they don't pay enlisted men that kind of money."

"But why would he kill Ron and Stacey, Kade?" she asked. "Or come after me? He's JAG, not a SEAL. They would've laughed in his face if he'd been the one threatening them."

True. "Because before he was JAG, he was CIA."

"What?" she squeaked. Kade winced. "But . . . but that's not possible."

And she was losing it.

"I'm on my way," he said, glancing down at the speedometer. Pushing ninety in a thirty-five. At least traffic was light. "Ryan's neck-deep in this shit. Get out of there. Tell him anything."

"Okay, I'm downtown, at—"

But she was cut off, and the next voice on the line was most definitely not Kathleen's.

"I'm sorry, but Kathleen can't come to the phone right now," Ryan said. "She'll have to call you back later."

Kade clutched his phone so hard, the edge bit into his fingers. "You lay a finger on her, and I personally will make sure it's the last thing you ever do."

"Tell Kirk that if he wants to see her alive again, he should make sure he loses this case," Ryan said, then hung up.

Panic burned a hole in his gut, but Kade ignored it, instead pushing the accelerator down even further. He was still over fifteen minutes away. His one hope was that Ryan wanted to use Kathleen for leverage. Hopefully, that meant he wouldn't hurt her. The signal was still coming from her phone and it would continue to do so, even if Ryan turned it off.

Kade just hoped he hadn't left it behind.

He drove like a madman, weaving in between cars and into oncoming traffic at a suicidal speed. The thought occurred to him to call Blane, but that would take time away from trying to get to her, and he couldn't afford that.

He was only five minutes away when his phone rang again. It was an unknown number. Maybe it was Ryan, wanting to talk terms.

"Yeah," Kade answered.

"Help me!"

It was Kathleen, breathless and terrified.

"What's happening?" he asked.

"I don't know," she said. Her voice shook. "They shot Ryan."

"Who? Who shot Ryan?"

She was sobbing now. "I don't know! His head just exploded. And now they're after me."

Kade could tell she was close to hysterical, and hysterical people didn't last long when someone was after them. If he could just get her to calm down for four more minutes . . .

"Take it easy," he said. "Breathe, Kathleen. Keep it together. I'm coming for you."

But she didn't reply to him. Instead, she said, "God, Frankie, you scared me!"

Kade frowned.

"Frankie?" he heard her say, the relief now edged again with fear.

"What's going on?" Kade asked. "Who the fuck is Frankie?"

But she either didn't hear him or couldn't answer, because all she said then was, "What? What do you mean? No!"

The line went dead.

CHAPTER FOURTEEN

Kade's Mercedes squealed to a stop in the parking lot of the restaurant. He slammed it into park and didn't bother to close the door as he vaulted out. He was inside seconds after that.

"There was a girl in here," he said to the maître d', "just minutes ago. She left with a man."

The guy frowned at him, giving him a once-over. "I'm sorry, sir, but we have lots of couples coming and going."

It took a tremendous amount of self-control not to wrap a hand around the man's neck and shake the information out of him. Kade bit back his frustration. "This girl is hard to miss," he said. "Long hair. Reddish-blonde. Petite little thing. Big blue eyes."

At his description, the man's expression cleared. "Ah, yes," he said with a nod. "Very polite young lady. She and her escort left nearly ten minutes ago, I believe."

"Did you see where they went?"

The man shook his head. "I'm afraid not."

Suddenly, they both heard a scream from outside. Kade had his gun in his hand before he hit the door.

A family was standing in the parking lot, a woman huddled with two small children and a man who stood in front of them. They were all staring at something. As Kade got closer, he saw the body of Ryan Sheffield lying on the ground. His head was a pulpy mass of blood and gore. The family seemed frozen in shock as they stared.

"IMPD," Kade lied as he pushed past them, but the family got out of his way.

Kneeling down, he examined the wound, then the damage to the truck where it seemed the shooter had missed. Low on the door—he must've been firing at another target. Kathleen, Kade guessed.

But where was she now?

Holstering his gun, Kade pulled out his phone. The GPS was still active and heading away at a rate of speed that said she was in a moving vehicle. He hurried to his car.

"Wait!" The maître d' had grabbed onto his jacket. "You're leaving?"

"I'm in pursuit," Kade said. "Call nine-one-one." Shaking off the man's hold, he got back in his car and shot out of the lot.

Kathleen's kidnapper was headed back toward downtown. Kade dialed as he drove, sending through his Bluetooth so he could watch the screen for Kathleen's signal. When Blane answered, Kade didn't sugarcoat it.

"Kathleen's been kidnapped."

Blane didn't waste time on shock or stupid questions. He'd had enough training as a SEAL to leave emotions aside and just deal with the facts.

"When?" he asked.

"Fifteen, maybe twenty minutes ago," Kade replied. "He's got her in a moving vehicle, headed southwest."

"Who is he?"

"Unknown." Kade gave Blane a brief rundown on what he'd found out about Ryan Sheffield and how he'd taken Kathleen. "But then she called me, said she needed help, that someone had killed Ryan and was trying to kill her."

"She called *you*." It was a reiteration of fact, but edged with something else. Maybe Kade had been wrong about Blane being able to leave emotion aside, because he sounded surprised and angry.

"Yeah, she called me," Kade retorted. "Does it fucking matter who she called? The point is, the bad guy has her, and if he killed Sheffield, then someone else has a dog in this hunt that we don't know about. Ryan wanted to use Kathleen as leverage. I don't know what this guy wants."

"She called him Frankie?" Blane asked.

"Yeah. Has she mentioned anyone by that name to you?"

"Not a word."

Kade glanced at the tracker. "They're heading into downtown. Lots of people and places, but the tracker is working."

"You've got a *tracker* on her?"

Oops. "Thought for sure I'd mentioned that," Kade muttered.

"You didn't."

"Don't get all pissy. It's coming in pretty fucking handy right about now," Kade said. "You're welcome."

Then the signal was gone.

Kade stared at the screen in disbelief. "No."

"No what?" Blane asked.

Kade restarted the app, waiting for it to zero in, but it showed nothing. Kathleen's signal was nowhere to be found.

"I lost her," he said. His voice sounded strangled to his ears.

"You *what?* You *lost her?*" No mistaking the fury in Blane's voice now.

"The GPS stopped transmitting," Kade said, thinking furiously. "He either destroyed it, or they went somewhere the signal can't reach. A basement maybe, or someplace with concrete walls."

"Your tracker can't reach from a basement? It's not much of a tracker then, is it."

Blane's bitter anger set Kade's teeth on edge. "I didn't know she was going to be kidnapped," he snapped. "Just meet me at my place as soon as you can."

"Why? What are we going to do exactly? You have no idea where she is."

"I don't know, but I'll think of something." Kade ended the call.

He was on his computer when Blane came through the door, still in his suit from work.

"Anything?" Blane asked, shrugging out of his jacket and tossing it onto another chair.

"I'm searching for anyone she might've known with the name Frank or Frankie. People working at the courthouse, other law firms in the area, the bar, tenants of her apartment complex . . ." He trailed off. "But so far . . . nothing."

Blane shoved his hand through his hair, pacing the floor behind him. "It can't be someone she's known very long, or she'd have mentioned him to me," he said.

Blane's cell rang and he pulled it from his pocket. Glancing at the screen, he stopped in his tracks and raised his gaze to Kade's. Their eyes met in mutual understanding.

"It's her phone," Blane said.

"But maybe not her."

"Keep him talking," Kade said, swiveling back to the computer. He began typing, running a trace back from Kathleen's cell company to what tower was closest to her current location.

Blane answered on speaker. "Kat, where the hell are you?"

"I have her," a male voice said. "I thought you m-m-might want to s-s-say goodbye."

He sounded young, younger than Kade would have thought, and the stutter was very pronounced.

"Who is this?" Blane asked.

"The man who's going to k-kill K-K-Kathleen. Then I'm going to k-kill you and K-Kyle. Do you want to listen?"

Kade's fingers faltered at the keys.

There was silence on the phone and Kade could hear Blane's harsh breathing as he stood behind him.

"No! Stop!"

Kathleen, yelling. Then a scream filled with pain, abruptly cut off.

"Kathleen!" Blane yelled. "What the fuck are you doing to her?"

"She will pay for what she is," Frankie said.

The coldness of his voice sent a chill through Kade. He'd dealt with murderers before—hell, he *was* a murderer—and they all had that same note in their voice where you just knew there'd be no hesitation and no regret for their actions.

The trace was nearly complete, narrowing it down to two towers.

"I am going to hunt you down and kill you."

Blane's icy words echoed in Kade's ears. *And if he doesn't, I will,* Kade silently vowed.

"I'm going to shoot her and let her bleed like my father bled. Then I'm going to burn the hair she's so proud of. Then if she's still screaming, I'll cut her throat."

The stutter was gone now, the voice one of a madman. A lunatic. And that lunatic was going to kill Kathleen, maybe within moments.

"No, please." Kathleen's strangled plea filled the room. Neither Blane nor Kade moved. They didn't speak. They just listened.

The feeling of utter helplessness was one Kade hadn't felt in years. It nearly drove him mad, hearing her beg for her life, and him, unable to do a damn thing about it.

"Any last words, Kat?" Frankie sneered.

Kade had a wild, insane hope that she'd say something to him. Anything. Even if she just said his name—

"Can you hear me, Blane?"

Kade's eyes slid shut.

"Yeah, babe, I can hear you," Blane gently said.

"Blane . . .his name's Frankie. He's driving a city cab, about five seven, twenty years old, hundred-fifty pounds, clean shaven—" They heard the crack of metal against bone and Kathleen cried out in pain.

"Kat!"

"Time's up," Frankie said.

A gunshot sounded and the air Kade breathed froze in his lungs, choking him.

Kathleen screamed in agonizing pain. It tore through Kade worse than anything he'd ever known. In that moment, he had no doubt that if he could have, he would've given his life in exchange for hers.

"I'll see you soon, Kirk." There was a clatter, then the line went dead.

Neither of them said anything, and Kade knew they were each taking a moment to steel themselves against the panic and rage they both felt.

Kade spoke first.

"The trace was near where the GPS signal disappeared," he said at last, hardly able to recognize the sound of his own voice. "I couldn't get any closer, and it sounds like he destroyed the phone, so there won't be any more signals."

"But she gave you information," Blane said. "He's twenty, five seven, drives a cab."

A memory struck Kade. "Holy shit," he breathed.

"What?"

"I know this guy. I met him. One of the cab companies I looked into when Bowers disappeared. There was a kid. His name was Frankie." He'd struck Kade as odd at the time, but with nothing else to go on, he'd ignored the feeling.

Kade pulled the company up online, then called their listed number. A moment later, he'd hung up and turned to face Blane.

"His name is Franklin Randall Wyster. He moved here a few months ago."

"When his family brought the suit against Kyle," Blane added. "Of course. He said on the phone that his dad had died. His dad was James Wyster, killed by SEAL forces on a raid into Iraq."

"Looks like there's more we don't know about the Wysters," Kade said, hitting the print button on his computer. "Here's a news story on an honor killing a couple of years ago. Frankie's fifteen-year-old sister." He handed the papers to Blane. "The father and son were never prosecuted."

"So the family's Muslim, the dad changes his name to Ahmed el Mustaqueem, and he flies off to Iraq to fight for the other side," Blane said. "He gets killed by SEALs, then his family sues for wrongful death since he was technically an American citizen and a non-combatant."

"And it seems Frankie was anxious to take matters into his own hands, killing everyone involved with the case and his father's death," Kade added.

"Including Kathleen," Blane finished.

Their gazes met in mutual understanding and dread.

"Where would he have taken her?" Blane asked, stepping closer to peer over Kade's shoulder.

Kade swiveled in the seat to face the computer screens, pulling the map from one monitor to center on all of them and zooming in to where he'd last seen the GPS.

"It could be anywhere within this radius," he said, outlining the block with his mouse. "Unfortunately, this is heavily populated, so it's a little like a needle in a haystack. But hey, if you want to start busting down doors and searching, I'm in."

"We can't do that," Blane said. "Someone would call the cops and we'd get arrested."

"You want to call the cops anyway?"

"No. We have no proof except our word that he's involved, and it'll take too long. Kathleen doesn't have that kind of time."

The reminder made Kade's stomach churn. "I'll start running through real estate records," he said, "see who owns what. If one of the places is abandoned or for sale, he could be there."

"How long is that going to take?"

"Don't you think I'm going as fast as I can?"

Blane shoved his hand through his hair again. "I know. I'm sorry. I'm going to head that direction, so you can just call me when you know and I'll already be there."

Kade heard the sound of Blane slipping his Glock from its holster and the ammunition clip ejecting as Blane checked the rounds before slamming it home again.

"Okay," he said. "Just wear a vest. This lunatic wants to kill you, and I hate funerals." He didn't look up from the screen. Kathleen was already in serious danger, perhaps dead or dying. Kade didn't need Blane to die tonight as well.

"All right," Blane said. "Call me when you find something."

Not if, but when. His trust that Kade would come through was daunting and Kade hoped it wasn't misplaced.

"Will do," he said. He heard Blane leave through the front door, but his concentration was already back on the information scrolling down his screens.

~

It took too many nerve-wracking hours for Kade to find the right house, and he was only able to do so because he'd cross-referenced the owners of the properties with recent airline passenger lists and saw that one house was currently unoccupied due to the owners being out of the country. That's the address he told Blane on the phone, and that was the address he was currently breaking into.

Blane had taken the front while Kade was approaching from the rear. The guy may or may not be alone, so he crept silently down the empty hallway.

Someone cried out and Kade froze.

Kathleen.

Backtracking, Kade peered around a doorway into the kitchen and that's when he heard him.

"Kirk. Did you c-come looking for your whore?"

It was Frankie. His back was to Kade and he had a hold of Kathleen. Relief flooded Kade. She was still alive.

Moving soundlessly, he stepped into the kitchen, his gun held out in front of him and aimed at Frankie. But he couldn't shoot him. The bullets might go right through and hit Kathleen.

"I'll k-k-kill her first, then I'll kill you."

He was talking to Blane, who stood beyond Frankie, his weapon trained on him. Kade knew Blane could see him, but he didn't given anything away, not even so much as a flicker of his eyes in Kade's direction.

"You can't get both of us," Blane said. "You shoot her, I kill you."

Frankie laughed. "S-s-stalemate."

"I'll put down my gun—"

"No—" Kathleen protested before Frankie yanked her backward, cutting off her words.

"I'll put down my gun," Blane continued, "and you let her go. I'm the one who's going to get Kyle off. Remember, he's the man who shot your dad. I'm the one you want."

Frankie didn't answer. Kade saw exactly where Blane was going with this. His arm was steady, his aim sure. He waited.

"Do we have a deal?" Blane asked.

Frankie nodded. "P-put down your gun, K-K-Kirk."

Blane carefully bent and placed his weapon on the floor. Kade knew Frankie would aim for the chest. It was doubtful he was a good enough shot with a handgun to hit anywhere else on Blane, especially not at that distance.

And he was right.

When Blane stood, Frankie whipped his arm up and away from Kathleen, firing into Blane's chest and knocking him backward onto the floor.

"No!" Kathleen screamed. Her knees gave way and Frankie didn't bother holding her up any longer. She crumpled to the floor, which gave Kade a clear shot.

He squeezed the trigger, putting two bullets center mass on Frankie. Kill shots. Frankie went down.

Kathleen was staring at him in wide-eyed disbelief from where she lay on the floor. Kade holstered his gun as he rushed toward her. She was struggling to get up and get to Blane, who was trying to get his breath back from where he lay.

Crouching down beside her, Kade pulled her into his arms. "Hey, take it easy," he said.

She looked like hell. Blood and dirt coated her face, along with bruises that marred her flawless skin. Her hair was matted with more dried blood and her clothes were dirty, with one sleeve torn off and wrapped around her leg as a tourniquet. The bullet wound in her thigh was nasty, blood easing from it. It had to hurt like a motherfucker.

"Blane—" she gasped.

"Shh. Don't try to talk," Kade soothed. He couldn't believe she was alive. He touched her cheek, which was too cold from blood loss. Holding her as close as he dared, his eyes roamed her body, looking for any other wounds. She was cradling her hand. One finger was swollen and by the way it was bent, likely broken. Kade's lips pressed together. He should've just incapacitated that fuck and used the knife strapped to his ankle to flay him alive.

"But Blane—" she said again.

"I'm fine, Kat. I'm right here." Blane had recovered and now crouched on the other side of her. She whipped her head around to stare at him.

"Call nine-one-one," Blane said.

"I'm on it," Kade replied. Handing her over to Blane was hard to do, but she needed medical care, so he was exceedingly gentle as he passed her into Blane's arms.

Though he returned in moments, Kathleen was unconscious by the time he got back. Kneeling next to Blane, they waited in anxious silence for the three minutes it took for an ambulance to arrive. Jumping up when he heard sirens, Kade hurried to open the door.

Paramedics came inside, toting heavy cases of equipment. Blane reluctantly moved aside, letting one of the men handle laying Kathleen back on the floor.

"Can somebody tell us what happened?" the paramedic asked.

Blane gave him a quick rundown. Another EMT had spotted Frankie's body and stepped toward it. Kade shook his head and blocked the man's path.

"He's dead," he said. "Work on her." He pointed at Kathleen.

"How do you know he's dead?" the EMT asked, sidling sideways to try to pass Kade by.

"Because I shot him. Trust me, he's dead. Now go work on her." He was getting seriously pissed and it must have shown because the guy looked hard at Kade, then backed down, turning to crouch next to the guy cutting the tourniquet off Kathleen's thigh.

The cops were there, too, and Blane told them in concise terms what had happened. One of them glanced at Kade.

"Why is Dennon here?" he asked, gazing suspiciously at Kade, who gave him a thin-lipped sneer in return.

"I hired him," Blane said, "to help with this case. His presence is legit."

Blane's tone brooked no argument and the cop gave a reluctant nod, jotting something down on his notepad. He turned away and went to where his partner was examining Frankie.

Fifteen minutes later, they were loading Kathleen onto a stretcher and into the back of an ambulance. Blane climbed inside and Kade made to follow, but the EMT stopped him.

"Sorry. Only have room for one passenger," he said briskly.

"I'll call you," Blane said to Kade.

Kade stepped back and the doors slammed shut. The sirens started again and the ambulance took off down the street. He watched it go.

She was okay. Kathleen was going to be all right.

It finally hit him and he had to lean against the building, relief and leftover adrenaline making his limbs shake.

"Hey! Tell dispatch to send someone to collect two bodies," the cop called out to his partner, who was at the patrol car, talking into a radio.

Kade glanced back at the door and saw the cop disappear back inside. Curiosity aroused, he followed him.

"Where's the other body?" he asked.

The cop was picking up casings from Frankie's gun. He looked around, saw Kade, and went back to what he was doing.

"In the basement," he replied curtly, offering no further information.

Kade rolled his eyes and stepped around the cop and over Frankie. Kathleen had been heading through the kitchen, which must mean the basement was . . . there.

An open doorway was on the far side of the room, and through it he could see a flight of stairs. He headed over and slowly descended. There were fresh blood stains on the stairs. Kathleen's blood.

The basement itself was dank and musty, the hard-packed wooden floor covered in dust. There was an open doorway with a transom window above it. A strong smell emanated from the room. Kade crossed to it and peered inside.

A man's body, obviously dead for several days, lay on the floor. Maggots swarmed around his face and an empty eye socket.

Bowers. It had to be.

Kade spied the remains of Kathleen's phone on the floor, crushed, and he felt a wave of horror wash over him. Frankie had kept Kathleen *here*, with the dead body, for six hours? How the hell had she gotten out?

Just imagining her being here—shot and hurting inside a freezing-cold room that had no source of heat, with only a decomposing corpse for company—had his hands fisting and rage building in his veins. But he had no outlet for all that fury. Frankie was dead. Kade couldn't kill him again, though he wished he could.

He left, hurrying up the stairs and not saying anything to the cops as he passed by. They got out of his way pretty damn fast and moments later he was in his car. He had to blow off some steam. The rage at what she'd gone through, and the bitter disappointment that she wanted Blane at her side—not him—was eating him alive.

Though he supposed he could take comfort in the knowledge that she obviously thought he was a better choice to call if she needed help, since she'd called him instead of Blane when the chips had been down. It was a small consolation.

Kade pulled up to a bar in a part of town where the cops didn't bother responding to calls anymore. He was looking for a fight, and this was as good a place as any.

Inside was dimly lit, with about two dozen people scattered around the room. Heads turned when he walked in and Kade could almost feel the menace in the air, which suited him just fine.

There was an empty seat at the bar and he slid onto the stool. That put his back to the room, but there was a mirror behind the bar, giving him an unobstructed view of everyone and everything behind him.

Catching the bartender's eye, he tossed a hundred-dollar bill on the counter. "Vodka, neat," he said, "and keep it coming."

The guy was slow to wander over, but he snatched the money quick enough, the bill disappearing into his shirt pocket.

"We're all out," he said. His gaze lifted briefly to look over Kade's shoulder.

Kade glanced in the mirror. Four guys were heading his way.

"Then I want my money back," Kade said. He saw one of the guys sliding on a pair of brass knuckles.

"What money?" Reaching under the bar, the bartender pulled out a baseball bat.

His sneer turned Kade's simmering rage into a pool of ice-cold fury.

The guy swung the bat at Kade, who reached up and caught it mid-swing. It hit his palm with a loud slap. Kade gave it a sharp jerk, pulling it out of the guy's hands. He hadn't been expecting it and hadn't reacted in time. Kade shoved the bottom of the bat right back at the bartender, nailing him hard in the face. There was a crack of bone and the bartender was down for the count.

A glance in the mirror showed him the men had paused in surprise, but they were over it.

The first one came at him before he had time to turn around. The bat was still parallel to the floor and Kade reversed its direction, shoving the tip behind him and catching the first attacker in the jaw. The bat was hard wood, heavy enough to withstand the impact of a baseball flying at nearly one hundred miles an hour. Compared to that, the guy's bones could've been made of glass for what it did to him. He went down, which left three.

Kade spun on the stool, gripping the bat with both hands, but not like a batter would. It took too long to swing a bat—you needed both hands to wield one, and swinging it left your body entirely vulnerable, which was why it wasn't his first choice as an offensive weapon.

But it'd do in a pinch.

He held it with both hands like a battering ram, which is exactly how he used it on Brass Knuckles. There was a reason why they were illegal—they could do a lot of damage with only one hit. So the answer was . . . don't get hit.

Kade shoved the bat at Brass Knuckles, punching the air right out of him and breaking some ribs. The guy doubled over, his buddy flanking Kade with a knife. Kade whipped the bat up, striking the forearm of the guy slashing the blade toward him, which did two things—it deflected the blow, and broke the man's radius bone.

He yelled in pain, his hand reflexively opening to drop the knife, which Kade caught.

The guy in the middle seemed frozen in shock. Kade's hands were full of weapons, but he had no room to maneuver. The guy was too close. So he whipped his head forward, striking the other man's nose with his forehead. The blow was fast and brutal. Blood spurted from the man's crushed nose and his eyes rolled up in his head. His knees collapsed.

Brass Knuckles had finally caught his breath and swung for him, the light catching on the wickedly lethal weapon. He was a big guy and there was a lot of force behind that swing. If it landed, Kade would have a broken jaw, lose some teeth, probably have a concussion, and maybe a cracked skull. Brain damage and death were also possibilities.

Kade dropped the bat and leapt forward, off the stool and into the guy's space. Now his punch was too badly aimed to land with any kind of force and his arm glanced off Kade's shoulder.

Grabbing his wrist, Kade twisted and ducked under the guy's arm, using the momentum to slam the man's hand down on the wooden bar, palm up. A second later, Kade swung the knife, burying its point into the center of the guy's palm and pinning it to the bar. Brass Knuckles yelled in pain as the blood began to flow. Grabbing the back of the guy's head, Kade slammed him headfirst onto the bar. The yelling stopped immediately and Kade dumped his body over the barstool he'd just vacated.

Kade turned to see the crowd had gone silent. No one moved forward to help the four men, which was too bad because that had felt pretty damn good. He was breathing hard, his heart pounding with adrenaline, his senses heightened as he waited for another threat. But none came.

Rounding the bar, he saw that the bartender was still out cold. Reaching down, Kade retrieved his money, then grabbed an unopened bottle of vodka.

"Thanks for the drink," he said to no one in particular. Then he was out the door and gone.

CHAPTER FIFTEEN

"Hey, it's me," Blane's voice mail began. "The doctor came back, said she's going to be fine. They got the bullet out of her and she needed some blood. She'd lost a lot. A couple of inches higher, and he would have hit her femoral artery. She's banged up, scrapes and contusions, and a broken finger. Other than that, she's okay."

Other than that.

Kade took another swig of the now half-empty bottle of vodka as he sat in his car, staring up at the glowing windows of the hospital. He'd listened to the voice mail over and over again, the inventory of her injuries like an accusation. He should've been there, should've protected her. He'd let Blane down.

He'd let her down.

Kathleen hadn't asked anything of him, and the one time she had, Kade hadn't gotten to her in time. She'd endured a psychopath, a corpse, and a deadly injury for six hours before they'd found her.

They'd been the longest six hours of his life.

The vodka burned going down, joining the acid tearing his gut up from the inside out.

He didn't recall making the decision to go inside the hospital, just found himself walking the deserted corridors in the middle of the night. Passing an empty nurses' station, he walked around the counter and navigated the software they'd left open on the computer screen until he found Kathleen's room number.

A few minutes later, he had silently entered her darkened room and stood, drinking in her still form on the bed. A shaft of light from the window illuminated enough for him to be able to see her face, sound asleep.

Moving slowly toward the bed, his hand lifted to touch her, and that's when he saw the blood on him. Brass knuckles guy—Kade must have gotten blood on him when he'd used the knife. The reddish brown stained his hand, a stark contrast to the pale skin of Kathleen's cheek.

He jerked back. It was a good reminder. Kade had blood on his hands both literally and figuratively. He should no more be allowed to touch her than he should be allowed into heaven—not that he believed in such a place.

But he *did* believe in hell, and not just the hell-on-earth kind, but the real deal. Because he was dead certain that's where he was destined to end up. It was the only place people like him deserved. And perhaps part of that hell was wanting something so badly—something so pure and good—and knowing you'd never, ever have it.

Going into the bathroom, he quietly closed the door before he washed his hands, carefully erasing the evidence of the brutality he'd meted out tonight. Too bad that, for him, brutality was more than skin deep. It went to his bones, right down into his soul.

He caught sight of himself in the mirror. There was a bruise forming on his forehead from where he'd smacked that guy. Other than that, he didn't have a mark on him. He was almost sorry. It seemed he should pay for Kathleen's pain with some of his own.

His eyes looked . . . empty. He wondered what, if anything, Kathleen saw when she looked into them. Did she see what he saw? A bleak wasteland of darkness that would only drag her down into the depths with him?

Returning to her bedside, he watched her, and maybe she sensed a presence because she suddenly woke with a gasp, then struggled to sit up.

Kade lightly clasped her shoulder, the bones too fragile beneath her skin. "Take it easy," he said. "You're okay. You're safe."

At his voice, she relaxed back against the pillows with a sigh. "Where am I?" Her voice was a hoarse whisper that made him wince.

"Indiana University Hospital," he said, wondering how much she remembered of her ordeal.

"Hate hospitals."

"That's what Blane said. But you needed to come here. They had to remove the bullet from your leg and you'd lost a lot of blood." No sense sugarcoating the ways in which he'd failed her.

"Thirsty." Now *that* he could do something about.

Grabbing a cup off the table, Kade filled it halfway with water, then helped Kathleen sit up so she could drink it.

"Thank you," she said once she'd finished it, and her voice was clearer now, and stronger.

"No problem," he automatically replied, helping her lie back down.

"How'd you find me?" she asked.

"I put a tracking device inside your cell phone after the first time you disappeared on me," he said. "I wasn't about to lose you again." He swallowed, then said the fear he couldn't help expressing. "Though it seems I nearly did."

She didn't reply to that and silence descended. After a few moments, she asked, "What time is it?"

"Around five a.m.," he replied. "You were missing for over six hours. We would have gotten there sooner, but the asshole must have turned the phone off. It stopped sending a signal. All we had to go on was about a square-block radius." It seemed he couldn't stop the rationale, the defense of how long it had taken to get to her, as if he was begging her to understand why he'd failed.

"How'd Blane know about Frankie's dad?"

"He was with me when Frankie called. I heard what you said, the description you gave. That was enough for me to track him down. Frankie was Franklin Randall Wyster. Son of James Walter Wyster, aka Ahmed el Mustaqueem."

She said nothing, so he went on.

"Frankie and his dad allegedly committed an honor killing a couple years ago. The victim was his daughter, Christine Wyster. She was fifteen at the time. They were never prosecuted."

Her body shuddered at that and Kade had a flash of regret for telling her. She empathized too much, could feel others' pain too deeply.

"I thought Ryan was the one who killed those people," she said, "but really it was Frankie."

"Frankie may have killed them, but Ryan was the one threatening them into changing their testimony. I don't know who he was working for, but I'm going to find out."

Kathleen was quiet again for a few minutes, her eyes slowly blinking, as though she was finding it hard to stay awake. The heavy-duty drugs she was on must have been kicking in.

"Why do I feel funny?" she asked, the words slurring slightly.

"Painkillers."

She blinked again, this time a few minutes passing before they reopened, and Kade wondered if she even realized she was dozing.

"Knew you'd find me."

Her words were hard to make out, soft and slurry, and they felt like the feathery touch of forgiveness.

"Six hours was a long fucking time, princess," Kade rasped. He couldn't stop himself from touching her this time, grasping her hand gently. His palm was much larger, swallowing hers.

Her lips lifted slightly in a smile even as her eyes stayed shut.

"Go to sleep, Kathleen," Kade said, smoothing back her hair. They'd cleaned her up, washed the blood and gore from her, and the strands were soft. "You need your rest." He released her hand and her eyes suddenly flew open.

"Don't leave," she said, and wonder of wonders, she reached for him.

Kade sucked in a breath and swallowed the heavy lump in his throat. "I'm not going anywhere," he reassured her, taking her hand in his again.

She relaxed, seeming content with that, and her eyes drifted closed.

So that's where Kade stood, at her bedside, her hand in his, for the next three hours.

~

Blane reappeared with the change in the morning shift. He paused when he spied Kade.

"I didn't know you were here," he said.

Kade unobtrusively slipped his hand from Kathleen's and stepped back. Glancing over his shoulder at Blane, he shrugged. "I'm still on bodyguard duty, right?"

Blane clasped his shoulder, giving him a squeeze. "Thanks. I'll take it from here." He drew up a chair and sat down just as a nurse walked in. Kade took the opportunity to slip out the door.

He was nearly dead on his feet. He'd been up straight for over twenty-four hours and felt it. Driving in a daze, he found himself pulling into Kathleen's parking lot rather than his own. Surprised, he sat there for a minute, then got out and went into her apartment.

Tigger ran to greet him and Kade refilled his food and water bowls, then stood in the kitchen, staring at nothing. He tossed his jacket on the couch, then let his feet take him into her bedroom.

She hadn't made the bed, the sheets and blankets still pushed into a huddle from where she'd slept. Kade had a brief flash of Blane and

Kathleen making love there, but he shoved the image aside. Instead, he pictured Kathleen sleeping, the way he'd seen her each time he'd stood over her—a black-clad monster guarding something rare and precious.

Falling into bed, he stretched on his stomach, pressing his nose into the pillow and inhaling the scent of Kathleen. The knot of guilt and self-loathing inside him eased. Peace—only with her, only because of her—and he slept.

～

Kade tried not to think about her for the next couple of days, instead devoting himself to tracking down every tie Ryan Sheffield had within the CIA and any other government agency. He was finally rewarded late one evening. It had only been one call, which had lasted a total of ten seconds, but the number was unmistakable. He'd seen it on his own caller ID too many times to recognize it for anything other than what it was.

Keaston.

Blane didn't know, might never know, how warped and corrupt his uncle was. Maybe he didn't want to know. The man had been like a second father to Blane over the years, despite his antipathy for Kade, which he'd always been careful not to show around Blane.

Kade needed more evidence, hard evidence, before he could breathe a word of this to Blane.

Toggling a key on the keyboard, Kade flipped between applications, pulling up the screen currently displaying Kathleen's medical records. One of the first tests they'd done was for pregnancy, which had turned up negative.

Too much relief had flooded him at that news, followed by guilt. He hadn't been able to bring himself to say anything to Blane, so Kade didn't know if he was relieved . . . or disappointed. He wondered how he would've felt if it'd been him. It seemed such a foreign concept—being a father, having a wife, making a family. An ephemeral dream . . . an impossible dream.

Kathleen was being discharged today, and Kade wondered if Blane would take her home or to his place. She needed additional care, so he couldn't imagine him leaving her alone. He'd bet Blane would find some way of getting her to agree to stay with him. Mona would be able to help her out, and she'd be close at hand for Blane to do some serious groveling.

Kade had no doubt that Blane would work his magic and be back in Kathleen's good graces all too soon, which was how it should be. They belonged together, Blane and Kathleen, and it only showed what a sick fuck he was that Kade was in love with his brother's girl. It was just better not to think about it.

Which lasted until about eleven or so.

Blane's house was dark and quiet when Kade let himself in through the kitchen door. His steps were silent as his memory provided the path to avoid the stairs that squeaked. He paused outside Kathleen's door, wondering if he'd find her inside, or if Blane already would have gotten her into his bed.

To his ashamed relief, she was in her bed . . . alone. And sound asleep.

He closed the door and stood near the bed, drinking her in. It felt oddly familiar and soothing, to watch her again, like he was settling back into a comfortable routine.

The room was bright enough from the moonlight pouring through the slats in the blinds for him to see her clearly. He didn't think she was aware of him, then she spoke.

"Kade."

It was like a blessing and a summons, drawing him toward her without any thought or will to resist. She reached to grasp his hand once he was close. Warmth flooded up his arm.

"Didn't mean to wake you, princess," which was exactly how she looked tonight. She wore a filmy white cotton nightgown, and even though the neckline was modest and the sleeves long, it was the sexiest thing he'd ever seen. Her hair was a wash of muted gold on the pillow, her eyes wide and trusting as she gazed up at him.

"It's fine," she said, sitting up. "Are you all right?"

The concern in her voice brought an acute edge to the guilt in his conscience. "You're the one with a gunshot wound and you're asking me if I'm all right?"

She didn't reply. Moving over, she tugged his hand, her request unmistakable. But sitting next to a pajama-clad Kathleen, in the middle of the night, on her bed—in his brother's house—was a bad idea. It would probably never be a *good* idea, but right now, with his feelings so razor sharp, it seemed like a particularly bad choice. Which of course didn't stop him from sitting, but he tried to stay as far away from her as possible. Her hand was still inside his, warm and soft.

"Thank you for coming after me," she said.

As if he needed to be thanked.

"We were nearly too late," he said. Didn't she understand the enormity of his failure?

"I'm fine, Kade." She smiled, transfixing his already mesmerized gaze. "I'll heal. I survived."

The thought of her injuries made the banked rage inside boil back to the surface. His hands tightened into fists before he remembered he still held her hand. He didn't want to hurt her, so he forced himself to relax.

"He died too quick after what he did to you."

Losing her, the reality of it, hit him hard. She wasn't his to keep, but he'd still see her, even if she was with Blane. But he'd almost lost her permanently from his life, and he couldn't take that. He could handle being friend-zoned, just as long as he could still talk to her, be with her in some small way. It was more than he deserved.

She opened her mouth to speak, but he suddenly didn't want to hear what she had to say. She'd probably defend him, but she was wrong.

He pressed a finger to her lips to quiet her, which was also a bad decision.

Her lips were soft and full, the warmth of her breath fluttering against his skin as he quieted her. She stared at him, her eyes so wide and so blue, it almost hurt to look into them. Once he started touching her, he couldn't stop. His hand moved to slip under her hair and curl around the back of her neck.

"You even look like a princess," he murmured, thinking out loud. "White gown, blonde hair tumbling over your shoulders, blue eyes so wide and innocent. All you need is a knight in shining armor to come to your rescue." Instead, she had him. A pitiful substitute.

"You came to my rescue, Kade."

He grimaced. "Blane's the white knight. Not me."

"Sometimes knights wear black."

She was gazing at him and he was lost in her eyes. What had that meant? She thought he was like Blane? A good person? She was delusional, but he didn't want her to stop looking at him like that, like he was her whole world, so he said nothing.

Suddenly, she winced.

"What? What's wrong?" Had he unintentionally hurt her? But she shook her head.

"It's nothing. Probably just time for another pain pill," she said.

Kade got up and retrieved a glass of water from the bathroom, then gave her a pill from the prescription bottle on the table. Once she'd swallowed it and lay down, he had no further excuses to stay, so he rose to go.

"Wait," she said, latching on to his sleeve and stopping him. "Where are you going? Are you going to your place?" She sounded vaguely anxious.

He nodded and could have sworn he heard her let out a long breath.

"Do you mind . . . I mean, if it's not too much trouble—"

She wanted something of him, but was hesitant to ask. If she only knew there was nothing he'd deny her.

"What do you need? Are you still in pain?" he asked.

"No. I just . . . don't want to be alone." Her voice was small and slightly embarrassed. "It's . . . dark," she continued. "Just until I fall asleep. Then you can leave."

Kade had slept for years with the closet light on and the door cracked, unable to bring himself to embrace full darkness while he slept. There were too many things that could hurt him—had hurt him— and always they found the cloak of darkness to be their best ally in an ambush. He heard the fear behind Kathleen's request, and didn't require further explanation.

He lay down next to her on top of the covers.

She turned toward him, scooting closer until she was nestled right up against him. He closed his eyes, memorizing the feel of her body pressed against his. She hadn't asked Blane to guard her from the nightmares inside her head—she'd asked him. That thought burrowed inside his chest and wound its roots through his heart.

Though she was quiet, he could tell she wasn't sleeping, not yet, and a question that hadn't been answered came to him.

"Kathleen."

"Yes?"

"How did you get out of that cellar?"

Her reaction was immediate, the pliant softness of her body stiffening next to his. When she spoke, it was in a horrified whisper.

"I used Brian's body as a ladder."

She had the same feeling in her voice that he was quite familiar with—the regret and horror of what you would do to save your own life. The will to live is strong. It takes a lot for someone to give up and accept their fate. Kathleen hadn't buckled. Despite the hopeless circumstances, she'd done the unthinkable . . . because she'd had to.

She was fucking amazing.

Wrapping his arms around her, he pulled her closer to him. "Shh," he said, smoothing her silken hair. "You did what you had to do. He wouldn't have wanted you to die there, too." Her body gradually relaxed again, melting into his as he held her.

"Those men didn't deserve any of this," she said.

"Nope," Kade sighed. "They were just pawns. Bowers and Freeman were threatened into changing their testimony, then killed by a fanatic looking for revenge."

"And Stacey," she said, her voice sad, "caught up in it just because of who she loved."

Kade wondered if it had occurred to her that the same could be said of herself. She'd been a target—had nearly died—because of Blane. But Kathleen was smart and he bet she'd figured that one out on her own.

They lay there for a long while, and she seemed content to let him hold her and keep touching her hair, his fingers sliding through the long strands. Her head was against his chest, listening to his heart beating, maybe. It was soothing. Peaceful. Kade could lie for hours like this, just holding her. It didn't matter that there were layers of fabric and blankets between them. He was sure this would be the last chance he'd get to hold her like this, and he didn't want it to end.

The clock downstairs tolled the hour. Midnight. Her voice came softly out of the darkness.

"Merry Christmas, Kade."

"Merry Christmas, Kathleen."

She fell asleep soon after that, the pain medication taking effect, but Kade didn't leave, though there were many reasons why he should. At the moment, none of them seemed important enough to propel him from the bed.

She nestled closer in her sleep and his arms instinctively tightened around her. He could smell her hair and the clean scent of her skin. Closing his eyes, he committed this moment to memory. Chances were good it would never happen again, and it was worth taking the time and effort to never forget it.

He didn't sleep—he didn't want to waste this time by sleeping it away—so he just lay there, staring at the ceiling and breathing in Kathleen.

It was the best gift he'd ever gotten on Christmas morning.

The sky was just beginning to lighten when he extricated himself and slid from the bed. He took one long last look at her sleeping before easing out of the room. Turning away from the closed door, he glanced down the hall. Blane was standing outside his bedroom, watching him.

Kade stiffened. Guilt rose like nausea and it felt as though Blane had caught him red-handed doing something wrong. Which he hadn't, not really.

Unless you counted falling in love with his girl.

Blane started walking toward him so Kade met him halfway.

"What were you doing in Kat's room?" Blane asked. His voice was modulated. Trying not to wake Kathleen, Kade guessed.

"Just checking on her," Kade replied. He raised an eyebrow. "Nothing wrong with that, is there?"

"No, I'm just surprised. Since when have you cared about any of my girlfriends?" An edge of accusation was in his tone. Barely present, but there nonetheless.

"Kathleen's not your girlfriend." The possessive retort came instantly, without thought, a reaction to the jealousy that had struck him at the term *my girlfriend.*

Blane looked at him.

Kade shrugged, struggling to make it sound nonchalant when he said, "She dumped your ass, remember? And I don't see her sleeping in your bed tonight."

Blane's eyes narrowed. "I'll win her back."

Kade gave him a thin smile. "I'm sure you will, brother." He turned to go, anxious to put an end to what was rapidly becoming dangerously close to a confrontation.

"How long were you in there?"

Blane's question made him pause. Kade glanced back around. Debated lying. Decided not to.

"All night." He paused, then added. "She asked me to stay."

Blane was an expert in controlling his reactions, but Kade knew him better than anyone, so he could read the anger and dismay those words produced.

"You call her *princess*," he said. "Why?"

"It's just a nickname," Kade hedged. "You call her *Kat*."

"That's different. I know her."

"Do you?" He took a step closer to Blane. "Do you really? Because it looks like you only see what you want to see."

This time when he turned and walked away, Blane was silent.

Chapter Sixteen

Kade glanced in the rearview mirror and pushed his fingers through his hair. He'd slept all day before rising in time to dress for Christmas dinner and drive back to Blane's. He was tense, his stomach in knots, and he wanted to see Kathleen.

He had to say good-bye.

No way could he stick around, that was patently obvious. He wouldn't be able to stay away from her. And neither could he watch as Blane seduced her once again, then no doubt dumped her in a month or two once the challenge was over. He'd seen it happen too many times to want to have a front-row seat when it happened to Kathleen.

He was nearly out of the car when he hesitated, then reached back in and grabbed something from the glove box and dropped it inside the pocket of his slacks.

Mona insisted they dress for Christmas dinner, so he was wearing a black suit, but he refused to wear a tie, opting instead for a black shirt he left open at the neck. It reminded him of what Kathleen had said to him last night.

Sometimes knights wear black.

He wondered if she'd remember saying it.

He heard voices and laughter as he walked down the hall to the library. His feet wanted to move faster, hurrying him toward Kathleen, but he forced his steps to a measured pace. The anticipation made it that much sweeter when he stepped into the room and saw her.

She was easy to pick out, standing somewhat apart from everyone else, gazing out the window with her back to him. Kade took a moment to admire her.

She wore a black velvet dress that clung to her body, accentuating the curve of her waist and flare of her hips. Her hair was a warm blonde cascade of curls and waves down her back.

He didn't think twice, he just headed straight for her.

"Penny for your thoughts," he said, once he was near.

She turned, her exquisite blue eyes widening in surprise, then lighting up with pleasure. She smiled and he stopped breathing for a moment. She was so beautiful, it made his chest ache to look at her.

"You're here," she said, sounding almost breathless.

She looked as happy to see him as he felt on the inside, but dared not let show. Still, he couldn't help the small smirk that curved his lips.

"Stating the obvious," he teased. "Let's hope that bullet to your leg didn't affect your brain." His hungry gaze drank her in, from the pink of her lips to the deep swell of her cleavage, the black a vivid contrast to the pale ivory perfection of her skin. She held an empty martini glass between lax fingers.

"Looks like you could use another drink," he said, using the excuse of taking her glass as an opportunity to step closer to her. He leaned down. "I know I do."

It seemed the most natural thing in the world to take her hand in his, slotting their fingers together as he walked her to the bar set up on the sideboard. The empty sugar-encrusted glass wasn't her style, but he guessed Mona had given it to her. Setting it aside, he took two old-fashioned glasses and filled each with ice. Grabbing the bottle of vodka, he poured a healthy shot in each, then topped it with tonic and handed her one while he took the other.

"To your continued good health," he said, clinking his glass against hers.

Blue eyes on his, she took a sip. Kade avidly watched the way her lips formed to the glass, the movement of her throat as she swallowed, and how her tongue swiped at the damp fluid left behind.

"Glad you could make it, Kade."

Kade had seen Blane's approach, and he didn't miss the way his arm slid possessively around Kathleen's waist. Jealousy sank its claws in deep and Kade took a long swallow of his drink, fighting the insane urge to shove Blane away from her. If he kept looking in her eyes, he could control it, so he didn't look away from the clear, pure blue.

"Wouldn't have missed it, brother," he said.

Keaston's wife, Vivian, stepped inside their circle, giving him a hug, which he allowed. Sliding her arm through his, she chatted with him as she led him away from Blane and Kathleen.

Kade listened with half an ear, his attention focused on Kathleen as she and Blane talked quietly. She was smiling up at him in a gentle, adoring way that made Kade's stomach churn. He tossed back the rest of his drink, then excused himself from Vivian to go pour another.

Dinner was torture. He sat down and across the table from Blane and Kathleen. Blane was at the head with Kathleen on his right. Kade drank more than he ate, emptying too many glasses of wine. But no matter how much he drank, he still felt stone-cold sober, which sucked. He wanted not to care that Blane whispered in her ear, making her smile. Or that he kept touching her—her hand, her arm, the back of her neck underneath her hair.

He poured himself another glass of wine.

It felt like the night was never going to end and Kade glanced at his watch for the umpteenth time as he followed everyone to the family room. His earlier pleasure that Kathleen had seemed glad to see him had evaporated. She'd been polite, that was all. Blane had been right—Kathleen was nice. Of course she'd want to be on good terms with her boyfriend's brother.

Kade poured himself an after-dinner scotch, deciding at the last second to pour one for Blane, too, especially when he heard Keaston talking to him.

". . . it's not often—ever, actually—that I've seen you take the kind of risks you've taken lately, Blane."

"What do you mean?" Kade heard Kathleen ask.

"Robert—" Blane rarely used Keaston's first name, and when he did, it was never good. Kade uncorked the scotch and poured another shot into Blane's glass.

"I suppose he hasn't told you," Keaston interrupted, "but it took considerable effort on Blane's part to free your friend and her parents."

Kade turned around in time to see Kathleen's face fall.

"You may very well have placed yourself in an extremely vulnerable position," Keaston continued. "You now owe some very powerful people, Blane."

Considering how Kade suspected Keaston had his fingers involved in using Sheffield to get Blane to throw this case, the subtle warning wasn't lost on him. And apparently neither was it lost on Blane.

"That's enough," Blane said. Kathleen flinched at the anger in his voice, drawing Kade's eye. She was pale, the pink flush of her cheeks gone, her mouth pinched with worry. Her body was stiff and she'd drawn into herself, as though Keaston's words had made her smaller somehow. It made Kade angry. She'd been enjoying herself before, even if it had been with Blane rather than him, and he wanted to see her smile again.

"Now it's Christmas," he said, handing Blane the drink he'd poured.

As he'd hoped, Kathleen smiled a little and he heard Mona chuckle. The tension in Kathleen's body eased as she glanced over to him. Maybe it was his imagination, but he thought he saw a flash of gratefulness in her eyes.

Kathleen and Blane started talking in an undertone again and Kade forced his gaze away, emptying the scotch in his glass with one long swallow. It burned going down, but not enough to rid him of the ache that only intensified the longer he was in the same room with Blane and Kathleen.

"Play something for us, Blane," Mona said.

"Oh yes, please do," Vivian added.

"Only if Kathleen sings," Blane replied.

That got Kade's attention and he turned around from the sideboard where he'd been filling his glass yet again.

"No, I can't possibly," Kathleen stammered. She was blushing and it was good to see some color in her cheeks again.

"Of course you can," Blane said. "You have a beautiful voice."

"Yes, she does." It was out of his mouth before he'd realized he'd spoken, and he was suddenly aware of a burning desire to hear her sing again. The night she'd done her Britney Spears impression was burned in his mind.

Her eyes met his and her cheeks turned even redder, making him wonder if they were thinking of the same thing. She'd sung, and then he'd kissed her. God, she'd tasted good. Those little pigtails in her hair had made him think of doing things to her that would make her blush hard . . . then come even harder.

Blane coaxed her into joining him and a few moments later, was playing the introduction to "The Christmas Song." Her voice was a pure soprano with the texture of warm honey, and it spread over and beneath his skin, soothing his soul. She leaned gracefully against the piano as she sang, her body gradually relaxing until she looked up and their eyes met.

Everyone else melted away and Kade was only aware of her. She didn't look away and it seemed as though she was singing directly to him . . . for him.

Although it's been said many times, many ways . . . Merry Christmas . . . to you . . .

The moment was shattered by applause and she started, breaking their gaze. She smiled shyly at the praise, waving away the compliments.

People began to leave and Kade put off his own departure, trying to figure out a way to have a few minutes alone with Kathleen to say good-bye. Blane had hardly left her side, as though he could read Kade's mind.

She disappeared while he was saying good-bye to Mona and Gerard, leaving him and Blane alone. They didn't speak, just sat across from one another, sipping on identical crystal glasses with amber fluid. There was tension between them, which was so unusual, Kade wasn't sure what to do about it. Part of him wanted to reassure Blane that he wasn't going to try and steal his girl. The other part of him wanted nothing to do with making any such promise.

Kathleen returned in a few minutes, saving the awkward silence, and handed them each a package.

"Merry Christmas!" she said, settling onto the couch.

Kade was so surprised, he didn't know what to say or do. No one besides Mona and Blane had ever given him a Christmas present. Years ago, his mother had, of course, but he'd had no relationships that lasted long enough to develop an attachment that would prompt a gift at Christmastime. And now Kathleen had done just that, though by the look of it, she'd given the same gift to him and Blane. He couldn't decide if that was a good thing or a bad thing.

"Well, open them," she prompted, since it appeared the same thought was going through Blane's head, as he'd made no move to open the gift she'd given him either.

He and Blane unwrapped the gift at about the same pace, and Kade was left staring in astonishment at what he held.

It was Lake Winnipesaukee. It had to be. A small painting depicted the lake on a moonlit night, the waters dark and still. It was beautiful, and thoughtful, and completely unexpected.

"It's Lake Winnipesaukee," she explained to them somewhat anxiously. "Blane said you two used to go there when you were young. I thought you might like it, hoped that it would remind you of good memories you share."

Kade glanced at what Blane held. It was the same painting, only done in daylight with bright sunlight glistening off rolling waves.

The gifts were so apt, so fitting, that it shamed Kade. She was amazing, beautiful, generous to a fault—commissioned paintings weren't cheap—and he'd cheapened her worth by trying to work out any way he could possibly be with her. She was above him. So far removed from him it was like an angel in the heavens watching him grovel in the dirt.

It was suddenly hard to swallow.

"You hate it," she said, sounding utterly crestfallen.

"No, absolutely not," Blane said. "It's beautiful, Kat. I hadn't realized you'd remembered that story."

Kade cleared his throat. "What story?"

Blane glanced at him. "The time we were diving and I couldn't find you."

The memory came back, crystal clear, and Kade laughed. "Ah, yes. You were supremely pissed off."

"More at myself than you," Blane said.

"Thank you, Kathleen," Kade said, making her smile in delight. He now had a new treasured possession.

"I guess it's time for my gift then," Blane said, reaching inside his jacket. Pulling out an envelope, he took it to Kathleen, sitting by her on the arm of the sofa.

"But you already gave me something," she protested.

Kade wondered if he wanted to be there for this, but considering it came in an envelope, it couldn't be that personal. And he was right.

"You got me front-row tickets and backstage passes to the Britney Spears concert?" Kathleen squealed, gazing at the papers in her hand.

"What else would I give her biggest fan?" Blane asked with a grin.

Her biggest fan. Guess that explained the Halloween costume. Kade wondered if she still had it.

Kathleen hugged Blane, which caused the smile on Kade's lips to fade. It wasn't that personal, but it'd been a helluva gift. No way could he top that. Then Blane handed him the perfect opportunity.

"Just don't expect me to go with you," Blane said.

"That's fine," Kathleen said, sinking back to the sofa. "I'm sure I can find someone else to go with me."

"I'll go," Kade said.

"Really?" Kathleen wasn't looking at either of them, so intent was she on studying the tickets and passes. "It's in July."

"Absolutely."

Blane glanced quizzically at him. "Why would you do that? You suddenly a Spears fan?"

The concert was in July. It was December. Seven months was an awfully optimistic time frame for Blane. Odds were he'd be long gone from Kathleen's life by the time spring rolled around, much less summer.

"I don't mind taking Kathleen to see her favorite pop star," Kade said. "In the middle of the summer, I'm thinking it'll be steaming hot, right, Blane? We'll have a few drinks, enjoy the show. Maybe Kathleen will even wear her Britney outfit again."

God, he could see it now. *Sweat trickling down between her breasts, the heat of her skin if he pressed his hand to her bared abdomen, the heated wetness between her legs* . . . fucking heaven on earth. If Blane wanted to give that up, that was his call. But Kade wasn't going to hide the fact that Kathleen wouldn't be alone for long once Blane dumped her.

Blane was glaring at him, anger clenching his jaw. Kade merely twisted his lips in a smirk. The tension was back tenfold between them, so much so that even Kathleen felt it. She glanced up from the tickets.

"What? What's wrong?" she asked.

"Nothing, Kat," Blane said, finally glancing away. "I think I'm going to call it a night. May I help you upstairs?"

And that effectively ended Kade's hopes of getting Kathleen alone. He was absolutely certain that there'd be no sneaking into her room tonight, not after Blane had seen him leave this morning.

Kade got to his feet as Kathleen approached him. Stretching up on her toes, she wrapped her arms around his neck for a hug. Kade automatically slid his arms around her waist. Even though he didn't like people touching him, it seemed the rule didn't hold for Kathleen, who of course had no idea.

"Merry Christmas," she said, giving him a squeeze.

Blane was watching. He and Kade's eyes met. Neither of them blinked or looked away as Kade hugged Kathleen in return.

"Merry Christmas, princess," Kade said softly in her ear, brushing a kiss to the top of her head.

Blane helped her upstairs and Kade watched them go. He could tell by the way Blane touched the small of her back that Kathleen's room would be empty tonight.

Why he stuck around, he didn't know. Maybe because he was a masochist and just wanted to torture himself. Thank God he couldn't hear anything. The house was too big and Blane's room too far away for that. But he didn't need the soundtrack—he could see it all inside his head.

He drank some more—he didn't know or care what it was exactly—and tossed aside the jacket he'd worn. He never did feel right in a suit. It was as if his body knew it hadn't been born to wear them, like Blane had been. The shirt felt too tight and confining, so he unbuttoned it and rolled back the cuffs.

Sitting in a chair in the darkened room, Kade stared into the fireplace. The tree was still lit in the corner. The only sounds were the crackle of the fire and the clink of the ice in his glass as he drank.

He became lost in thought as he sat there, his imagination painting images of Kathleen with him instead of Blane. It took on a dreamy quality, the alcohol finally doing its job and muddling his thoughts. But rather than dulling his need for her, it only made it grow and sharpen into a double-sided blade that dug into his gut.

Kade didn't know if he was dreaming or awake when Kathleen floated into the room, ethereal and lovely in her white nightgown. She walked to stand in front of the fireplace, the flames clearly illuminating her body through the thin fabric. The sound of her soft sigh reached his ears and Kade squeezed his eyes shut for a moment, forcing away the alcohol-induced lethargy so he could take advantage of this unexpected opportunity he'd just been handed.

"I thought no creature was supposed to be stirring," he said, startling her.

She turned around, squinting to try to find him in the darkness. "I didn't realize anyone was still up," she said. Her voice was hushed, as though afraid she'd wake someone. Blane, perhaps? Had she left his bed and come in search of Kade? A wild hope rose in him at the thought and he stood, set aside his empty glass, and walked over to her.

The fire lit her from behind, making her hair glow and her eyes seem luminous, as though lit from within. In his half-inebriated state, Kade could almost believe she had a light inside her, shining from her soul through her eyes.

"It's so not a good idea for you to be down here," he murmured, and he didn't know if he was talking to her or himself. Self-control seemed a distant memory.

"Why?" she asked, studying him. "Are you drunk?"

"I wish I were. It would be easier." Or maybe it wouldn't. Alcohol only made him more acutely aware of what he didn't have, and would never have.

"What would be easier?"

"Leaving."

Her eyes widened. "You're leaving again?"

Was he imagining the dismay in her voice because he wanted it to be there?

His lips twisted. "Duty calls." He needed to gather more evidence on Keaston before presenting it to Blane—or simply going behind Blane's back and confronting Keaston himself. No need to disillusion Blane unless absolutely necessary.

"What duty?" she asked.

"Something I found on Ryan's phone. I need to look into it."

"Did you find out who he was working for?"

"Maybe," he hedged. "If I'm right—and I really hope I'm not—then it affects Blane in a major way. I have to find out the truth."

"Protecting Blane," she mused quietly. "You're a good brother, Kade."

Good. A word that should never, could never, be used to describe him. Her view of him was skewed by her own goodness, painting him in strokes of integrity and loyalty, which was so far from the truth as to be laughable. He was drawn in shades of black—menacing, remorseless, deadly. Whereas Kathleen . . . she was pure gold.

"I don't know if that's true anymore," he said. The thought of gold reminded him, and he reached into his pocket. "I didn't have a chance to give you my present."

Taking her hand in his, he turned it palm up and deposited his mother's locket on a new chain he'd bought. The jeweler had polished the antique locket to a brilliant shine.

She seemed stunned, staring down at the necklace. "Kade, you didn't have to—"

"I wanted to," he said, cutting her off. Reaching down, he opened the locket. She gasped.

"How . . . how did you . . ." She stopped speaking, just stared at the tiny photo of her parents Kade had copied and placed inside, covering the photo of himself as a child beneath it.

"Turn around," he said, taking the necklace from her.

She turned and lifted her hair so he could fasten the clasp. The necklace was perfect, the locket nestling right above her cleavage. She placed a hand over it.

Kade didn't want to stop touching her, so he rested his hands on her shoulders. Their bodies were close, nearly touching, and he inhaled, savoring the scent of her one more time.

"I wish you would stay."

He barely heard her whisper, then she turned back to him, raising her eyes to his. He'd give her anything if she asked, but staying . . . staying might just kill him.

"I can't," he said roughly. "Do you think I'm blind? Blane wants you back. If I stay, I'll have to watch you and him together. Don't ask me to do that." Blunt honesty wasn't usually his thing, but the instinct for survival was strong. If she wanted him to stay, he'd be helpless to deny her, but it would drive him insane.

She didn't ask him to stay. She did something even worse. She started to cry.

"Dammit," Kade cursed under his breath, his hands cupping her jaw and brushing at her tears. She just stared at him with her wide blue eyes, the crystal rivulets tracking down her cheeks faster than he could wipe them away. "Don't cry, princess, please," he begged. The sadness in her eyes was something he'd put there, and he hated himself for it.

"When will you be back?"

"In time for Britney," he said, desperate for her to stop crying and smile at him. He didn't want her tears to be the last thing he saw of her.

"Please," she said, her voice broken and barely discernible. "Please be careful. Don't get hurt. Don't die."

He couldn't handle this. She sounded like . . . like she needed him. *Him.* Kade Dennon. Assassin, hacker, lawbreaker, and all-around shitty person.

"I didn't know you cared," he said, testing the waters.

"You know I do."

He hadn't known, hadn't dared to hope that she felt something for him, even if it was just worry for his safety. It was less than he wanted, but better than nothing, and he held tightly to it.

If he didn't leave now, he wouldn't leave at all, and he'd fight Blane tooth and nail for her.

Kade wrapped an arm around her shoulders and pulled her close. Her arms went around his waist as she burrowed in close to him. Her hip fit perfectly in his palm, the warmth of her skin seeping through the thin cotton of her gown.

He wanted to kiss her so badly, it was a burning need in the center of his chest, but he didn't. Because if he did kiss her—here, under his brother's roof—it wouldn't stop at just a kiss. There was too much attraction between them for it to only be a kiss, too many feelings bottled up inside him, and he didn't want to do that to her. It was bizarre and inexplicable, but he felt as though he'd tarnish her gold with his touch. And he wanted her to stay gold.

Letting her go was more difficult than not kissing her, and when she opened her mouth to speak, he pressed his fingers to her lips.

"Shh, don't say it," he said. He didn't want this to be good-bye, though it might very well be the last time he saw her. He was usually gone for months at a time. She could move away as quickly and easily as she'd moved here, especially when Blane broke her heart.

He prayed she'd keep that hopefulness and optimistic view of the world after that happened—he hoped Blane wouldn't tarnish the gold in her soul either.

Kade pressed his lips to her forehead for a long moment. An act of benediction and blessing when usually bestowed, though tonight it felt as though he was drawing from her. Strength. Protection. Warmth. Affection.

Sliding into his jacket, Kade kept his eyes on her, committing the sight to memory. His mother's locket shimmered against her skin, and he couldn't think of a better place to leave the best part of himself than resting against Kathleen's heart.

Grabbing his coat, he turned and left the room, wishing he could return to the warm circle of her arms. But wishing was more useless and pointless than hoping. Instead, he walked outside into the bitter cold. Alone.

ABOUT THE AUTHOR

Photo © 2014 Karen Lynn

Tiffany Snow has been reading romance novels since she was too young to read romance novels. After a career working in the information technology field, Tiffany now has her dream job of writing full time.

Tiffany makes her home in the Midwest with her husband and two daughters. She can be reached at Tiffany@TiffanyASnow.com. Visit her on her website, www.Tiffany-Snow.com, to keep up with her latest projects.